Totally Bound Publishing books by P. Stormcrow

The Playgrounds
The Words to Bind
The Will to Serve
The Heart to Lead

Collections
Rules of Summer: The Knots that Hold
Some Like it Haunted: The Fae Effect
Love's Bloom: Dear Elliot

The Playgrounds

THE HEART TO LEAD

P. STORMCROW

The Heart to Lead
ISBN # 978-1-80250-956-4
©Copyright P. Stormcrow 2022
Cover Art by Fiona Jayde ©Copyright June 2022
Interior text design by Claire Siemaszkiewicz
Totally Bound Publishing

THE HEART TO LEAD

Dedication

For the inspiration behind Lani.
I hope you enjoyed the fictional shoe collection I
gave you.

Chapter One

Lani McMillan curled her lips into a smile of amusement when the town car the hosts had hired for her pulled up to her destination. A masquerade party to celebrate a renewal of vows... She had been to enough weddings and celebrations in her lifetime, but this was a new twist. As she emerged from the vehicle, she smoothed the long black dress with a thigh-high slit and adjusted the teardrop diamond pendant hanging on a white gold chain just below her collarbone.

Her stilettos clicked against the stone steps of the venue as she walked. The happy couple had rented a sprawling heritage estate thirty minutes out from the city. Laughter spilled out from the opened windows, lights illuminating the entire place against the setting sun. As she approached the door, she settled the Colombina mask over her face, covering her eyes and cheeks. She brushed her fingers over the midnight lace, trailing over a row of black and silver beads before she tilted her chin up. With a last check to ensure that her red curls remained pinned in a loose knot above her head, she readied herself. *Showtime.*

"Good evening, Ms."

"Evening." With inherent grace, Lani presented the invitation to the suited gentleman at the door who was sporting a much plainer version of her own mask. In fact, most staff seemed to wear the same face covering, like it was part of the uniform.

"Excellent. Welcome to the party, Ms. McMillan."

Lani gave him a polite smile and dipped her head before entering. The hosts, prominent members of society, had spared no expense in celebrating their renewed love for each other in the most public way possible. A large crystal chandelier dominated the expansive foyer. Below it, water gurgled from a fountain.

To both her left and right were smaller reception areas, each lit by their own rows of mini chandeliers. Music from a string quartet drifted from the distance, and it was what helped Lani decide which direction to go.

An abstract ice sculpture stood as a centerpiece, hinting at two figures embracing. Lani's lips curved into a bittersweet smile. When the couple had arrived at her office all those months ago, they could barely tolerate sitting next to each other, with nothing but betrayal and hurt wedged between them. They had come a long way, and it made her happy to have had a hand in that as their relationship counselor. Since the accident three years past, she had dedicated herself to helping people find second chances, something she herself had never gotten. Death was the cruelest Mistress of them all.

"Champagne, Ms.?"

Lani tore her gaze away from the sculpture to flash the waitstaff a small smile and took the glass in hand. Most other guests were already in masks, enjoying the additional air of mystique the costume pieces provided. As she sipped her bubbles, savoring the sweetness, she scanned the room then stopped as she beheld a particularly delicious specimen. He wasn't towering tall, perhaps half a head or so more than her and her four-inch heels. Powerful muscles strained against the black suit he wore. Although the plain staff mask covered a part of his face, it only brought out his square jaw and chiseled features further. With dirty blond hair spiked up and faded down on the sides and back, he could almost pass as a male model.

Their eyes met, her hazel to his steel gray, and Lani inhaled. Something sparked between them, and though he dressed like any other security staff at the party, Lani knew she would have no problem picking him out of a crowd anywhere. He held her gaze, neither of them willing to look away first until he reached for the wire and earbud in his right ear. With a polite nod of acknowledgment toward her, he moved aside. Duty called.

Lani suppressed the urge to seek him out so that she could twine his tie around her fingers and pull him close. She shook her head. *If only this was that type of party instead.*

"Oh my, is that you, Lani?"

She turned to the older woman, readying her professional smile. "Diane," she greeted and accepted the hug that followed. Another one of her clients. This social circle had made her business very lucrative over the years and funded the move to the new office she adored, not to mention her growing shoe collection.

Soon, she had amassed a small group of men and women around her.

"Ladies and gentlemen, if you will, the ceremony is about to begin." Another staff member ushered them deeper inside the house, where they had set up the hall similar to a more traditional wedding venue. Lani had to admire the bouquets of flowers that lined the aisle. Although lavish decorations adorned the room, nothing was over the top. If she had to design her wedding, though, she would have it more subdued, smaller. That chance, however, had long passed. Commitment was not for her anymore.

The couple exchanged their vows with beautiful heartfelt speeches, and soon all the staff herded the guests upstairs once more to another banquet hall. Out of the corner of her eye, Lani glimpsed that same security guard from before. When he stayed within her field of vision, she realized with a start that he was hovering.

Seated with the same group she had been speaking with at the reception, Lani made polite conversation but, to be frank, she was growing tired. From the beginning, she'd had no illusion that this was anything but a work function, an opportunity to network. These people with their yachts and mansions were not her kind. She worked for a living, for one thing. Still, what she wanted was to curl up at home with a mug of tea and process the melancholy mounting within her, to stare at the photos of the last man she'd ever seen a future with—a man who had passed away three years before.

Perhaps coming here was a mistake.

At least dinner was delectable. From the appetizer of crab and shrimp cakes molded into heart shapes to the aromatic lobster bisque then to the main course of miso-based black cod, the seafood option she chose took her on a journey of oral delight. Then there was the chocolate mousse… Lani had to refrain from retrieving her phone so that she could take photos. Her close friend, Luna, would have wanted pictures.

Soon, dinner gave way to more festivities as the doors opened to a dance hall with a band set up on stage. Lani's eyes lit up before she remembered she had brought no date with her. Had she known, she might have cajoled Darryl or Jacob to come with her. A small sigh of regret escaped her lips as the music began.

Others at her table had already excused themselves to join the growing company of dancers on the floor as the band struck up their first song, a stately number. Left alone with her thoughts, she cast a longing glance at the door.

"Lani!"

Great. With another smile plastered on her face, she rose from her seat to find the hosts approaching. She allowed Sharon to pull her into a hug.

"Oh, don't you look fabulous!"

Lani smiled. "Thank you. Nothing compared to you, though. Just like a beautiful blushing bride."

"Isn't she?" Eric wrapped an arm around his wife and pulled her to him. "We're glad you could make it tonight."

"Of course. I'm so happy for you both." Lani wasn't sure if it was a shot of envy that twisted her gut.

"We wouldn't be here without you. Thank you."

Pride came with swiftness to replace that envy — pride in her work, pride in having been able to help.

"I may have guided, but you two put in all the effort."

The couple turned and beamed at each other before another woman approached Eric. It was the perfect opportunity. Lani smiled and inclined her head. "If you'll excuse me." With the soft murmur, she made a quick escape.

Five steps. That was as far as she got.

"Leaving already?"

The deep baritone came from her left, and she spun on her heels to face its owner full on.

He kept a respectful distance, but up close, his gaze held an intensity much more than the one they had shared earlier across the crowd. The impulse to pull him to her, to fist his hair this time, returned, and she had to clamp down on her dominant instincts. This was not the place for the Domme in her to come out and play.

"Perhaps," she replied instead, accompanied by an enigmatic smile.

He stepped closer, and she quirked a brow in response. This one was bold. She liked it.

"A dance before you go?" He offered her a calloused palm. As far as pick-up lines went, he lacked sophistication, and Lani wondered if it was something that the man may not be used to. Still, she had been lamenting the lack of a partner earlier.

"Sure, why not?" She gifted him with a brilliant smile, placed her hand in his and allowed him to lead her to the floor.

It was the kind of dance that had him place his hand on the small of her back, and for her to put hers on his shoulder. They held each other's gaze, neither willing to back down again, as if resuming their earlier interrupted contest of wills. Lani registered the subtle tension in the muscles rippling under the suit.

"So, how much time have you bought yourself, sneaking off duty?" She could not help but tease. He seemed so very serious.

A slight rise and fall of shoulders. "My shift for the night ended fifteen minutes ago. If they need me, they'll call."

"I see. And yet you're still here." Lani found her smile growing wider.

"So are you, despite not being in the mood."

At that, she raised a brow in question but allowed the silence to stretch on.

Her mysterious partner sighed before turning them around in a spin in time to the music. He was a skilled dancer and led well enough. Lani had not expected that for a man of his size and demeanor. And that she let him lead at all was a bit of a miracle in itself.

"You smile and play their games, but there's something you're sad about...like you're in mourning."

Her heart skipped a beat, but neither her steps nor her smile faltered. Instead, she followed his lead, allowing him to twirl her again. Only when he caught her in his arms once more did she give a small laugh in response. "Very perceptive, Mr....?"

"Nathan." He nodded at her praise. "It's my business to be."

"I see."

"If I may, since both of us have a lack of reason to stay, would you like to get out of here?"

Lani thought she heard a tinge of hope in his tone, but the desire she saw smoldering in his eyes overshadowed any hints of it.

Bold indeed. But the prospect of spending the night sulking alone did seem rather bleak. Lani knew what Nathan was offering and found it to be palatable — maybe beyond just palatable. It had been a while since she had scratched that itch, even if it wasn't to play as a Domme. Besides, she was curious about all those lovely warm curves she felt beneath his suit.

"Mm-m, I believe I can be persuaded."

"This way then," he whispered in her ear, then stepped back to lead her out of the party into the darkening night.

Chapter Two

When they entered the car, Nathan ripped the mask off his face. Beside him, the beauty remained sitting, poised yet relaxed. He knew she was gorgeous beneath that delicate thing of lace and beads, but something about that serene confidence she exuded drew him to her like a moth to flame.

"Where to?" He failed to keep the huskiness out of his voice and cursed himself for being so transparent.

"Your place should be fine." Her answer came with the swiftness of certainty, though it no longer surprised him. She struck him as the type who knew what she wanted. No playing coy. And it was sexy as hell.

He nodded once more and straightened as they pulled out of the parking lot. Her gaze was on him, heating his skin as she studied him. Nathan was well aware that many women found him attractive, although he did not understand why. Some days, despite the years away from the army, he felt like just another clone, a poster child of how a military man should look. Still, he hoped that what she saw now was pleasing enough.

Silence filled the car, but it was a relief to Nathan that she wasn't a chatterbox. Not one for much conversation himself, he focused on the driving, taking the most efficient route possible. At every stoplight, he stole glances at her and hardened at the thought of the night they had ahead of them. *Christ, what is it about this woman?*

As he pulled into the underground garage of a downtown luxury apartment building, he caught her turning to look out of the window from the corner of his eye. Mild surprise registered in her features, and he had to suppress a smirk, glad to have impressed her.

He led the way from the car up to the modest eighth floor he lived on. As the minority partner of the security firm, he managed to sustain some luxuries that made life comfortable, but not the more opulent lifestyle the other two owners of the business enjoyed.

When they entered his apartment, she hummed in approval but did naught else.

"Would you like some wine? Or coffee?" He shrugged off his jacket and rolled his sleeves up, only to startle when she stepped up and placed a hand on his arm. Rarely did he meet anyone who could move with so much stealth, especially in stilettos.

"Let us not harbor any illusions that this is any more than what it is." Her voice was soft, and the echo of sadness etched in the curve of her lips made him hesitate, while a desire to protect, to wipe away the cause of such emotion rose within him.

Nathan shifted to remove her mask and cup her cheek with his large hand, almost covering one side of her face. With his view of her unhindered now, part of him wondered at her delicate feminine features and at the way his rough calloused hand had to struggle to remain gentle against her smooth skin. "And what is this?" It came out as a hoarse whisper.

She smiled at him, a smile of both fondness and abolishment that told him he should know better than to ask. Without another word, she leaned in to brush her lips against his. *So soft.*

A low growl rumbled in his chest, and he pressed closer to deepen the kiss. Nathan shifted his body to turn toward her in full, sliding his hand down from her cheek to cup the graceful curve of her neck, stroking along the contours until he came to rest against her pulse, fluttering beneath his thumb.

Her hands did not remain idle as she raised them to undo the buttons of his shirt, popping each one open with deft skills while never breaking the kiss. When she parted her lips and tasted him with a small flick of her tongue, he moaned and slid his hand to the back, where he found what kept her dress together.

It became a race to see who could get whose clothing off faster. She won the first round, sliding his shirt off until it forced him to withdraw his hands from her so he could shrug it off. His toned muscles must have distracted her enough that he managed to undo her zipper next, peeling the garment off her. As the black number pooled at her feet, he groaned and broke the kiss so that he could feast visually on the wondrous body encased in a matching dark lace bra and thong. This woman oozed sex appeal, and his cock twitched inside his slacks.

She did not shrink at his scrutiny. Rather, she watched him in return with knowing eyes while she unbuttoned and unzipped his pants, taking advantage of his stunned state. His cock sprang free as she tugged at his waistband — he had gone commando today — and he sucked in a breath as she traced her forefinger along the outline of his shaft.

Her gaze never left his as she leaned in. In her tall heels, there was almost no need for her to raise herself as she brushed her lips by the tip of his ear. He shivered as she found one of his sensitive spots. Up close, the scent of her arousal was intoxicating.

"Enjoying the view?" The whispered words slipped past every single bit of control he had and he groaned again, this time with a nod as he took advantage of her closeness to unsnap her bra from behind. He slid the piece of lace down, his hands trembling with excitement as if he had never done such a thing. Once he freed her breasts from their confines, he cupped them both, one in each hand, and kneaded them with delight. He grinned like a kid in a candy store at her first moan and, wanting to hear more, he lowered his head to wrap his lips around the left nipple to suck and tease.

As she threaded her fingers through his short hair to hold him closer to her breast, he spun them until he could press her against the kitchen counter. It made her arch farther backward, and he slid his hand down to the small of her back, caressing there as he switched to the other side with his lips. Her moans filling the air were music to his ears, and he grew even more ravenous to sample her.

She must have had similar thoughts as she pressed her hands against his shoulders, pushing with insistence for him to lower himself. He licked and nibbled his way down until he kneeled before her. Skipping her center to tease, he caressed her foot, still in those sexy heels, and trailed his fingers along her calves, admiring the taut muscles leading to softer thighs. Something about being on his knees before her made his cock throb with eagerness but he never rushed his own pleasure to leave a partner unsatisfied, and he was damn sure he wouldn't start now. Parting her legs, he nipped and kissed a path up toward the lace-clad prize he had hoped for all night.

"Yes, that's it," she whispered in encouragement, stroking his hair with a sigh of contentment. She seemed in no rush either, and he took enjoyment from a woman experienced enough to know that anticipation made fulfillment later all the sweeter.

When he reached the apex of her thighs, he couldn't resist any longer and stuck his tongue out to press the fabric against her slit, pressing inward. She trembled in return, and he held her by her hips, steadying her.

"So beautiful," he groaned, the words muffled by his reluctance to pull away again. As she leaned back against the counter, bracing her hands against the surface, he nudged the strip of cloth off to one side to get a better taste of her bare flesh. He lapped at her dripping nectar, sweet against his tongue, over and over until she cried out with want, pulling his hair.

The thong, so seductive before, was now annoying him. In a gesture of impatience, he yanked it down and resumed his pleasure, thrusting his tongue into her in three quick strokes before withdrawing to circle her clit. He repeated the pattern as he hooked one of her legs and settled it on his shoulder to gain better access. Nathan needed more of her.

When she braced herself against him, moving a hand to cup the back of his head, he parted her folds with his fingers. Her body tensed, and he changed tack, pushing a digit then a second into her as he prodded her stiffening nub with his tongue. He traced every line of tension up to her face with his gaze, watching her eyes close, her lips parted in gasps of pleasure. Every little sound urged him on, made his movements more aggressive. He crooked his fingers to find the spongy patch that was her G-spot and rubbed and pushed against it until she buckled in climax, pulling him in even closer.

He kept up, letting her ride out her orgasm until her hold on him loosened. When he eased back on his haunches at last, his face glistening with her juice and a Cheshire cat grin tugged his mouth upward.

"Oh my." She opened her eyes and looked down at the sight he apparently made. While he continued to trace idle figures across her hips, she stroked his hair, relinquishing that seemingly almost-painful control over him. Breathless, she smiled and reached down to wipe his chin with her thumb.

Mesmerized by the sexual haze that clouded her hazel eyes, Nathan remained kneeling until she held his shoulders, exerting a gentle pressure to pull him up. He shook his head a little, as if to shake off the hold she seemed to have on him and cupped her face once more.

"I need—"

She kissed him, cutting off his words before leaning back. "Show me your bedroom."

He swallowed hard and nodded, offering her a hand. She placed her smaller one in his and stepped out of the puddle of clothes onto the ground, her heels now making clacking noises across the hardwood floor. With every step, his cock seemed to harden to the point of becoming almost painful.

His bedroom, similar to the rest of his apartment, was sparse in decoration. A brief fantasy flitted through his mind, and he wondered what touches a woman like her would bring if she lived here with him. He shook his head, discarding the ridiculous idle thought.

Still holding her hand, he sat down on the edge of the bed, pulling her close to stand between his legs. He busied himself tracing her curves, from the small of her back down to the rear where he kneaded her buttocks. Guilty of being an ass man, he found hers to be a most wonderful shapely one.

"My turn."

He groaned when she sank to her knees, taking his pants all the way down with her while he obliged by lifting his hips to help. With a teasing smile, she licked the head of his cock with the flat of her tongue then traced along the shaft with its tip. Nathan gripped the sheets, and he struggled to not thrust upward. "Fuck."

"Language," she teased and reached to take his balls, squeezing just hard enough as a warning without actually hurting him. A shudder ran through his body, then he buckled as her warm mouth enveloped his cock.

Rather than more swearing, he let out a deep breath, and for the next few minutes, he focused on trying to keep still, even as she hollowed her cheeks and bobbed her head up and down his shaft. He reached behind her and freed her hair from its loose bun, just so he could watch the cascade of red curls fall around her as she sucked him with the most skillful mouth he'd ever had the pleasure of being in. Fuck, he would not last long at this rate.

As if sensing his closeness, she withdrew and swirled her tongue once more, moaning on purpose so that the sound vibrated around his sensitive flesh. It was not yet enough to push him over the edge but it was damn close, and he let out a deep groan, sure she was teasing him as she leaned back to stroke along his shaft with too-gentle touches.

Where had this sex goddess been all his life? No, she'd made it clear what this was. Could he tempt her to stay?

All he could do, however, was moan in agony blended with ecstasy as she lifted herself up once more, keeping the teasing contact with just her fingertips. Unable to hold back, he pulled her close, burying his face against her soft stomach, dotting kisses across and lowering until she pushed his shoulders backward.

"Condom."

He startled as she took a step away. "Right." His glance fell on the bedside table, and he reached over to pull one out of the drawer. Before he could rip the package, she snatched it from him and did it herself.

Her gaze held his, studying his expression with an intensity he did not expect as she rolled the condom onto his cock, inch by agonizing inch. He surged forward and caught her lips once more in a searing kiss, swallowing her gasp.

They parted and, without another word, she moved to straddle him, lowering herself. He cupped her rear once more, supporting her descent as she let out a soft sigh of satisfaction.

"Ride me." His voice was husky with need as he rolled his hips. She clenched around his cock, squeezing him as she sank all the way — tight and wet. Nathan struggled to keep his mind clear enough to give her what she deserved.

"Patience, darling," she whispered in his ear as she settled against him. As if to emphasize her caution, she traced the ridge of it, then down along his jaw. When she reached his neck, she nipped and sucked, and when he groaned in protest, she rolled her hips against him.

"Ride me," he insisted again through clenched teeth. If she thought he would beg for it, she had another think coming. Two could play at this game. He parted his knees farther to spread her wider, and he tucked his hand in between them, crowing on the inside in triumph as he found her clit with his thumb.

Her eyes flew open, and her mouth forming a small O in surprise. He had her now. He rubbed the swollen nub. But she held still, to his growing frustration, although she spasmed within. *Fuck. Stubborn woman.* She was close. He could sense it…

"Move." After a moment, he relented. "Please." He was just being polite.

It seemed to be what she was looking for. With a long, drawn-out moan, she lifted herself, using his shoulders for balance and purchase, then slid down again. Soon, they'd established a rhythm, moving as one as they pushed each other to mutual release, with Nathan determined to hold back until she found hers. In a desperate attempt, knowing he wouldn't last much longer, he moved his head in, grinding and capturing a nipple with his lips, sucking hard. She arched and dug her nails into his flesh as she shuddered in a glorious orgasm.

Almost with relief, he released himself with one strong thrust while keeping his arm wrapped around her, pouring his seed into the condom. A growl rumbled from his throat before he slumped forward. She leaned against him, languid as she buried her face in the crook of his neck. He nuzzled her, caressing her back in soothing touches.

"Stay with me tonight," he whispered in her ear, although he could not see her expression. There was a moment of hesitation as she lay against him, her shoulders rising and falling, but when the nod of assent came, he curved his lips into a smile he did not understand.

Chapter Three

His gentleness surprised her. Used to administering aftercare as a Dominant, Lani had to admit that she enjoyed being pampered during their time in the shower together. And when they retreated to the bed, she did not resist as he pulled her in for a cuddle, even though he was rather affectionate for a one-night stand. More than once, however, he had tried to steer the conversation to more personal questions. Still, Lani evaded them all. She wanted no attachments.

But long after he fell asleep, she remained awake, questioning what she was doing in this bed. It was not her policy to stay. Perhaps this was just scratching an itch, a biological imperative she was subconsciously following. Lani's gaze landed on Nathan, watching the way his chest fell and rose in repose before she eased his thick, heavy arm away from her. A breath of air escaped her lips as she succeeded in the maneuver without waking him, and she pushed herself to sit up, giving up on her quest for the elusive creature that was sleep.

Before retiring for the night, she had retrieved her phone, and now, on a whim, she grabbed it from the bedside table. Surprised by the notification that lit her screen, she sat up straighter.

Still awake?

Her friend, Jacob, was messaging at this hour? Lani frowned, recalling the day before when she'd had lunch with his sub, Luna, and how she had run out with tears trailing down her face. *Crap.* She should have texted Jacob right away after that. But part of her had thought that whatever was happening, they had to work it out themselves without her playing the middleman all the time. It was the only way their relationship was going to grow stronger. Still, if either of them reached out, she would always answer, and this was no different.

Sort of. I am, but Nathan isn't.

Why did she mention her one-night stand? Lani berated herself in silence, but it was too late to take it back.

Okay, I'll stick to text. Luna came by.

Her stomach dropped.

You okay?

Yes. Something's not right.

What do you mean?

Given how late it was he was texting, 'something not right' was an understatement. But she needed more information.

Luna said Bryan offered her stability.

Lani almost bolted from the bed, her hands trembling suddenly. She bit her lower lip hard and typed back with furious speed.

What?!?!?!?

We need to figure out what's going on. Luna fed me some bullshit line about me jerking her around, and that's why she turned me down. If that was really it, she wouldn't have looked so damn happy when I first offered it. And this thing with Bryan is too coincidental. I'm not buying it.

Right, Jacob had grown a set of balls at last, enough to offer Luna a long-term contract. Lani had all the confidence in the world that he would have eventually, but she was still relieved that it had finally happened. Those two were meant for each other. What neither of them had expected, though, was that Luna would turn him down. And now to choose Bryan instead? The ex-Dom that Lani was certain had abused her one way or another? None of it made sense. Luna was loyal to Jacob to the bone.

Nothing added up.

Beside her, Nathan stirred, and Lani froze. He mumbled something unintelligible and slung an arm back across her hip. The gesture knocked the cell out of her hand and sent it spinning off the bed until it landed on the floor just out of reach with a dull thud. *Cripes, he's strong.*

Lani remained still, listening for signs of him falling into a deeper slumber. The light on her phone screen flickered, then darkened. When Nathan's breathing evened out once more, she moved his arm away again and slipped out of bed to pick up the device.

What did you say to her?

She typed then stood there, waiting for a reply. When none came, she let out a small sigh. Jacob needed her help right now. Her gaze wandered to the sleeping figure once more, moonlight spilling from the window to highlight the face that relaxed and softened in slumber. There was something there akin to vulnerability that called out to the Domme in her.

Lani shook her head. He was a complication she did not need. Decision made, she let herself out of the bedroom, careful to not wake him. She'd rather skip the awkward explanations and goodbyes.

In the kitchen, she gathered her clothes and slipped each piece back on with efficient and precise movements, opting to leave her hair down. She checked her phone again. There was still no word from Jacob, but now she brought up the app to call for a Lyft. That done, she swept her focus across the apartment one last time before she grabbed her purse and let herself out, closing the door behind her with as soft a touch as she could manage.

She walked down the hall with purposeful strides, her chin set high. This was no walk of shame. Lani had no regrets and no problem with one-night stands. As a sex-positive and pro-kink counselor, she understood all too well how conventional and traditional values often made women in particular feel guilty about casual sex.

Sometimes it wasn't easy to embrace one's sexuality and celebrate it for itself. *A shame.*

Home first and a change of clothes. Perhaps a few hours of sleep before she would barge her way into her friend's residence. Lani could picture in her head which drawer at home she had kept his spare key.

* * * *

By the time Lani jumped into the car and began the drive toward the apartment building, the sun was just rising above the horizon, spilling forth shades of orange across the concrete. As she zipped along the empty streets, well ahead of rush hour, her mind could not help but run over the events of the previous night. Despite trying to rein in her Domme instincts, the sex had been damn hot. And when he'd kneeled before her, everything in her had screamed to exert control. Even when she played with a trained submissive or helped another Dominant train, no one had quite intrigued her to this extent. *Too bad we met at a work function.* With a bemused smile, Lani wondered if he was a closet sub — or was he even aware of how he'd said 'please', so full of want but unwilling to take without permission?

That line of thought distracted her from the more pressing and much less pleasant one. Lani let out a small sigh as she made a turn onto a side street. Three years before, Luna had taken the leap to sign Jacob's standard limited-time contract, to commit to her training with him as a submissive. To this day, Lani never regretted the push she'd given her friend. She had learned then to never take the people around her for granted, that they could be there in one moment and gone the next. It was a hard lesson, one she was still paying for today herself and would do so for the rest of her life. And she didn't want Luna to make the same mistake. So what trouble had Luna gotten herself into now? Lani's forehead creased with worry.

Then she arrived.

Lani considered the buzzer, staring at it before shaking her head. To be honest, she wasn't sure if Jacob would let her in. Sometimes the man would shut out everyone and try to shoulder the world himself. She supposed that was the flaw of most Dominants. Lani perked up. So she would not give him a choice. That was why she'd brought the spare set of keys, anyway. She could already hear him call her 'pest', and despite the gravity of the situation, the anticipation of his reaction widened her smile.

With the keys in her hand, Lani breezed through the front lobby and headed up in the elevator. Purpose propelled her to the apartment unit, and, without a moment of hesitation, she fitted the key to the lock and opened the door.

It was quiet in there...almost too quiet. Lani wondered if Jacob was still asleep. Well, if he was, it was time to wake him up, as he should be by now for work.

"Hello?"

No answer. Tucking the keys in her tote bag, she set it down on the dining table. With a clacking of more sensible heels across the laminate floors, Lani lengthened her stride, taking her toward the rooms down the hall. *Ah-ha*. Artificial light spilled from under the crack of the closed office door.

"Jacob?" She pushed on the handle, eased it open and poked her head in.

He was a mess. Lani *tsked*, though the sound under her breath was inaudible. The man's eyes were red from lack of sleep, and his hair stuck every which way, like a rat's nest. It looked as if he had been pulling at it all night. He hadn't even dressed for work yet and was clad only in a pair of sweatpants. This was serious. She had never seen him this shaken, and it worried her all the more. With a small shake of her head, as if it would shed her own fears, she affected her calm, matter-of-fact demeanor.

"Have you slept at all?"

He groaned. A normal response. That was positive.

Stepping into the room, the whiteboard that hung on one wall drew Lani's attention right away. "Oh my," she exclaimed with a breathless gasp.

"What are you doing here, Lani?" he muttered.

She picked up the embarrassment in his voice but chose not to acknowledge it. The effect this was having on Jacob would have appalled Luna if she knew. But then again, that was why her friend had asked her to watch over him before she'd run out of the restaurant in a hurry, wasn't it? Some pieces of the puzzle fell into place.

Lani took a step toward the whiteboard to study it further. The thing looked like an evidence board out of some TV cop show. Information about Bryan and his various relationships filled the space. In one corner, someone had drawn a box around a winking smiley with the word 'Gotchya' scribbled beneath. Lani recognized Luna's handwriting. *Poor man.*

Let's fill in what blanks I can.

"I think you're not wrong."

She studied the myriad of emotions that flitted across his face, recognizing relief amidst the grimness. Then came the panic as realization dawned on him that being right meant Luna was in real trouble. *Well, now's not the time to spare the man his feelings.*

Lani grabbed a marker as she began adding her own notes. She chose each one with an abundance of caution. "Before Luna ran out on me at lunch yesterday, she was distraught. She asked me to take care of you, no matter what it took or what happens, and she was desperate for me to agree. That's the behavior of someone who cares, and from what you told me, inconsistent with the reasons she gave you for leaving."

The last bit of info added on the whiteboard, Lani capped the market, surveyed her handiwork then turned toward Jacob. "So if our wayward sub is truly in trouble, what do we do?"

A ghost of a smile graced Jacob's lips. *Good.* Now that he had a purpose, he would regain some of his confidence and Lani knew he would move heaven and earth to protect what was his.

"We dig. And I suggest we start at the club."

That made sense. Although Bryan had access to Luna in more ways than one, according to the board, the fetish club they both frequented would be the easiest place for them to gather more intel. The community was insular, and both of them had solid enough reputations to have some clout. She nodded, glanced at her watch and walked toward the door. "I'd better get to work. I have a client appointment in thirty minutes. I'll meet you at The Playgrounds tonight."

"Thanks, Lani."

Lani looked over her shoulder and gave him a small smile. "Of course."

Halfway down the hall, Jacob called out from behind. "Hey, who's Nathan?"

Damn it.

She composed her features into a more neutral expression, her shoulders rising and falling in a casual shrug. "No one, just someone I hooked up with last night."

"Lani…"

The worry in his voice was evident, and she sighed. "I'm fine. We've been over this. You have enough on your plate as is. Go get ready for work. I'll let myself out."

Behind her, he grumbled, and she chuckled to herself. Without waiting for a reply, she walked down the hall, grabbed her bag and left the apartment to begin her day.

Chapter Four

The dream was still roaring in his ear when he bolted upright on his bed, drenched in his own sweat. He turned his head this way and that until his waking mind sorted itself out. This was home, his home — not the battlefield, not the war.

With a groan, Nathan covered his face with one hand then ran it upward, threading through his hair. He dropped his other one to his side, the coolness of the sheets brushing against the calloused pads of his fingers. He frowned. Why did he expect it to be warm?

The woman! Memories of the evening before flooded his mind, replacing the immediacy of the dream. He searched across the room before he threw back the covers. Not bothering with such things as pants, he plodded out to the hall. Heavy steps echoed with thuds as he checked his apartment. Nothing. The only clothing that remained puddled in the kitchen was his. She had left without a goodbye.

Nathan cursed under his breath. He hadn't gotten her name. Unreasonable anger surged within him. It was bad enough that, according to his ex, he couldn't hold down a relationship to save his life. Now he couldn't even keep a woman in his bed for one night.

What the fuck was wrong with him?

"All you care about is your job. You haven't bothered to take a good, hard look at yourself, so how can I expect you to know me? To know us? I'm sick and tired of pretending everything's okay. I'm done."

Those had been Stacey's last words, spoken with more sadness than anger before she'd stalked off to bed. The next morning, he'd found her gone, along with ten years of marriage. Even switching jobs and getting therapy during their separation period has proven to be too little too late. He suspected she had long hooked up with someone else who could meet her expectations and desires. *Lesson learned.*

A lesson that still stung and he seemed doomed to repeat all over again.

His gaze fell on the mask lying with all the innocence in the world on the floor, tucked in the L-shaped corner between the cabinet and the counter. She had forgotten it there like some damn glass slipper. With a gentleness that contradicted his size, he stooped to bring it up, his fingers caressing the curves that had hugged her cheeks previously.

"It was a one-night stand, idiot. What did you expect?" Nathan shook his head and tossed the mask onto the counter without looking. He needed to stop mooning over her like a lovesick cow. This wasn't his first casual encounter—just perhaps the first he had asked to stay, interested in something more. They had explosive chemistry, he was sure. But maybe she didn't feel the same.

Oh well. No use dwelling. He shrugged, despite being alone in the apartment, as if to shake off the melancholy. He had an appointment today with a new client, and his partners had too much on their plates to deal with it, so they were sending him instead, no matter how bad he was at being the face of the company.

Shower then slacks, a clean crisp white shirt and a tailored suit… He gelled his hair back then checked his watch. There was enough time for a drop by a café to grab a quick bite for breakfast, but just barely, before the meeting. He thought that all club owners were night owls, but not this client. Nathan had to admit that the whole deal piqued his curiosity.

An hour later, he sat in his car outside the nondescript building where the warehouse district began. The occasional truck drove by with their early morning deliveries, but the one he was about to enter stood in quiet stillness. In the evening, when all else shut down, he didn't doubt the place would come alive.

Nathan left his car and locked it with a quick press of a button. The sound echoed in the empty parking lot, but he paid it no heed. Straightening his suit, he entered the premises. It was brighter than he imagined, past the check-in and coat-check areas. Spotlights illuminated what he presumed to be the usually darker dance floor, lounge and bar. His steps rang across the cavernous place.

A set of heels clicked behind him. Nathan turned around to behold the sight of a tall woman. Dressed in a tailored suit of her own, she dipped her head in a cordial greeting. "Mr. Pelletier?"

"Yes, Nathan is fine." He extended his hand toward her.

"Dominique." She extended a slender hand to take his, and they shook. Nathan sorted the facts in his mind. Dominique was one of the two owners of the only fetish club in town, known as The Playgrounds. According to Wilson, she deferred to the other owner often.

"Please, this way."

He followed the woman across the room and up two flights of stairs. Brief glimpses as they passed the second level aroused his interest, but he knew he would get to know the space, eventually. *Part of the job.*

Down the hall lined with closed doors and moments later, Dominique knocked on the last one.

"Come in." The voice pitched a little lower than he'd expected but was cultured, with a hint of a lilt.

Nathan followed once more, surprised by the sight of the tiny blonde who rose with elegance to greet him, her hand extended. This time, he was the one who took it and shook.

"Erica."

"Nathan."

The woman sat back behind the large desk, and like a well-choreographed dance, Dominique moved to another chair, which was already placed in a corner.

"Please, have a seat." Erica gestured toward the one opposite to her. Nathan had the fleeting impression that they were examining him as he eased into the posh Herman Miller. Regardless, there was an undercurrent of something going on, a display of power, perhaps, though he couldn't put a finger on exactly what yet.

"Thank you for sending the contract ahead. We've reviewed all the materials and would like to go over a few points."

For the better part of the next hour, both women demonstrated how sharp their minds were with shrewd questions that ranged from details on services offered and to their operations and personnel involved in each area. By the end, even Nathan's mind flagged, and gratitude welled in him for the mental fortitude his military training had afforded him to have lasted this long.

"Thank you for your forthcoming answers. I believe that is all the questions we have." Erica spoke with briskness as she gave a brief glance toward Dominique, who remained silent. She turned her attention back to Nathan. "If you would?"

He pulled out the folder that held the stack of documents that detailed the contractual terms from his bag. Since they had already proven to have read every line, he flipped it to the areas highlighted for their signature on both copies. His face remained expressionless, but inside, he breathed a sigh of relief as they each graced the papers with their John Hancock's.

"Welcome aboard." Erica swept one elegant hand over her desk, her palm up.

"Thank you, ma'am." The response was second nature to him, but he couldn't quite figure out why Erica lifted a brow with a spark of interest in her eyes.

Before Nathan could ponder much more on her reaction, Erica nodded at Dominique, who held another file folder toward him.

"As requested by your colleagues, I have prepared the schematics of our current security system and our up-to-date members list, including probationary members."

Right. While The Playgrounds was an open club, only registered guests could use the second and third floor facilities, though the visitors might observe. The only way a non-member was allowed to use those facilities was if another full-fledged one invited them as a play partner. Nathan accepted the papers and flipped through the pages for a quick review to ensure everything they had requested was there.

It was a world consisting of structure and rules that puzzled and fascinated him. Although Wilson and Daniel had insisted that this was just another job, another client, Nathan could not help but wonder if they had somehow bitten off more than they could chew. During his time on the force, he had learned that to protect, he must understand not only the setting but the game and the players themselves. And right now, none of them knew enough.

He skimmed down the names that made up the members' list. One name stood out and his brows knitted as he tried to figure out where he had seen it before. The ghost of a memory teased the edge of his consciousness, but his mind refuses to produce an answer.

"We trust that your firm will handle this information with the utmost confidentiality?" Erica's voice cut through his thoughts, and he snapped his head up from the papers to see both women studying him.

"Of course, ma'am." If Wilson were here, this would be where he'd flash her one of his reassuring smiles. But he wasn't his partner, so Nathan only bowed his head again, though one last thing… "Would it be possible to get a quick tour of the place before I go?"

Dominique looked toward Erica, her head tilted in inquiry. When Erica nodded her approval, the taller woman rose from her chair. "I'd be happy to show you around. Please, come this way."

It wasn't until they had both left the room with Dominique closing the door behind her that she spoke again. "Back here is where the offices are." She gestured to each closed-off room then strode with purpose toward one in particular. "This is what we consider our security office."

When Nathan placed his hand on the handle, Dominique nodded. He pushed the door open, enough to take in the sight. Screens of camera feeds around The Playgrounds covered the opposite wall. There were other various pieces of equipment lying around, set up by the previous company, and he made a note to ensure that their tech guys would come in to do a more detailed inventory. Although the room was small, it would make a decent command center when needed.

"Thank you." And he meant it.

She gave him a brief smile and continued with the tour. "Down here are the private rooms for members and their guests. Each has a security feed that they can choose to keep on both video and audio, on audio only or turn off completely." They strolled down the hall at a casual pace. Nathan's fingers itched to open a door, but professionalism stayed his hand.

They made their way down the stairs, pausing on the second level. Unlike what they just visited, this entire floor was laid open in one big, open space, set up like a gym—a very perverse gym.

"Our public dungeon. Many of our patrons enjoy a bit of exhibitionism, and it gives those who are curious a chance to observe."

Again, he found Dominique studying him and cleared his throat when he felt a flush creeping up from beneath his collar. What was up with him?

"I think it may be beneficial for you and some of your staff to come back one evening when the place is in full operation. It would be best to acclimatize early on to the variety of activities that go on around here." For the first time, a wry smile graced the Amazon's lips and Nathan had to return with a sheepish grin.

"That is some excellent advice. I will speak with the team about it once we review the information you've given us."

They made their way down to the bottom level, and Dominique pointed out each of the areas more akin to the usual night club. What was of particular interest was the lounge.

"When we first set it up, we had intended it to be for people to just relax and mingle. We can also turn the dance floor into an open stage and the lounge into audience seating space. But informally, members available for play started using it as a waiting place. Submissives gather and sit here to show they are seeking a partner."

Nathan blinked, trying to process. Research from previous nights had bolstered his knowledge, but since he was so new to the concepts, it still took him moments to put meaning to the words. He needed more intel.

"Dominique, I noticed you seemed deferential toward Erica…?" Nathan left the sentence hanging, then realized how blunt he'd sounded. It was a flaw of his — or so Daniel and Wilson told him.

For the first time, Dominique laughed. It was not an unpleasant one, amusement lighting up the serious face. "Ah, very observant of you, Nathan, especially for someone not of the lifestyle. Yes, Erica and I are business partners, but she is also my Domme." She gave a small shrug, although her expression softened with fondness at the mention of her partner. "It's common knowledge here."

"I see." Nathan filed the information away in his head.

With a lingering smile, she gestured across the floor. "It may not be conventional, but this place? It's our baby and our home. Help us keep it safe, Nathan."

That he could understand, and he nodded with firm resolve. "We will."

Chapter Five

Lani tapped her pen against the file she was studying, poring over the details of another client who had contacted her office for her services. The backlog of requests seemed never-ending, and she rubbed her forehead with a sigh of weariness. She wanted to help them all, but not everyone was a fit, and she was a one-counselor show, even with an assistant. Each case took a good chunk of time to assess and research before she could deem whether she could actually do much for them.

Take this one, for example. With a history of mild PTSD, depression and anxiety, he should see a therapist or a psychologist rather than the counselor she was. But he had provided references from previous practitioners she recognized. The few phone calls had verified that his care providers thought he had progressed enough to move to a lighter approach to tackle more specific areas.

Joseph Pelletier — war veteran, ex-cop, divorced. He'd stated in the questionnaire that she had all potential clients fill in that he wanted to focus on understanding himself to improve future relationships. Most guys, especially ones who fit his profile, lacked such self-awareness — or at least were reluctant to admit such vulnerability upfront. The fact that he did so intrigued her.

An initial meeting wouldn't hurt. Lani placed the folder in the 'will see' stack. Ophelia, her assistant, could tackle scheduling this bunch tomorrow.

Quitting time. Lani pushed herself back from the desk and stretched with a yawn. The last few nights have been exhausting, dropping in The Playgrounds to help Jacob investigate when she could. Tonight, however, she was going to have some fun instead.

Her lips curved into a smug smile.

Hours later, Lani strolled into the club, clad in a black corset with flourishes that showed off red lining beneath, a pair of matching panties, garter and stockings ending in seven-inch platform heels. A casual wave came from a fellow Dominant, polite bobs of heads from some subs who recognized her. From one corner, a familiar figure waved.

"Declan lovely, how are you?" They exchanged hugs and a light kiss on each other's cheeks.

"Lani, good to see you."

Blond-haired, blue-eyed Declan was a Dom who was a few years younger than her and Jacob and also a regular of The Playgrounds. Unlike the more stoic security guard she had fucked the other night, he was all smiles and charm.

Wait! Why am I still thinking of him?

Filing that thought away for further examination later, Lani turned toward the collared sub beside him. "And this sweet thing?"

The girl gave her a small smile and looked up before casting her eyes downward. "I'm Tara, Ma'am."

Lani reached out and with one forefinger and tipped the sub's chin up to her. "Ah, no need to be shy, sweetie."

Tara blushed, highlighting the smattering of freckles across her cheeks.

"Oh, Declan, I can see why you just had to claim this one. She's adorable."

At her compliment, Declan glowed with pride, but when he turned back to Tara, his entire demeanor softened. Lani kept a squeal from escaping, seeing how smitten her friend and student was. And by the way Tara met his eyes with adoration, Lani was certain she felt the same.

In the end, Declan tore his gaze away while Lani waited with all the patience in the world. He rubbed the back of his head, a sheepish grin to show that he was aware what that smirk on Lani's face meant.

"Well, shall we get started?" Lani offered the gracious save.

"Yes." Declan straightened at that while Tara stiffened beside him. He turned to his sub, one hand on the small of her back. "You okay, kitten?"

Tara gave a shaky nod. "Just a little nervous."

Lani smiled at that. "There's no need to be. Position training is not difficult, and we'll take into account what your body's limits are." She began to walk, leading them toward the third floor where she had already booked them a private room. "Always keep in mind that Declan and I want you to succeed."

"Remember, like we discussed. This is the reason I asked Lani to help. She's the best around these parts at this."

She glanced back to see Tara breathe out her tension. *Good girl.*

The room's theme was red, but it was a subdued, deep tone that spoke of opulent luxury rather than garish incitement. Dark mahogany planks covered the room while a strip of velvet cushions lined the walls at waist level. Various pieces of equipment hung on the wall, but Lani paid them no heed. Instead, she strode with purpose toward the electronic panel next to the door.

"Declan, clear the floor and bring a pillow over to the center."

She heard the shuffling of furniture as the dear boy jumped to the task. With a soft hum beneath her breath, she studied the controls to ensure that both the audio and video feeds were on. It was nothing unexpected, as Declan and she had already discussed the logistics of this session.

"Now." Lani retrieved a riding crop from the wall and lifted a brow when a tremor coursed through Tara's body, even as the sub stood in the middle of the room. It confirmed that she was into a bit of pain, as Declan had mentioned before. *Interesting.* As Lani circled her while Declan parked himself off to one side to watch, she noticed Tara shifting her weight from one foot to another, her hands on her thighs, moving her thumbs back and forth.

"Stop fidgeting." Lani's voice held a sharper edge now, giving her inner Domme free rein.

Tara froze. Declan had already done a marvelous job with the girl.

"Now, I believe your Dom prefers to use hand signals to tell you what position he wants you in, so I will name each one. Let him show you the corresponding gesture, then I'll describe the pose. Understood?"

"Yes, Ma'am."

She nodded her satisfaction. "First, rest position."

Declan moved into view and held his hand out, palm flat downward.

"Rest position is the most basic one but one of the hardest to maintain for long periods of time. It does, however, get easier the more you practice." Lani gave Tara an encouraging smile. "From standing as you are now, lower yourself and focus on folding your body. Remember, part of this is cultivating grace. Kneel with your toes down, then lean back to sit on your feet. Keep them and your knees together. Hands should lay relaxed on your thighs." Lani repeated the hand signal and watched as Tara followed her instructions.

As a first attempt, it was not bad. Lani corrected subtle angles—elbows in, head tilted upward to look up. Once satisfied, she stepped back, letting the girl get used to holding the pose.

Declan moved closer and stroked his sub's hair. Lani's heart ached at the intimate gesture. She remembered doing the same when August had mastered the position. He had been so quick to do so, too. She cleared her throat. This was not the time for a trip down memory lane.

"Next is rest-display. The only difference is to part your knees and arch your back more." She nodded to Declan, who gave the signal, his palm still facing down but this time with his fingers spread wide.

They ran through two more poses, both standing, then practiced flowing from one to the other. For the untrained eye, Tara was executing each one well, but Lani was a perfectionist, and when the angle was incorrect or the transition did not happen in the right order, she would flick her wrist to issue small lashes with the riding crop. Pain was an excellent teacher. And by the end, when Tara started getting the hang of it for real, Declan began feeding her little pieces of chocolate fudge shaped like kitten paws as treats. The carrot and the stick. Each was just as important.

* * * *

On Dominique's advice and after much discussion with Wilson and Daniel, Nathan and Wilson had taken a skeleton crew to The Playgrounds that night to acclimatize the staff who would work this contract, cautioning and coaching them to not gawk like tourists.

Wilson had taken one of the more senior guards downstairs to circulate and observe, leaving himself and the two techies in the room. Much of what they were discussing was mumbo-jumbo to him, but he followed enough to understand that they were arguing about which upgrades they thought the system needed.

"Hey, let's focus on making what we have on hand work for us first, okay?" There was still a probationary period for them to get through, after all.

"Yes, boss."

Nathan had to chuckle at the sigh of resignation from Carla, but he hid it well by turning his attention to the panel of screens that were lined along one wall. Most rooms were empty this evening, and he contemplated sending the techs out next so they could get over their culture shock, too. At least patrons seemed to be using the public dungeon tonight, according to the set of cameras that monitored that area.

Movement flickered on the far-left screen, drawing his gaze. Three people had entered a private room. Were they going to have a threesome? Rule was no full penetration, though. But he supposed that there were plenty of other things they could still do within the confines of that rule. Curious, he remained glued to the feed.

Wait! There was something familiar about one of them. His heart pounded as his eyes widened. He watched as the woman in the ridiculously tall heels crossed the room, retrieving a riding crop. Dressed in a corset, panties, stockings and garter belt, she oozed sex and dominance. Dear sweet Jesus, it was her. His pants tightened.

All chatter faded from his mind as she spoke to the other two, a male and female, though Nathan paid them little heed. Instead, everything in him zeroed in on the goddess he had slept with the other night. He cursed the inferior quality of the security feed and had to agree with Carla that an upgrade was necessary. Then again, his brain had no problems filling in the details—her pouty lips, for instance. He remembered them on his own, then later around his cock, teasing him to an almost-painful hardness...like now. *Shit*.

When she touched the girl, just correcting her poses, Nathan realized she was instructing her. The one on her knees was clearly a submissive. The guy? Perhaps another Dom. And his one-night stand? There was no doubt that she was a Dominatrix. Wait! Was she a pro? Did she do this for a living?

Oh fuck. I slept with a Dominatrix.

"Hey, boss, what're you watching?"

The nearness of Jasper's voice jolted Nathan's spinning thoughts. *Shit, when did he creep up from behind?* The shorter guy peered over his shoulder, and Nathan resisted the urge to elbow him. He liked his personal space.

"Damn, that's hot.

The initial desire to nudge the tech away morphed into the appealing idea of hauling him by the collar and tossing him out altogether. Instead, Nathan growled, a low rumbling sound in his chest. "Jasper, this is a job. Stay professional or do I have to take you off this contract?"

Jasper swallowed hard. "No, boss. Sorry," he muttered and turned away from the camera to return to his seat.

Like Nathan had any right to talk. He was just fortunate that he stood close enough to the console that neither Jasper nor Carla could see the tenting in his pants.

On the screen, the redhead he knew was using the riding crop. Her strikes were light and brief, used for more correction on the poses than for inflicting pain or pleasure. Nathan wasn't sure if it was relief or disappointment that welled up in him over the fact that nothing sexual was going on.

And I'm chastising Jasper?

At that moment, the door opened, and Wilson walked in. The knots in his stomach loosened a smidgen.

"How is it out there?" He kept his voice steady by some miracle.

"Interesting." Wilson himself looked a little dazed. The older man with some graying at the temple and silver shot in his well-trimmed beard rubbed his face. "I think it may be best if we repeat this exercise and make sure all our staff go through it."

"Yeah, I agree." He glanced at the exit. "I'm going to grab some air."

"Okay."

No one paid him any attention as he escaped from the small, cramped room and down the halls. His wandering gaze strayed of its own volition toward the room he knew she was in, but he forced himself to move past it and down the stairs until he made his way to the bar.

"Hey, Nathan, right?" The bartender approached after a few minutes of him standing there, working on steadying his breathing.

It took a minute for him to recall his name. "Yeah, Darryl?"

"Good to meet you, man. Welcome to the team."

They shook hands.

"Can I get you anything?"

How he wished he could order a beer right now. No, he'd needed something stronger in his state.

"Water. On the job."

Darryl nodded and moved away to return moments later, sliding both a glass of water filled with ice and a bottle fresh from the fridge. "One for the road."

"Thanks." Nathan downed the drink, letting the cold liquid cool the fire stoked within him. He lingered, leaning against the bar, watching the club's members and patrons come and go. Down on the first floor, it was harder to pick out who the regulars were, but he picked up certain patterns of behaviors. Those familiar with the scene focused more on socializing and were more relaxed and casual with their postures, while those unfamiliar with the establishment gawked and giggled a lot more.

Rather than fixating on one area, he swept his view across the expanse of the club, making more mental notes.

"I need a guide," he mumbled to himself.

"Sorry, man. Wish I could help, but I'm too anchored here." Darryl followed his gaze out across The Playgrounds, but Nathan, distracted, didn't respond. Instead, he stiffened

She was there, sidling up to the bar on the other end.

Darryl must have seen her, too, as he moved away with an, "Excuse me."

Well, now what?

Chapter Six

"How did it go?" Darryl strolled over to her other side of the bar as Lani slid into one of the plush cushioned seats.

"Excellent." Lani eased back and crossed her legs in smug satisfaction.

"You look like a cat that just ate a canary."

Lani laced her fingers together and stretched her arms out. "All in a night's work. Declan chose well, and they are coming along nicely as a pair."

Darryl chuckled at that, taking the towel slung over his shoulders to wipe the surface down. Lani understood it was more of a habitual motion, geared to keep his hands busy. His bar was always sparkling clean.

"Funny how about a month ago, Tara was sitting at this spot drowning her sorrows when she hooked up with Declan. Guess you never know who you may meet or run into."

Lani raised her brow at that comment. She knew that both Darryl and Jacob, her closest friends, had been hinting at concerns over her.

"Well then, if it worked out for her, give me a lychee-tini."

"Lani, you know that's not what I meant." Darryl pursed his lips together.

"I know, I know." Lani waved a hand in the air. "You think someone's going to show up out of nowhere, make me fall hard and forget all about August." She rolled her eyes.

"No one wants you to forget about August. None of us have, Lani, but—"

"No, Darryl, I get that. I understand you guys are worried and that it is coming from a place of love, but everyone goes at their own pace, and I have mine. Besides..." She gazed downward, "we have more pressing matters. Have you picked up anything about Luna?"

"I may have a lead but not sure yet. I'd rather wait and see how Jacob wants to play it."

Lani nodded. It made sense.

"Hi." It was a familiar voice and coming from right behind her.

She spun around, her eyes widening as her entire body tensed. This was the very last place she'd expected to run into her one-night stand.

From the corner of her eye, she spied Darryl raising a brow in question. She shot him a quick glare, only for him to grin and mouth almost soundlessly, "Remember Tara."

Careful to not let Nathan glimpse her childish behavior, she stuck her tongue out at her friend, who then only laughed and walked away. Spinning back around, she mustered her most cordial smile possible. "Nathan, how are you?"

The man's face was not an expressive one, but Lani still picked up on the flicker of emotions that played across in the minute twitches of facial muscles, the way his brow furrowed ever so slightly, indecision warring in his eyes. She had thrown him off. *Excellent.* The last thing she needed right now was a confrontation.

She noted how he worked his throat before speaking. "Good. Busy night."

"Oh?" Lani allowed the silence between them to stretch on.

"Yeah." Nathan unscrewed the water bottle in his hand and took a heavy gulp. "I'm on duty tonight. Upstairs." Then he winced. "Security, I mean."

A shot of disappointment stabbed through her, and she struggled to keep surprise away from her face. Was she hoping he was working in some other capacity? That would be too good to be true. No, he was here because he was a member of the new security firm Erica had hired. She had heard about that but just didn't expect her most recent one-night stand to be part of the package

"You?"

The question surprised her, and she raised a brow. She could choose to take it as an insult, but she would hear more before she decided.

"Sorry," he mumbled, and looked away. Gone was the confidence from the other night, and Lani realized how completely out of his element he was. "Just, I saw, on the camera earlier..."

Laughter bubbled up, and she laid a hand on his arm, even as he flushed in embarrassment. She could see how someone with little experience in the scene could interpret what had happened. "Ah no, my dear boy. That was a favor for a friend. It's called position training."

"So you're a—"

"Domme, yes." She curved her lips upward in amusement.

Nathan swallowed again and Lani couldn't help but lean forward, closing the distance between them. "Is that a problem?"

"No, Ma'am." His answer came without missing a heartbeat. Their eyes met, so close that all it would take was one of them to close the inch of a distance for their lips to meet, each obviously unwilling to be the first to move aside. It seemed they were forever challenging each other in staring contests. Was he aware that he had called her using a title a sub would use for a Domme?

"I see you've met Lani here."

Well, so much for staying anonymous.

Nathan broke away to turn to Darryl as the bartender pushed a glass toward Lani. Her cranberry lychee liquor cocktail. God, she needed it. She only hoped that Darryl had gone more heavy-handed on the alcohol.

She wondered what Nathan was going to say.

"Yeah, we've met."

"Oh?" Darryl inclined his head in Lani's direction, only for her to return the expression with the most innocent smile she could muster.

"Brat," he muttered under his breath, but she caught what he'd said, regardless. It made her beam all the more.

Nathan must have heard the word, too, as he looked from Darryl to her and back again, furrowing his brows once more, as if working through another piece of the puzzle. The poor boy was like a fish out of water.

"Hey, if you're looking for a guide, Lani could help. She's been in the community for a long time and knows pretty much everyone at The Playgrounds."

Lani shot him a dirty glare. Darryl was trying to set her up...again. Little did he realize what had already transpired between them.

Nathan, however, looked at her with fresh interest. "I would appreciate if you could spare some time to show me around. I'm growing more familiar with the club physically, but I lack context to put accurate meaning to what I observe."

It was more words than she'd ever heard out of him. Lani studied Nathan in a new light. The intelligence, the self-awareness and the absence of ego made for a very attractive package for a sub, even if it came from a place of professionalism.

But she didn't have the time, and she couldn't afford the attachment that somehow, she knew in her gut, would form. Luna and Jacob were much more important right now, and this new complication was the last thing she needed.

So she was already shaking her head when her lips parted. "My services don't come cheap."

Why did I say that?

"I can speak with my partners about putting you on the payroll as the firm's consultant," Nathan offered.

Behind the bar, Darryl laughed. "I think she meant you'll owe her a favor. And her favors get pretty pricey in different ways."

Lani struggled to not blush herself. *Damn this man. Damn Darryl.* It was true, though, that she had no interest in another job. But why the hell did she hint that she might help?

Nathan considered for a moment before nodding. "That seems fair."

"Careful, man. An open favor like that…"

Lani was still staring into Nathan's steel-gray eyes, watching them darken. She had a retort for Darryl, but the words seemed to have fled her mind.

"She can ask me for anything in return." His gaze held hers once more.

Oh my.

The image of him kneeling before her the other night surfaced unbidden from her memories.

"Well then." Darryl grinned, then looked to the other end of the bar. "Ah, look, a customer." And with that, he moved away again.

Lani made a mental note to smack him later.

"I suppose we have a deal." Her voice had lowered to a hushed whisper, but as close as they were, he obviously had no problems hearing her — or perhaps he read lips.

"Yes."

Stillness hung between them once more, both of them oblivious to the busyness of the club. The tension was almost palpable, and a familiar thrill shot up Lani's spine. As a Domme, she recognized something in him, and she wanted to peel back all the layers and pretenses to see more of it.

But for now, she had to fulfill her side of the bargain.

Lani evened out her breathing. "Where do you want to start?"

It was enough to jolt him out of the trance he had put them under. He dropped his gaze and surveyed the sea of bodies beyond the bar instead.

"How would you read the dynamics here?" he asked.

Spinning her chair around, Lani allowed her eyes to wander from the lounge to the far corners before she shook her head. Friday nights were always busy, and tonight was no different.

"It's about a regular night. You've got your usual flood of tourists." She paused in her speech to nod at the dance floor. "They like to gravitate toward the dancing. It's something they're familiar with, at least until they get over the culture shock. A few of the braver ones will wander upstairs to gawk and giggle. Our dungeon monitors keep a close eye on those in case they become disruptive or disrespectful."

"By tourists, you mean those who are not in the lifestyle?"

Lani confirmed with a small noise. "We've been getting a lot more of that kind since those books came out. The movies brought even more of them in."

"Ah."

"What about those?" Nathan jerked his chin toward the lounge.

"Did someone explain to you that the bottoms like to go sit there to indicate they're looking for a play partner?"

"Yeah. Dominique mentioned that."

"Well, you can tell which ones those are by a few signs. They prefer to remain alone. Even in groups, they're preening more and they're always keeping a look out around, even when they are talking to each other."

Lani tilted her head back to watch Nathan study the lounge. "What about her? She doesn't have the posture of a submissive."

Her gaze traveled along the trajectory Nathan pointed out. *Ah. Cassie.* The man's powers of observation astounded her. *A fast learner.* Lani's lips curved upward. "Cassie's a switch. She's asking for play likely as a bottom tonight, but you're right, she can't quite hide her leanings toward dominance, either. It's an interesting challenge for any top."

"Doms...enjoy the challenge?" Now the question came at a slower pace, as he grew hesitant once more. The fluctuation threw her off, making it hard for her to gauge where his discomfort lay.

"Some. Not all Dominants are the same, and we all have different preferences in subs."

Another pause.

"And you?"

Lani laughed and reached up to pat his cheek. It was such a natural gesture to her, but the touch seemed to startle both of them such that her laugh faded in an instant. She shook her head as she attempted to recover the camaraderie building between them. "That's for me to know. Why? Interested?" The last she asked, quirking her lips in mischief, but inwardly she wondered at why she was being so flirty with someone she'd, minutes ago, had no desire to see again. Or that's what she had been telling herself.

There was a perceptible change as Nathan's eyes widened, but the rest of his face remained stoic as ever. "I'm...curious."

He left it at that. Was he wondering about the lifestyle on a personal level? About her? Lani bit her tongue to stop herself from asking further.

It was, however, time to experiment. Lani spun around to retrieve the glass of red liquid and held it up to her lips for a sip before speaking again.

"Well, dear boy, if you want to satisfy your curiosity, you may need to take the risk and jump down that rabbit hole."

"I see." Nathan's gaze flickered toward the stairs. "And would that be something like the position training that you were teaching earlier?"

Surprised by his answer once more, Lani inhaled and told herself the warmth she felt building in her belly had nothing to do with the man that, probably subconsciously, was dropping hints that he wanted to offer himself to her. "Oh no, it would be much more hands-on than that."

She noted the sharp intake of air and the heat that emanated from his body. Tempted as she was to lower her eyes and see if her words had aroused him, Lani kept her gaze above the waist. Ah, there was a flush creeping up from beneath his collar. *Excellent.* If he wanted to dance, she would push further.

"Let's take a little walk around, shall we?"

Nathan swallowed hard and Lani crowed in triumph. The night was becoming even more interesting than she had expected.

Chapter Seven

They climbed the stairs together, with him following her the entire time. It had been a long while since someone had positioned themselves behind her that way. Lani reminded herself that he was not a sub — but he sure acted like one, confusing her senses.

The dungeon was more active tonight than she had expected. Over half the stations were being used, and the sounds of moans and yelps mingling with murmurs and chatter filled the air. The two monitors had their hands full, circulating and trying to keep watch over any potential misconduct.

Behind her, Nathan coughed to clear his throat. When Lani spun around to face him, she noted the slight slack muscles in his expression and the glaze over his eyes. *Culture shock or subspace?* Lani placed a gentle hand on his elbow, her voice filled with concern. "You okay?"

Nathan shook his head. Lani studied him as he shrugged the daze off. *Impressive.* "Reading about the subject is nothing like being in the middle of it."

She chuckled and patted his arm. "You've been doing research, then."

"Yeah." He still sounded a little faint, his voice quiet. Lani leaned in closer to catch his words.

"I figured it wasn't a standard contract, and we needed as much intel as we could get beforehand." He exhaled in a slow sigh. "It's hard to differentiate between fact and fiction, though. For every helpful link, there seemed to be five others to porn sites, and I'm sure those are oh-so-realistic." His voice dripped with obvious sarcasm, even as a wry grin accompanied the twinkle in his eye.

It took Lani a second to catch on, but laughter spilled from her lips. This was the first time she'd experienced his humor, and she found she liked how his smile lit his face up and youthened him. It warmed her body a different way and eased the confusion that swirled inside. Her shoulders loosened and tension drained from her as she made a quick decision to focus on enjoying herself and the company at the moment.

"Have you been able to talk to the dungeon monitors yet?"

His forehead had now creased with a frown. "No, but it's on our list. We've been busy focusing on the equipment. Erica and Dominique hired us mainly for our tech set-up, and personnel are more on an event-basis."

Again, the Goddesses, as the owners of The Playgrounds had been nicknamed, showed their savviness. Contractors from a security firm wouldn't know what to look for during play unless they were in the lifestyle themselves. They could act as bouncers for entry, but not as dungeon monitors up here.

"You should touch base with them soon."

Before Nathan could reply, a scream nearby startled both of them. Next to her, his body tensed before he surged to motion. Lani tightened her hold on him in a firm grip, not that she had the strength to rein him back if he wanted to continue onward. Yet, it was enough. He came to a grinding halt, and both of them looked at the source of the shriek.

From the corner of her eye, Lani saw his face turn crimson when he realized the sound was not of pain or terror but rather of a woman in the throes of an intense orgasm. *Oh, the poor boy.* But this was too much fun to pass up, and she leaned in to whisper in his ear.

"I don't remember you being quite this red when you made me scream the same way the other night."

He let out a small groan and shifted his weight. Lani dropped her gaze and realized with delight that he was trying to hide the fact that he was adjusting himself. An absurd sense of self-satisfaction settled within her.

"You'll be the death of me," he muttered back.

"Darling, I've got moves you haven't even seen yet." She winked, flicking one finger under his chin. Though meant to be a teasing gesture, she paused when he captured her hand and held it to his chest.

"And will I get a chance to see them?" His eyes darkened, his voice thick with desire.

Lani should have known Nathan would ask sooner or later, but the question still caught her off guard. She raised a brow at him, letting the silence stretch on. When he said nothing more, she sighed.

"Nathan, I'm a Domme, and I'm not exactly relationship material at this point, either."

He shrugged. "Nor am I." He rubbed the back of his neck. His eyes flickered to the scenes unfolding behind her. "I'm not asking for commitment."

"Then what?" Until he could articulate what he was interested in, she would not make the first move. She was not in the habit of persuading someone unsure of the lifestyle to play.

He kept one hand wrapped around hers and placed his palm over her cheek. The tender gesture threw her off balance again, and she sucked in a breath to steady herself. What was it about this man that continued to shift the earth beneath her every time she thought she'd found her footing with him?

"Can we keep taking it as a casual thing? Just two consenting adults?"

Two consenting adults scratching a mutual itch. Her mind completed the sentence for him. "No strings attached."

He nodded in acknowledgment.

She frowned as she considered him and the proposal he'd laid before her. It was a more attractive offer than she expected. "I'm a Domme." It was important that he understood the implications.

Nathan parted his lips to speak, but Lani shook her head. He closed his mouth once more to listen.

"I'm a Domme," she repeated for the third time. "This means the things that turn me on have a power component to them. This may not be compatible with your likes."

It was Nathan's turn to shake his head. "I understand what you being a Domme means, and I would never ask you to change who you are." He lifted and dropped his shoulders again. "As for compatibility, we seemed to have done fine the other night — unless you disagree?"

Though still uncertain about how they would do even as play partners long-term, there was no doubt the attraction was there in abundance. "You sure you know what you're getting into?"

"No," Nathan replied. Again, his honesty was refreshing. "But I'm curious to find out."

She laughed under her breath and drew his hand from her cheek to hold his knuckles up to her lips, gazing up at him through her lashes. "Brave boy. Very well. We'll see how deep down this rabbit hole you want to go."

From the corner of her eye, she glimpsed a young man staring at the two of them, his hands in his pockets. When their eyes met, he darted his gaze away, his face red with embarrassment.

"I think someone's looking for you," Lani murmured.

Nathan threw a quick glance over his shoulder and groaned. "Jasper."

She withdrew her hand from his grasp and let go of him, albeit with some reluctance. "Give me your phone."

She punched in her number when he relinquished the device. "Text me when you're off. If I'm free, I'll send you a location and time."

With that said, she rose to place a light kiss on his cheek and sauntered off.

She found Jacob sitting at the bar, his face pale and drawn. Darryl's lips were tugged downward in a perpetual frown.

"What happened?"

Rather than answering, Jacob's tightened his grip on the glass in his hand, and he lifted it to down the contents. His gaze flickered toward Darryl, who gave a small nod.

"I just finished talking to Cassie. She's been playing with Bryan."

Lani checked to see Darryl's reaction. Sure enough, the grimace was there.

"She said he's obsessed with making Luna his. Had some plan to do it, too, according to Cassie."

The pleasant heat that had filled her from her encounter with Nathan evaporated at those words, replaced by a chill that seeped into her bones.

"Blackmail?" Lani whispered the word, voicing what was surely on all their minds. She hated laying out the possibility between the three of them, but it seemed to be the most plausible rationale for Luna's recent behavior.

"Yeah, but what does he have over her?" Darryl asked as he absent-mindedly wiped the bar down.

"I don't know, but I have a stack of Luna's writings describing her time with Bryan. I'll see if there's anything I can figure out from those." Jacob choked back the rest of his drink and stood. "I should head out."

Lani frowned. "You shouldn't be driving right now. Come on. I'll take you home and take a cab from your place to mine after."

It spoke to the other Dom's mental state that he agreed without a peep of protest. Clearly deep in thought, Jacob only replied with half-hearted attempts at answers to her entreaties for conversation, and at last, she gave up on trying to get his mind off Luna altogether. With a last admonishment to rest, she left his apartment.

In the darkness of a cab's backseat, she stared out toward the passing city lights, furrowing her brows with worry for her friends. Helplessness threatened to blossom into equal parts despair and frustration. For a Dominant, the lack of control was the worst feeling in the world and Lani racked her brain, trying to figure out what more she could do short of somehow tying Bryan down and whipping him senseless. Although her tastes did not run along the sadistic streak, a perverse pleasure at that thought caressed her spine.

God, she needed to blow off some steam as much as Jacob did.

Right on cue, her phone buzzed with a message from an unfamiliar number. She glanced down as the screen lit up.

It's Nathan. Are you still around?

She smiled at the words. So simple for a man, so layered.

I left. On my way home.

Would you be interested in meeting up tonight?

The grin continued to play over her lips. She did just admit to herself that she needed to blow off some steam.

I'll give you a choice. The Playgrounds or your place?

When she didn't get a reply right away, Lani had to resist the urge to cackle out loud. No sense in frightening the cab driver.

My place. If you'll stay the night this time for real.

Ah-ha. So he was a little sore about that. She had been wondering if and when it would come up.

I'll arrive at your place in thirty and we'll see. Maybe if you're a very good boy.

Oh, I can be good. Very good. I'll be waiting.

A message with his address and buzzer number followed the last one, and Lani allowed herself the luxury of admitting to the flush that was blossoming across her cheeks.

Exactly thirty minutes later, dressed down to a simple blouse and skinny jeans, paired with a more modest pair of heels, Lani stood in the elevator with a tote bag slung over her shoulders.

As soon as the doors opened, Nathan greeted her. Her eyes widened in surprise, but she quirked her lips upward as her gaze fell on the proffered arm. She linked his with hers, laying her hand on it, and without another word, he escorted her into his home.

The apartment was dim, and it took Lani a moment to locate the light source. Candlelight flickered from thick wax candles that stood on a cerulean ceramic plate. He had also placed other small tea lights in other strategic places. For a casual fling, Nathan was putting in an awful lot of effort. Her heart ached and her grip on his arm tightened. Long ago, there was someone else that had put in such effort for her once.

Something must have shown in her face, for Nathan leaned down, concern furrowing his forehead. "You okay?"

Lani swallowed the lump in her throat and gave him a most brilliant smile. "Why, of course, darling."

The slight down-turned corners of his lips betrayed his skepticism, but he nodded, letting the topic go, much to her relief. "Wine?"

"Yes, I believe a glass or so will do nicely."

She needed it—just enough to dull the still-sharp edges of her memory.

Chapter Eight

They sat on the couch, a bottle of red between them, their knees brushing against each other's as they spoke. Unlike her, he still wore in his outfit from when he had been at the club earlier, a simple black shirt and slacks that was coupled with a silver tie, though now he had his sleeves rolled up.

"What did you think of The Playgrounds?" Lani swirled the red within the wine glass, inhaling the aroma with a slight smile of appreciation.

"It's…interesting…" Nathan trailed off.

Lani made a small noise of acknowledgment and gave him an expectant look.

"It was a bit of a shock to the system," he admitted. "I don't think I had any idea such a place existed before this contract."

She lifted the glass to her lips, smiling against it before tipping the contents for a sip.

"It's common knowledge only for those who know something of the scene already," she replied as she put the wine down once more. "But I want to hear. How did it make *you* feel?"

He shifted his weight with the pretense of setting his own drink aside. But Lani recognized the slight flush around his neck, how he was shifting his balance this way and that, trying to settle—which meant he was squirming while attempting to hide it. For a man who has been forthcoming about everything else, Lani found this behavior amusing.

"I am...unsure," he admitted, each word dragging out with slow reluctance. When all Lani did in return was raised a brow and make another noncommittal noise, he sighed and rubbed his neck. She came to recognize this as his tell for nervousness.

He still said nothing, darting his eyes away. With an exhale of her own, she reached out with one hand to take his, giving it a gentle squeeze. "Nathan, if we are to play, open communication and honesty both to yourself and me is important."

Using his name had the desired effect. He snapped his head up to meet her in the eye. She could almost see the inner struggle playing out inside him in those steel grays, wrestling between modest conventions and raw desires.

"I would be lying if I said none of it turned me on." There was that rueful smile.

Lani leaned closer, gazing up at him through her lashes, their faces inches apart. "Which parts?"

So close. He swallowed hard. The next words rushed out in a hushed whisper. "Control. The parts where control was given and taken."

It was enough for her for tonight. She had pushed further than she'd expected. Lani curved her lips into a smile for him alone, as if she was proud of his answer.

Without another word, she pressed forward and captured his mouth with hers. She kept the kiss light, teasing, licking and nibbling, and he moaned, holding still while she took her time to sample him, letting her set the pace. Was he aware that he was relinquishing control?

"Lani." Her name became a groan of desire and she decided she liked how it sounded. Ignoring the blatant plea, she worked her way down along his jawline and the curve of neck. When he lifted his hands to touch her, she gave them each a playful swat before taking a hold to guide them back to lie still in his own lap. She bumped against his obvious arousal, but she only grinned when he did not resist.

"Hmm, if my memory serves me right, your bed is much more comfortable, is it not?"

"Definitely."

She walked her fingers up from his stomach to his chest, and at last, Lani indulged, twining his tie around her hand. She rose from the couch and tugged at the makeshift leash with a smirk. "Come."

A thrill ran along her spine as he moved to obey. She kept her dominance light, almost teasing, and he seemed content to let her take the lead for now. As they reached the bedroom and neared the bed, she relinquished her hold on him, only to give him a gentle push. Again, with a bemused smile, he followed her silent commands, easing onto the mattress.

Oh, she would wipe that grin off his face and see him beg before the night was over.

Lani positioned herself to stand between his legs, tracing his jawline to under his chin. With two fingers, she tilted his head up toward her and brushed her lips against his once more with feather-lightness.

He raised his hands to pull her close by the hips and slipped upward under her blouse to caress her bare flesh. This time, she allowed him to touch her. The warmth of his palm pressed against her mid-back before he moved up to trace the outline of her shoulder blades, skipping her bra straps. "Christ, you're beautiful."

She loosened the tie with deft fingers but left it on him as she unbuttoned his shirt. It took little effort to make quick work of it and, as she tugged the collar out from its place, she slipped the offending garment off him. *All those lovely muscles to play with.* She reveled at how every touch elicited a tremble from him.

He inhaled when she lowered her head to line kisses up his jaw along to his ear. When he moved one of his hands to work her bra clasp, she nipped the ridge hard enough to draw a yelp from him, a sound that was more from surprise than pain.

"Not yet." Command rang in her voice and satisfaction settled once more within as he left its spot, resuming his hand's journey downward until he was rubbing along the small of her back.

"Better," she murmured in approval.

Rather than remaining idle as he explored her contours, she took every opportunity to run her hands over his chest, down his back. As she scraped her nails over his skin, he let out a slight moan and Lani made a careful mental note of that reaction.

"That's it, darling. Enjoy this. We have all night."

For a while, they remained this way, exploring and learning each other's body, experimenting to find the less obvious erogenous zones. As Nathan leaned forward to trail kisses across her collarbone and straightened to kiss up along her neck, Lani tilted her head back, her eyes half closed in pleasure.

He pulled her closer, urging her to close the gap between them. Instead, she gazed down at him and eased away just enough to catch his gaze with hers. As she held it steady, she reached down to undo his belt and pants until his hardened cock sprang free. She traced its outline and ended with rubbing the pad of her thumb in slow circles over the tip.

"F-f…" Nathan stopped himself in time from swearing as his shaft twitched against her touch with much less control. With a delicious smile and her eyes never leaving his, she wrapped her slender hand around his girth and slid up and down with slow, sure strokes.

"What are you thinking about now, darling? Are you remembering my lips wrapped around your cock? Or the way it feels to be deep inside me?" She leaned forward to kiss the tip of his ear. "Or were you wondering about what it would be like for me to ride you while you're bound and unable to move?"

The sudden jerk and spasm from his erection betrayed just how arousing the thought was. Lani lifted one still-jean-clad leg, bending at the knee to press down on his thigh. Her strokes grew faster as she tightened her grip. His breathing became more ragged, and he threw his hands backward to stabilize himself, fisting the bedsheets. Lani sensed his body tightening and slowed her pace, much to the consternation written all over his face.

And still the man said nothing.

She smiled at the challenge, the length of his hardness hot and pulsing against her hold. She rubbed her thumb along the underside, stroking back and forth, pausing to circle just under the head before repeating the pattern.

"Lani." He uttered her name through gritted teeth.

"Yes, darling?" She batted her eyelashes at him.

He growled at her.

She held still with a smirk, pressing her palm against the tip. When no words followed, she began rubbing in subtle circular movements. "Tell me what you want."

His throat muscles shifted as he worked on finding his voice. "You." He was hoarse with strain. "I want to see you, to taste you, to make you come again and again."

Heat coursed through her, wetness drenching the things she wore. Pleased with his answer, she dipped her head and rewarded him with a light kiss. "You may."

It became a flurry of movement. Her leg fell off his as he surged upward to unbutton her blouse. He didn't even make it all the way. As soon as he deemed that there was enough room, he pulled the top over her head and tossed it behind him. The jeans came off next as she wiggled to help.

Nathan slowed then, his breath deepening as his traveled his focus across her body, devouring her with his eyes. He followed with his hands and mouth, and this time, when he moved to remove her bra, she did not stop him.

The groan he gave as he captured a hardening nipple between his lips was that of a man dying of thirst taking the first sip of water. Lani dropped her head back once more, closing her eyes as he worshipped her body until moans spilled from her.

It likely spurred him on, and as he sucked and licked one then the other, he slid his hands down her sides until he was peeling off her thong. And when he touched the slickness between her thighs, parting her folds, his moan vibrated against her sensitive skin, adding to the pleasure. But he didn't stop. Instead, he continued his fingers' path, traveling upward to trace her slit, to circle her clit. And when he rolled the small bundle of nerves between his thumb and forefinger, she shuddered in ecstasy. It was almost too much. Lani bit her lower lip to keep her orgasm at bay.

Close. She was so close. *Not yet. Build the fire up more.* She wanted an inferno roaring in both their ears.

Lani pushed his shoulders away. It wasn't a light gesture, more a shove that caught him by enough surprise that he fell onto his back. She lost no time in tugging the rest of his pants off before crawling up the bed over him, swaying her hips with every movement.

She wasn't certain who kissed who first. They crashed their lips together in passionate fury, tangling their tongues with each other as her body melted on to his, flesh against flesh at last without a stitch of annoying fabric separating them. He kneaded her ass with a firm grip while his throbbing hardness pressed with desperation against her slit, soaked in her juices.

And still she hovered above.

When they parted, both panting from the searing kiss, they stared into each other's eyes, only for Lani to wink at him. "Not yet, darling."

"What?" Dazed confusion gave way to dread when he realized she would not permit him to enter her just yet. Lani crowed in triumph as she saw realization dawning.

She slid her body down along his. When her breasts brushed by his cock, his hips jerked. She chuckled softly as she positioned herself between his legs and scraped her nails upwards over his inner thighs until she cupped his balls.

She set to work with her mouth and tongue on his cock, but never sealing her lips around the shaft. That would push him over the edge, and it was not her intent to end things just yet. She ran the flat of her tongue along his length, then teased the weeping head, tasting his pre-cum while sneaking a peek up. Nathan had shut his eyes, his face contorted into something between ecstasy and torture, his hips bucking against her actions.

"Hold still or I walk away," Lani threatened and returned to her ministrations, one hand massaging each sac with tender care. The control the man had was admirable as he stilled himself to the occasional twitches. Only the whites of his knuckles as he gripped the sheets betrayed the difficult time he was having.

Satisfied that he'd received the message, she returned to the task, licking along the length, circling her tongue, anything but giving him the satisfaction of enough pressure for him to come. He fell to silence until only his harsh breathing accompanied the sound of her blowjob. Lani ignored the thrum in her own body, derived from the power she felt over his pleasure. He was at her mercy, just like the way she liked it.

"Tease." Frustration was a rumble in the back of his throat.

"Mmhmm." The word vibrated along his cock, which only made it worse for him.

"Come up here."

Lani laughed at the attempt to exert control. To teach him a lesson, she kept the tip of her tongue pressed against the head of his cock but quirked a brow at him.

"Please." He relented after a moment.

"Not good enough." She sank her lips around the tip, sucking. He hissed at the new bout of sensation and let out another growl when she withdrew.

"If you want more, you'll have to ask...nicely."

Like she'd promised herself earlier, she would see him plead.

Chapter Nine

If she weren't so damn good at what she was doing to him, Nathan would stare at her with incredulity. Still, his eyes widened at her ask. Until now, he had gone with her lead. After all, it was important to ensure that he had her consent every step of the way. But her last words went beyond that, and it was only now that he admitted it to himself. She wanted him to submit.

He growled at the thought, but his cock only seemed to harden in response. *Why?*

The stubborn streak in him urged him to grit his teeth and take it, but the things she was doing with her magical mouth held him on the edge of pleasure and torture. When she took more of him in, inch by agonizing inch again, his hips bucked beyond his control. She withdrew, quick as lightning, much to his chagrin.

Only when he resettled and mumbled a half-coherent apology did she resume touching him, once more only with her tongue, using the slightest of pressure. His balls tightened, but the light touch was not enough for him to come.

He wanted to swear, wanted to howl, wanted to grab her head and thrust into her warm, inviting mouth. Instead, he held himself still, taking the teasing for reasons he could not fathom. He rolled his head back and squeezed his eyes closed, torn between the need to orgasm and the desire to see to her pleasure first.

"Let me taste you." It would at least pull him away from the edge — or that was how Nathan reasoned it in his mind.

Lani paused and stared at him as if in careful consideration. The grin added a whole new level of dread.

"No."

A harsh groan left his lips.

She played over his balls with her fingertips, then rolled the heavy sacs in her palm. Christ, how long had she been toying with him?

"I know how close you are." Her whispered words slid over his sensitive member, and he shivered. "Ask, and I'll let you come."

Fuck. Why was this the hottest experience he'd ever had in his life?

Then there was no more time to wonder when her lips enveloped his cock once more, sinking farther than before. The primal part of him howled in triumph, thinking he would get the relief he needed at last. Instead, she held herself still there, unmoving. She did, however, move between scraping her nails along his inner thighs and massaging his balls. When she hollowed her cheeks out to increase pressure, then released in a teasing preview of what would happen if he caved, his resolve began to melt.

One more time. One last defense.

"Let me make you feel good. Let me make you come first. Please." His voice was hoarse as he opened his eyes to look down at the sexpot between his legs.

She withdrew from him and wrapped her fingers around his cock. Hope welled up in him. Her next words, though, squashed that quick enough. "Stubborn boy. Later. Right now, the only choice you have is how much longer you want to prolong the inevitable." She smirked, stroking his shaft at a languid pace. "I can play with you like this all night."

Perhaps it was her confidence, her surety, in leading this dance—or maybe it was the authority with which she spoke, but his resistance gave way to the ingrained habit of obeying.

"No." His throat thickened, and he whispered his next words. "Please. Make me come." He expected shame to fill him, but his cock only throbbed as if echoing his plea. His focus narrowed down to the cauldron of desires.

Lani pressed a kiss on the tip, and he moaned again in response. "Good enough for now." She lowered her mouth onto him and this time, kept a tight seal around his shaft. Immediately, she moved her head in a steady rhythm, sliding her lips up and down, leaving his shaft shining with wetness. She sped up, and while the sensations almost proved too much, he could not help but be drawn to the intensity with which she watched him. He reached down, holding the silken red curls away so that he could see every expression, every movement as she worked. The image of her between his legs seared into his mind, and he knew then that he would never forget this.

All too soon, the muscles in his body tightened. He tried to hold back, to enjoy this just a little longer, but it was futile. "I'm about to…" he warned.

She only moaned in response, the vibration against his cock proving too much at last.

With a roar, he came, exploding into her mouth. The release short-circuited his brain such that his vision darkened and his head spun until his hips arched, only to fall backward on the bed. As his eyesight cleared, he groaned, realization slamming into him when he glimpsed her lips still wrapped around him. She had not only kept her lips around him the entire time, but she had swallowed most of his seed.

When she eased her weight back and straightened to a kneeling position between his legs, he reached out with a shaky hand to cup her cheek and wipe away the trail of cum from the corner of her lips down her chin. The smile she gave him shook him to the core.

"My turn. Please."

Lani nodded, her eyes shining. It was all the permission he needed. He pushed himself up, despite the heaviness in his limbs, and without missing a beat, lifted her from between his legs and flipped her onto her back.

A new urgency filled him, and pushing her legs apart, he dove in straight for her pussy. Her scent only drove his hunger on, and he rubbed his fingers along her labia before parting her folds, delving deep into her core with his tongue. She tasted like the heaven he remembered from the last time, her moans a melodic reward for his efforts.

Mirroring her earlier endeavors, he flattened his tongue and licked upward to reach her clit. There, he teased the nub to hardness until she was squirming against him. He turned to study her as her eyelids fluttered, her body undulating with the pleasure he inflicted on her.

Nathan wanted — no, needed her to come. He shifted, rubbing his stubble against her slit, even as he pressed a thumb against her entrance, and she trembled with obvious delight.

"Yes, oh yes, darling," Lani murmured in between moans, sliding her fingers through his hair to encourage him — not that he needed any. He ate her like a man starved for eons…more. He wanted more of her still. He scooped one hand under her hips to knead her ass, pulling her tighter to his mouth. With his other, he found a nipple and rolled it between his fingers, even as he captured her clit with his lips and began sucking it.

She peaked with accompanying screams of passion that filled the air, even as she soaked him with her own cum. He groaned as his cock stirred, but it was not quite ready yet. Instead, focused on giving her the same bliss she had given him earlier, he slipped a finger in as soon as she relaxed a smidgen and made a come-hither motion to press against her G-spot. It worked, reigniting the fading orgasm. Her hips thrashed, and he had to tighten his grip to keep her close to his mouth.

In the end, Lani had to push his shoulders away with a gentle shove, giving one last shudder as she struggled to catch her breath. Nathan understood when enough was enough. He looked up at her, watching the way satisfaction seemed to relax her entire face. She glowed…and it was because of him.

She smiled down at him. "Come up here." He followed, and she reached up to wipe his chin. "Stay here."

Curious, he nodded and rolled to his side, propping himself up to watch as she slipped out of bed. After a moment, he heard the tap in the washroom.

Ah, she must be cleaning up. He should do the same.

Instead, she returned with a washcloth. "Lie back." Surprised, he tried to protest, only for her to shoot him a look. He acquiesced, easing backward, though he kept himself propped up on both elbows.

She began with his mouth, wiping away her own wetness on him, even as she placed light kisses along his chin. Then she moved lower, dabbing at his half-hard cock. He groaned as it stiffened under her administrations. He couldn't help it.

"Mm, ready for round two so soon." Was that appreciation he heard in her tone?

"Sorry… I just never had a woman do this for me." He ducked his head.

"*Tsk*, that's because you've never had a Domme. Aftercare is our job." She leaned down to kiss the tip of his cock, and he twitched with a newfound sensitivity. "And our privilege."

A Domme? Yes. "But I'm not your…"

"You're my partner in bed tonight." She cut him off and, setting the washcloth aside, she crawled up beside him. "Now hold me." She yawned. "And after a nap, we can try round two."

"Round two." Nathan echoed with bewilderment, but his body reacted on its own, lying down and pulling her tight against him.

"I told you I could go all night." With a sigh of contentment, she curled up in his arms and closed her eyes.

Silence settled in the room. Nathan heard her breathing even out and savored her softness against him. As sleep took over, a last thought floated through his mind.

He had submitted to every one of her requests.

* * * *

When sunlight filtered through the window, he cracked open his eyes. Relief flooded his system when he realized she was still there. A grin he hadn't felt in a while tugged at his lips and spread warmth all the way down to his toes. At some point, they had discussed them both being cleared health-wise, and with her on birth control, condoms were no longer necessary. They had gone at least two more rounds, bareback — two long, passionate sessions that had his body aching beautifully. He was right. Their chemistry was explosive.

In his arms, Lani stirred and nuzzled him, her eyes still closed. He refrained from chuckling, not wanting to wake her. Something in him wanted to stay in this moment forever, but knowing that was impossible, he settled with prolonging it for as long as possible. Later, he would make her coffee and breakfast if she would let him.

"Mm-m." Lani tilted her head back with hooded eyes, still only half awake. She reminded him of a sleepy kitten. Well, if one could call a tiger a kitten.

With a small chuckle, Nathan pressed a kiss on her forehead. "Good morning."

She yawned and rubbed the sleep from her eyes. "Morning." Then, as she grew more alert, she grinned. It was the same grin he knew he had on his lips.

And right on cue, his stomach rumbled.

She laughed and pushed herself up. With more reluctance than he expected, he released his arms around her.

"Come on. Let's get some food in us then we can talk."

Talk? Confusion swirled inside him. It must have shown as she patted his cheek.

"Open communication is important—what you liked, what you didn't like. We also experimented with power dynamics last night, and I want you to tell me how you felt about it."

Oh. He'd never had a woman who talked so openly about such things before. Shock froze him in bed.

Lani laughed. "Come on, darling. Food."

Right. Food. Maybe he'd be more ready for this talk after breakfast and coffee.

Then again, probably not.

Chapter Ten

It had been a long time since Nathan had cooked for a woman, and he found a deep, almost primitive satisfaction in doing so. Breakfast was a simple affair — bacon, eggs and toast — but there was nothing simple about the one who sat across the counter, already dressed in the spare outfit she'd brought with her, her eyes following his every movement. Nor did he find the swirl of complicated emotions within him any less confusing.

"Coffee?"

"Tea, please. No cream or sugar. Mint, if you have it."

He made a point of remembering her preference as he put on the pot. Soon she had a steaming mug between her hands as he finished cooking. He set the plate of food down in front of her, his nerves ratcheting up as she took the first bite. When she beamed in response and made a small noise of approval, the swell of pride he felt only added to that cauldron inside him.

Rather than trying to sort out his own thoughts, he sipped own coffee—cream, no sugar—then dug into the meal. It was only then that he discovered his hunger, and he finished his plate with more gusto after.

He was, however, dawdling with the last few mouthfuls when he remembered what was about to follow.

"Finish your food, Nathan," Lani chided, her voice breaking through the silence. Amusement danced in her eyes.

Shit. Caught. With a sigh, he polished off his plate.

"Good. Now"—Lani extended her arms in a feline-like stretch—"I know physically you enjoyed our night. But emotionally, I want you to talk me through where you're at."

Nathan's gaze wandered across the table, and he had to resist the urge to sweep up the plates, to use cleaning as an excuse to avoid answering instead of staying remaining in his chair, a fly caught in the spider's web. But instincts told him that if he wanted a repeated performance in the future, putting off this talk was not an option.

Silence stretched on. As he exhaled, he looked up, straightening with mild surprise when he found all the mirth from her had dissipated. Instead, poised with seriousness, she waited with patience. *If this is what it takes.* The tangled emotions rose to the forefront once more and his brows knitted. When he opened his mouth, he spoke with the only truth he had, even if it was going to cost him.

"I don't know where to start."

He expected her to walk away then, or at least to express her disappointment. Instead, she softened and nodded.

"That's fair. Let's begin with some simpler questions then."

Okay, he could try.

"Did you enjoy last night?"

Well, that was easy. "Yes."

"Did you enjoy being teased?"

This one was more layered, despite the simple words. He considered the question before speaking, each word emerging at a measured pace. "I enjoyed the build-up, more than if we had gone straight to trying to just get off." It was easier to admit that than he'd expected, similar to discussing an operation with objectivity, no matter how crude it sounded to his ears. Maybe that was the key — to be clinical about his observations.

Lani inclined her head in acknowledgment. "And did you enjoy following my directions?"

Hesitation held his tongue. Nathan understood the intent behind her question and his first instinct was to say no. Anything less would be to admit he enjoyed being ordered around by a woman in bed, and that seemed all kinds of wrong to him. But his thoughts returned to all the times he had followed a woman's authority and how much Lani inspired the same instincts in him. Perhaps it was prudent to start there.

"It reminded me of my time as a rookie. My partner was a more senior female detective and took the lead in many of the investigations we were on."

Lani rested her arms on the counter and leaned forward. "And I reminded you of her?"

"A little," he admitted. "But while I have no problems with women in positions of authority, it's different when it's in the bedroom."

"Why?" Lani tilted her head to one side.

Nathan flushed at her question, but he had no answer for her — or perhaps his silence was enough for her as she spoke once more.

"Let's return to the original question. Did you enjoy it?"

He sighed and rubbed the back of his head. No matter how hard he tried, he couldn't deny that last night was some of the hottest sex he ever had. "Yes."

"But you're conflicted."

Nathan nodded again, then startled when Lani reached out to place a hand on his arm and gave it a gentle squeeze.

"Social conventions that have been ingrained into us at an early age dictate certain gender roles and expected behaviors. But that is a conditioning, not necessarily who we truly are. I suggest you give some thought as to what you, as Nathan, want, versus what you think you ought to enjoy because society tells you to."

Her words hit him like a ton of bricks. He understood conditioning. After all, the military was all about that, and it had taken forever to train himself to stop being on high alert all the time. So how much did he refuse to submit because it sounded emasculating?

Well, it is. Isn't it?

Lani squeezed his arm again. "Do you want to call it?"

"No!" The answer came swift and sure.

"Nathan, I can't change who I am. And I have no desire to push you into something you're not ready for."

His throat thickened. "What do you mean?"

Lani withdrew her hand and folded her arms on the table, letting out a sigh. She fluttered her eyes closed for a moment before opening them again. "I pride myself on being able to read people. It's a useful skill to have as a Domme. Last night, you followed and submitted beautifully, even without being conscious that you were doing so."

Before he could protest, she held up a finger, commanding silence. He closed his mouth once more.

"You let me tease you, to play with you for over an hour, and didn't break from the role. You relinquished control of your pleasure to me, and my dominant side recognized it for what it was — submission."

His growing discomfort at the truth of her words must have shown as she stopped and gave him a small, sad smile. "But even the thought of you doing so makes you uncomfortable and contradicts the image you have of yourself. I can help you explore that submissive side of you…but only if you are open to accepting it as part of who you are."

"Help me, then." The answer surprised him, and he straightened. Why had he said that? Was he doing what he could to hold on to this woman, even if it was to indulge in her kinks? No. He could lie to himself and use her as an excuse, but he would be lying. She was right. He enjoyed following her lead in bed, giving her control over him. He flushed hot with shame.

"Nathan…" Was that pity in her voice? "If it helps, this is not something you need to announce to the world. What happens between us in the bedroom can stay just that. It does not invalidate who you are outside, nor does it have to bleed into the other parts of your life."

Knots of tension within him eased as he conceded to her point. "Thank you." His therapist would have a field day with this one. Perhaps that new counselor he was meeting with in a few weeks would help him sort this out more?

"Don't thank me yet, darling. You may regret going down this rabbit hole. But remember that no matter how much I exert control, the choice to follow and submit is always yours."

This was nothing like he'd imagined. But, held at the precipice of something he sensed could lead to a significant change in his life, a mixture of fear and excitement welled up within him. "Still… Thank you."

The smile she rewarded him with warmed him, as if he were basking in the sun. "You're welcome. Now I need to be off. Are you going to be okay?"

He scoffed, puffing his chest. "Of course. Are you?"

Lani blinked in surprise and gave a small laugh. "Yes. Thank you for a wonderful night and breakfast."

"You're welcome." He tugged his lips into an easy smile without conscious effort. She seemed to have that effect on him, despite his confusion about her as a Domme. He shifted as she stood up and moved to retrieve her bag for her.

At the door, she turned once more and rose to press a light kiss on his cheek. "If you need to talk through this more, text me."

"And if I need another round?" He raised a brow but could not hold back the mirth that was surfacing.

Again, Lani chuckled and brushed the pad of her thumb along his lower lip. "You can text me for that, too."

Long after he closed the door behind her, he stood rooted to the spot, staring at nothing in particular. He wasn't smitten. He wasn't in the position to be smitten. According to Stacey, he was too cold for that. At the very least, he was not relationship material.

Then why did he want one with Lani while he remained there like a lovesick fool?

Nathan grunted and put it all out of his mind. To facilitate that, he turned on the TV, intending to distract himself while he cleaned up. Instead, he froze, staring at the screen.

"And now for your early morning news. Today, Renard Dickson will be released on parole after serving five years in the State Penitentiary. Dickson was incarcerated after a high-profile trial after he was arrested for a string of luxury jewelry store robberies, along with two partners…"

Nathan turned off the TV and sat down on the couch with a dull thud. Why was he released so early? His mind flashed back to the case, interviewing the terrified and scared hostages, cornering the three criminals in their safe house, the ensuing gun fight all the way to the final day in court. Renard had tried to spit at him before they'd hauled him away after the verdict.

He stared down at his shaking hands and clasped them together. Renard was just another case, but other memories flooded his consciousness. The sound of gunshots roared in his ears and he ducked his head, his arms moving to cover himself of their own accord. Bile rose in the back of his throat.

A loud ring from his phone jolted him out of the shock. He straightened, staring at the name flashing on the screen. For a moment, he debated letting it go to voicemail, but it was rare for Wilson to call this early — and on a weekend, too. Pulling air deep into his lungs to pull himself together, he picked up.

"Wilson?"

"Morning, Nate. Did I wake you?"

"No, it's fine." His throat felt dry, and his voice came out hoarse.

"You okay? You coming down with a cold?" He could hear the worry in his friend's words.

"I'm fine. What's up?"

"Got some time today to meet up for coffee? There's something I want to talk to you about."

Nathan frowned, unsure what to make of this unusual request. It was his turn to ask. "Is everything okay? Is the family all right?" Wilson was the model father and husband, willing to do anything for his wife. And with a toddler and a second one on the way, he had been spending less time at work to focus on helping her through the difficult pregnancy.

"Yeah, Janice is doing fine, and the munchkin is being the usual little brat. We're good."

Nathan bobbed his head, only to remember Wilson wouldn't be able to see. "I don't have any plans. I can meet up in an hour."

"Sounds like a plan. Meet you at the café on Fifth and Broadway?"

"Yeah."

* * * *

An hour later, they sat across from each other, both sipping their respective coffees. It afforded Nathan the opportunity to observe his friend. Although Wilson wore an amiable smile, there was a slight twitch that hinted at nervousness.

With a sigh, Wilson set his coffee down. "Always liked the stuff they make here. Not as acidic as those hipster places."

Nathan nodded in agreement but did not reply, allowing Wilson the time to compose his thoughts.

Silence did wonders in conversations. He had learned that from Lani.

"How do you think the business with the firm is going?" Wilson opened.

"It's fine. We've got a few long-term contracts and a decent roster of clients to fill in the gaps. Keeps us busy, but we need to be careful to not take on too much. Growing too fast can bring its own problems."

Wilson bobbed his head up and down in agreement. "But you're enjoying the work?"

What was with everyone asking if he was enjoying things? Nathan nodded again, still uncertain where this was leading. Luckily, Wilson didn't press further. They had been friends for so long that he understood Nathan wasn't one to dwell on discussions of feelings.

"How much money do you have saved up?"

Wilson was jumping from question to question so fast it was giving him whiplash.

"Enough."

"Enough to buy my share of the company?"

Alarmed, Nathan leaned forward, eyes narrowing. "Wilson, what's this about?"

Wilson sighed and tugged at his beard. "It's Janice. With the new kid coming, she wants to move back home, closer to her parents, so we have more help. And to be honest, I can see the sense in that. Not having any family support sucks right now. I can't even imagine once the baby is born."

Oh.

"Yeah, so I want to sell my shares to you."

Nathan's brows shot up. "Me? Why not to Daniel?"

His friend shook his head. "Not if I want the company to live on without me. Like you said, it's important to take our time to grow. Daniel's too aggressive. He has big dreams, but they're not practical. With my shares, combined with your own current ones, you'll have controlling power over the company's direction."

"Daniel won't like that."

"I know, but we have time to work on him. It's not as if we're moving tomorrow. What do you say?"

It appears today was the day of tough decisions. "I need to think about it."

"Sure, of course. Just don't dwell on it for too long, okay? If you're not in, I may have to look for another buyer."

"Okay." Nathan stared at the liquid in his mug and wished for a moment it held something with a little more of a kick than caffeine.

Chapter Eleven

The night at The Playgrounds was not off to a good start. Lani paled as she watched the sickening exchange between Luna, Bryan and Jacob.

"Yes. You would do well to remember and respect the contract I still have with Luna."

Lani could pick out the anger seething beneath Jacob's words, and she readied herself to step in lest Jacob lose control of his temper. And when Bryan sneered, Lani just about stepped up to punch him in the face herself.

"Well, I suppose if I was in your shoes, I'd feel the same way. Of course I'll respect your decision." Bryan didn't stop there but leaned forward to murmur something to Jacob, who clenched his jaw. None of this meant anything good.

"I should be thanking you. You're right. The anticipation will make breaking in my new toy later so much more fun. Isn't that right, Luna?"

Would that Bryan just not shut up? Poor Luna. Her friend looked pale and sickly. Lani longed to pull her into her arms and whisk her away from the two males having their pissing contest—not that she could blame Jacob.

"Yes, Master Bryan."

"And you are so looking forward to being broken, aren't you?"

"Of course, Master Bryan. I know how much you enjoy me on that cross, and I'm so looking forward to pleasing you on it, just like I did with Master Jacob."

It was the worst acting Lani had ever witnessed, and it relieved her. Luna wasn't fooling anyone, and Lani could only hope that it was enough for Jacob to keep his cool.

"Please, wouldn't you like a drink? I would absolutely *love* one." Luna pitched her voice higher, and Lani hoped for her friend's sake that Bryan would miss how fake she sounded.

Fortunately, Bryan's ego lapped up the act. "A most excellent idea. Anything my future pet wants."

As the two walked away toward the bar, Lani turned her attention back toward Jacob, who was hunched over in pain. "Oh, Jacob." With a soft sigh, she stepped up and placed a gentle hand on the man's arm.

Under her touch, Jacob relaxed and rubbed his face as if to shake himself out of the rage she was sure boiled beneath. "How much of that did you pick up?"

"Enough."

"Something was odd about that conversation."

Everything about that conversation was wrong, but that wasn't what Jacob needed to hear right now. "How so?"

"Both Bryan and Luna mentioned the cross. I think he's obsessed with proving himself the bigger Dom."

"Not unlikely. He has a classic psychopathic and narcissistic profile, from what we've been able to gather so far." Lani tapped her lips in thought as she studied Bryan's interaction and the way Luna would flinch at his touch.

"Yeah, but why that cross?"

Lani shrugged in response. "You and Luna rarely played in public. That was one of those rare times, probably the only time Bryan has witnessed you two play, right?"

Her eyes narrowed as she turned her attention to Jacob. Some idea had come to his friend, but she could tell he wasn't ready to share yet. Her friend wasn't the type to talk unless he had already some of it figured out, and it was what made him an interesting client for her practice, too.

Well, meanwhile, she would buy him time. She drew to her full height, tilting her chin up. "Darryl and I have got this. We'll keep them in the public. You go do what you need to do."

"Thanks." Jacob nodded and Lani saw him swallow. *The poor man.* She had never seen him this shaken in their long years of friendship.

Lani threw a look over her shoulders, her lips quirking upward. "Don't. Wait till you see my bill."

"Pest."

Her laughter trailed after her, even as she squared her stance. As repulsive as Bryan was, Lani looked forward to the challenge, and she would reclaim her friend, come hell or high water.

"Luna, lovely!" Without waiting for a reply, Lani reached for Luna's hand and pulled her into a tight hug. From the corner of her eye, she glimpsed anger flaring in Bryan's eyes. *Good.* She would make that wannabe Dom pay tonight for messing with her friends.

"Lani!" Luna threw her a glance mixed with reluctance and gratefulness as she accepted the embrace — but not without a backward glance at Bryan.

"Bryan, evening." Lani beamed her most sickeningly sweet smile. She further relaxed as Darryl moved into view from his side of the bar.

"Lani, good to see you." As soon as she released Luna, Bryan leaned in to give her a light peck on her cheek. It made Lani's skin crawl, even as she grew more incensed at him touching her when she had not given permission. The nerve! He was lucky she didn't call him out on it in front of everyone. Instead, pretending that he had thrown her off balance, she stumbled and landed with the heel of her knee-high stiletto boots on his toes.

"Oh my, I'm so sorry." Lani gave him another beaming smile. Without waiting for an answer, she turned back to Luna. "Sweetie, I haven't seen you in so long! Come... I must dance with you." She linked her arm around Luna's. "Jacob already said I can have you tonight."

Out of the corner of her eye, she saw Bryan turn red with fury as the veneer of civility slipped. Oh, this was too much fun. Lani winked at Bryan. "I'm going to steal this popular pet away now." She turned around and pulled Luna along, keeping a firm grasp on the sub's hand.

With her back toward Bryan, she did not see him close the distance between them until she felt his hand on her shoulder, digging his fingers into her with a punishing grip. The last thing Lani expected was Bryan making a physical move, but as she turned around to confront him, another voice spoke.

"Is there a problem here?"

Lani froze at Nathan's voice coming out of the blue. It took a moment before she realized Bryan had already released his grip. She turned halfway, enough to see Nathan's hand on Bryan's arm, thunder in his eyes. Although Nathan was the same height, if not a little shorter than Bryan, there was something about the way he filled up space that spoke of a man who was trained to handle himself.

"No, no problem at all." The forced smile on Bryan's face as he held both his hands up was as fake as they came. Beside her, Luna pressed closer to Lani, and she wondered if her friend was aware of the fear she was emanating.

Nathan nodded once and let go of Bryan...but made no move to leave. Lani's eyes met Darryl's, and the bartender dipped his head in acknowledgment. *Smart man.* He must have called Nathan in as security.

In the end, Bryan shrugged and headed back to the bar. Beside her, Luna sagged in relief, but Lani couldn't take her eyes off Nathan.

"You okay?"

"Yeah. We're fine."

"Good." Nathan cupped her cheek and rubbed the spot where Bryan had kissed with the pad of his thumb as if it would erase what the bastard had done. He gazed upon her with desire and something else, something that Lani was not ready to put a name to.

"Thank you," Lani murmured but made no move to remove his touch. Instead, she placed a hand on top of his.

"I'll keep an eye on him. Be careful of that one."

"I will."

"I need to get back to work."

Was he waiting for her permission? *Good boy.*

"Go. I'll text you later."

Nathan took her hand in his and lifted it to his lips, placing a reverent kiss on her knuckle before stepping away. She tracked his retreat until he melted into the crowd.

"Who was that?"

Luna had lost some anxiousness, replaced by clear curiosity when Lani faced her. Lani grinned and winked at her. "Just the new security."

Before Luna could question her further, Lani took up Luna's hand again and tugged her toward the dance floor. "Come on."

* * * *

Hours later, they sat face to face at a table in a pub that was open late. Some color had returned to Luna's face, but once she grew still without music and dancing to distract her, she became sullen once more. Lani wanted to grab hold of her shoulders and shake the truth out of her, but alas, this required a more delicate touch.

"So, little known fact... They carry this rare microbrew cider that is just the sweetest."

Luna perked up at that and Lani hid her smile, turning to wave someone down to order one for each of them. as well as a good helping of fries, honey-garlic wings and dry ribs. As she ordered, Luna's eyes grew rounder until the waitstaff left.

"You're hungry. Did you eat dinner?" Luna tilted her head.

Lani's shoulders rose and fell in a nonchalant shrug. "Dancing makes me hungry." Or rather, it should make Luna hungry. She looked like she hadn't eaten in days.

The ciders came first, and Lani wasn't sure if she should be concerned that the first thing Luna did was down half the pint in one go.

She racked her brain, trying to come up with a subject that didn't remind them of Bryan, but that asshole had wormed his way into almost every aspect of Luna's life, according to Jacob's board.

"Slow down, sweetie. Enjoy the taste." This was nothing like the Luna she knew, who savored food with all the relish in the world. When Luna relaxed and set the glass down, Lani leaned forward. "That's a nice outfit. I don't think I've seen it before."

It was the wrong thing to say. Luna flinched and lowered her gaze to fixate on a spot on the table. Lani sighed inwardly. Bryan must have made specific requirements on how she was to dress. Why was she not surprised?

"Luna, you know whatever it is you're going through, I'm here for you."

An interruption came with their food's arrival. Luna stared at each platter, then drank more of the cider. Lani took a slower sip herself, studying the other for signs of hunger. When she made no move to eat, Lani placed a wing on a plate and handed it to her. "If you keep drinking like that on an empty stomach, you're going to regret it."

Luna had always been a lightweight, and it showed with the way her cheeks turned rosy. As she accepted the dish, she took the chicken with one hand and held it up for a small bite. At last, a little sigh escaped her lips. That initial morsel led to another, then another, and soon, Luna was cramming food and cider into her, taking a break only to order one more drink. Behind the glass of her own pint, Lani relaxed, satisfied that Luna had become more like her former self.

Luna eased back in her seat and gave her a genuine smile at last. "So who was that knight in shining armor earlier?"

It was not what she'd expected. Lani almost spluttered but swallowed the cider in her mouth in time. It took a second for her to regain her composure, and when she did, she allowed herself a smug smile while lowering her voice. "A playmate. That's all."

Yes, that's all. Or so she told herself.

"I'm glad. You deserve someone, Lani." There was hope in Luna's eyes, a hope she didn't want to acknowledge. "Being with someone doesn't invalidate your love for another person."

Who were the words meant for? Lani or herself? Lani wondered but recognized how they applied to her, nonetheless. Even if she ended up with another sub, it would never replace August in her heart. She knew that, at a logical level. Letting someone go didn't constitute a betrayal. How many times had she told a client that?

"And you, Luna?" she asked, keeping her tone soft.

Luna met her gaze with a sad smile, her eyes unfocused. "You know I'd never stop loving Jacob."

Lani reached out, offering a hand palm up. When Luna placed hers on top, she held the sub's and gave it a light squeeze. "I know, Luna. I know."

Chapter Twelve

He could have left it to the staff to do this, but for The Playgrounds, Nathan wanted to remain more hands-on, given it was a new contract—even if it meant working on a Sunday morning.

The crew followed him in, hauling various equipment. Last night, Erica had summoned him to her office and requested an urgent sweep for bugs on the second floor. He'd grasped the implications quick enough, and it had set him on edge ever since. It didn't help that not everyone who worked this contract was available on such short notice, so Nathan had to pull in others who had not been on-boarded yet.

The stillness of the club contrasted with the crowd and noise he'd experienced the previous night. Behind him, his crew also fell silent, but Nathan braced himself for the chatter to rise again when they reached the second floor.

"Good morning, Nathan." Dominique's heels clicked on the concrete as she crossed the empty space.

"Morning, Dominique."

"Thank you for accepting our request so last minute."

Nathan shook his head. "It's okay. These things happen and need to be acted on fast."

"Yes, I'm glad you understand. Is there anything I can do to help you and your staff set up?"

He cast a glance toward the stairs. "We'll be fine. Give us a few hours and I'll bring you a preliminary report."

Dominique smiled and dipped her head in acknowledgment. "I'll be upstairs in the office. Thank you again."

"You're welcome." Nathan turned back to his crew as she left them to their own devices.

"All right, guys. The focus today is on the second floor. There are lots of places to hide stuff, so when we do the manual sweep, make sure you check the equipment. Then we'll go over the space with a frequency counter and the two probes. I want one last round after that, and pay close attention to anything that looks like it's been moved recently."

A low murmur of assent followed as Nathan led the way upstairs. When the rest of the crew reached the top, he heard sharp intakes of breath behind him and again reminded himself that they should onboard more staff to ensure they had enough coverage for emergencies. Hindsight was always twenty-twenty.

"Some of these things look like torture instruments from a real dungeon," one of the newer guys whispered, and Nathan had to resist facepalming. He knew, on a surface level, that the kid was not wrong. The stocks, for instance, looked to be straight out of a medieval chamber. Still, how to explain all this? Not for the first time, he missed Lani's serene confidence. It was going to be a long morning.

"I heard some people refer to places like these as jiggle houses."

Okay, enough was enough.

Nathan spun around. The comment had come from Jasper, and he should have known better, having been here before. He straightened and stalked toward the tech. It took all his self-control to not haul him out by the ear.

"If you are so interested, you can start by reading appropriate material about it and talking to someone who actually knows the scene. Otherwise, we are here to do a job. Please refrain from commenting on things you don't understand. These are our clients, and we are professionals."

The others inched away. Jasper, caught, winced and stood, shifting his weight from foot to foot and hung his head. "Yes, sorry, sir," he muttered under his breath, cheek flushing with embarrassment.

He stared at the abashed tech and sighed. As he relaxed his pose, he placed a hand on the younger man's shoulder. The gesture must have startled Jasper, who snapped back up with round eyes.

"Look… I get how this place can throw all of us off a bit. But I want to make sure we show we are respectful of the establishment and the people in it, okay?"

Jasper nodded.

"And if you have questions, you come ask me." As soon as the words left his mouth, Nathan groaned on the inside. He was hardly an expert himself, so why the hell had he offered? His mind flashed him an image of Lani as an answer. She had offered to be his guide, and the least he could do was pass on some of that knowledge.

"Thanks, boss."

"Good. Get to work." Nathan took a step back as he surveyed the team's action, pleased to watch it all unfold. Now that most of them had gotten over the initial shock, they worked to unpack and set up like a well-oiled engine.

He joined in on the first sweep of the dungeon with conflicting emotions. On one hand, the utter lack of dust impressed him — *they must have an excellent cleaning crew* — but it made their jobs so much more difficult. At least the club had bolted down most of the equipment, which meant at least they didn't have to lift and check underneath.

The team had done this a million times, and they checked every nook and cranny, taking their time. Once the techs brought in the machines, Nathan nodded and stepped away to make his way upstairs to take a look at the security room.

He paused, his hand resting on the door handle as he picked up a male voice on the other side.

"So I started from that time you guys played in public like Lani told me to."

Nathan's brow raised at the mention of Lani's name.

"Oh hey, Lani." After a brief pause, Darryl spoke again. "So, as I was saying, I started with the footage from the dungeon. I couldn't be sure, but at some point, Bryan did pull out his phone and touched his screen before putting it back in his pocket. I couldn't tell what he was doing, but it couldn't have been the phone camera, since he never pointed his phone up. Could be he was even just hanging up on an incoming call, for all I could tell."

Another pause. Nathan was torn between barging in and remaining outside. Hearing only one side frustrated him.

"Not sure. I'll keep scanning subsequent videos to see if he's ever gone back to retrieve anything." Darryl's voice softened until Nathan had trouble making out the rest of the conversation.

He didn't want a confrontation this early in the morning and with the pleasant bartender. He could only hope that this would amount to nothing. He sucked in a breath, opened the door and stepped in.

Startled, Darryl turned, guilt flitting across his face.

"Hello, Darryl." Wariness crept in Nathan's voice, although he kept expression neutral.

"Morning." He rose from the seat in front of all the screens. "Here. Sorry if I'm holding up something. Erica said it was the only time I could go over the security footage."

Okay, that was a positive start. But checking video feeds was not part of a bartender's job description.

"What's going on?" This was also too much of a coincidence.

A moment of indecision passed over Darryl's features before it hardened. "It's personal."

"Is Lani in trouble?"

Once more, surprise widened Darryl's eyes before he shook his head, his brows furrowing. "No, but Lani's friend is."

With a frown on his lips, Nathan unclipped the walkie talkie at his belt and made a show of shutting it off, then placed it on the table. "Tell me, please. Is it that girl Lani was with last night when that man got too aggressive?"

Darryl's shoulders dropped and he chuckled, though the sound lacked any mirth. "You're damn good at your job, aren't you?" When Nathan didn't reply, he sighed and rubbed his face. "Yeah. That guy's name is Bryan. Bryan Walsh. We think he may have something over Luna...but it's just a suspicion."

Nathan wanted to ask for more of the story but sensed that the other man wasn't ready to trust him yet. *Fair enough.* "So you're checking the tapes to see if there's any possibility he recorded something?" *The last-minute request for the sweep.* The pieces were coming together.

Darryl nodded.

"And nothing so far?"

"No, though he took his phone out of his pocket at one point, but the angle is wrong for a photo or video."

Nathan's gaze wandered toward the screen. "I'm going to check in with the team...then show me."

For the next two hours, they pored over the videos, but Darryl was correct in his assessment. Nothing else even came close to that moment Darryl had described earlier. And the team also didn't find anything in their sweep, no remote bugs or recording devices Bryan could have triggered.

In the end, both men sat facing each other, confounded.

"He's on probation, isn't he?"

"Yeah. Jacob and I were monitoring that night when he went overboard with a sub."

Nathan winced, unsure what that would even look like — and part of him didn't want to know.

Darryl sighed and stood up from his seat. "Thanks for this. I owe you one." The bartender grinned, laughter in his eyes. "I'll put in a good word with Lani."

Shit. He felt the back of his neck grow warm, flushing red. How did the man know? Nathan schooled his face to a neutral expression, only for Darryl to lean forward closer to him.

"You are interested, aren't you?"

Christ. At least he didn't seem to realize how far they had already gone. He swallowed hard. "I am. I think."

As if satisfied by his answer, Darryl straightened. "Good. Lani deserves to have someone in her life." He patted his shoulder. "And you're a good man, Nathan. If you ever need to talk, come by the bar." With that, he left the room.

Nathan stared after the exit, then exhaled and rose to leave himself, locking the door behind him. By the time he made his way downstairs, the guys were already packing up.

"Hey, boss." Jasper approached, hesitation slowing in his steps.

"Yeah?"

"Here's the paperwork for the sweep. I had the guys do one more round of manual, just in case."

Nathan nodded, taking the sheathes of paper in hand. He still had to report to Dominique. "Thanks. Why don't you guys call it for the day and try to enjoy what's left of your Sunday?"

"Okay."

About to make his way back upstairs, Nathan stopped when he realized Jasper was lingering, his mouth opening and closing.

"You need something?"

As if given permission, the boy stepped closer and lowered his voice. "I was wondering if you could recommend any decent sites to read about this kind of stuff…" He cleared his throat. "I mean, if I'm working this contract, I should learn more, right? I've been hitting up Reddit, but if there's other...more... authoritative sources...?"

Laughter threatened to escape from Nathan at the irony of the situation. Hadn't he used the same excuse? Wasn't he still using that line? A ghost of a smile tugged at his lips. "Yeah sure, I'll shoot you some links."

The boy perked up. "Thanks, boss!"

Nathan allowed himself a small chuckle as he turned to the last task of the day and wondered what Lani would make of this.

Chapter Thirteen

That night, Nathan stared at his phone, hovering his thumbs with indecision. Already, he had typed and deleted the message three times without sending it, and his wishy-washiness was annoying even him.

Hi, it's Nathan. Do you have a moment tonight for a question or two?

Before he could second-guess himself yet again, he hit the send button then watched the screen. When no reply came, he sighed, set his phone aside and rose from the couch.

Beer. Book. About to settle in for some relaxation, his heart lurched when the device rang instead. No. It wasn't Lani. A sense of trepidation settled in his stomach.

"Hi, Julia."

"Hey ,Nate, how's it going? Did I catch you at a bad time?"

"No, it's all good."

His old partner on the force. They tried their best to keep in touch after he'd left, but between her workaholic life and his reluctance to dwell on the past, they both sucked at it, which made the call at this hour even more surprising.

"Look… I've got to run soon, but I wanted to check in. Have you seen the news?"

Ah. Nathan could almost see Julia in his mind, chewing on her lower lip as she considered how much she needed to tell him. But he already knew.

"You mean about Dickson?"

"Yeah. Word on the street is that he's swearing revenge. Apparently, time in the slammer hasn't been kind, and he's gone a little loco, though he had put up a decent act for his hearing."

Nathan drew air deep into his lungs. *Great.* This was the last thing he needed. "You going to be okay?"

"Me? Yeah, sure. I've got what I need." She paused and Nathan could hear someone yelling her name. "Shit. I have to run. Big case, things are nuts here. Watch your back and be careful, okay?"

At that moment, his phone buzzed. A message must have come in.

"I will. You, too."

"Roger that." Julia hung up and left him in silence once more.

He stared at the beer and part of him wanted to down the whole thing in one go, but his hands were already moving before his mind registered to bring up the text that had just come in. This time it was Lani.

Was in the shower. What would you like to know?

An image of water cascading down the curves of her body hardened his cock within seconds. He adjusted himself in his boxers and grabbed his glass to take a deep drink. It took several more moments before he got his breathing even again.

Would you be able to recommend some reading material on BDSM?

This was for Jasper — or so he told himself. Never mind that the boy had just asked about sites beyond Reddit.

That's a broad topic, and I think any introductory articles I send you would be stuff you've already read or know, since you've been doing research yourself.

There was accuracy in her words. He could pass along the few essays and blog posts he had found to Jasper, enough to teach him basic etiquette. But if he were honest with himself, he was looking for something deeper, and for that, he could not use Jasper as an excuse. So he forced himself to type back.

On dominance and submission then. Any sort of beginner's guide to what to expect out of a relationship like…

Nathan stopped typing, staring at the word he had just typed before hastily deleting the R-word to replace it with the something more generic. *What the hell am I thinking?*
He pressed enter and shook his head.

I've got some on hand that I can send you, but a comprehensive list will have to wait until tomorrow.

Of course. No rush. Thank you.

You're welcome. Take in what you read, and if there is something of personal interest, let's talk.

What could he say to that? There was no one around to see his embarrassment, and yet he flushed all the same. He had all but admitted to himself that this wasn't just for Jasper or even for research for the job. Still, he couldn't quite give voice to the real reason, so he opted for a simpler answer.

I'll keep that in mind.

He left it at that.

His phone buzzed moments later with a series of URLs. Some were Amazon book links, but a majority of them pointed to online articles. Nathan grabbed his beer and shuffled to his office where his laptop sat shut on the desk. With another slower sip of his drink this time, he settled in and booted up the machine for a night of reading on the computer.

Consent was the biggest differentiator between the lifestyle and abuse. *No surprise there.* But the myriad of forms in which someone could skirt the edge of consent intrigued Nathan. A relationship that involved power exchange required a much more heightened sense of awareness of where each other's limits were.

Trust. That was the opposite side of the same coin. With consent came an implicit trust in each other to respect those boundaries and to know when and where to push to help each other grow.

A particular phrasing in one article caught his attention.

In a twenty-four-seven lifestyle, a good Dominant knows how to keep a sub grounded, to care for them both physically and mentally, often by providing structure. But it's a mistake to think of a submissive as passive. In return, the submissive relinquishes control to feed that part of the Dominant, but also serves by lifting their Dom's world. It is just as much their role to take care of their Dominant as it is for their Dominant to take care of them.

A sub wasn't passive.

The realization hit him so hard, and he slumped against the back of the chair and sucked in a breath.

Grounding. Structure. To care and be cared for.

That. He wanted *that*.

Or was it too romanticized to be true?

Nathan needed to talk to Lani.

* * * *

The text arrived as she took her first sip of tea in the morning. Lani was busy tapping away, checking her calendar for her appointments of the day when the notification from Nathan came up. An unreasonable thrill coursed through her as she brought the message up.

Good morning. I hope I didn't wake you.

She smiled at his consideration and set her tea down.

No, I was already up.

I had some questions about some of the reading you sent last night.

Did the dear boy finish going through all the links in one night? She would have been more surprised if he didn't have questions.

Certainly. I'm happy to answer.

It'd be easier to ask you in person. Can I take you out for dinner?

She stared at the message, rounding her eyes as the seconds ticked by. The Domme in her purred a yes, but warning bells in another part of her brain were strident in their ringing. It was that wariness that led her to a crueler answer than one she wanted to give.

Nathan, we're not dating.

She inhaled, then exhaled with careful slowness to ease the tightening in her chest. It was best to speak plainly sometimes — or so she told herself.

The message he returned with was the last thing she expected.

No, but would you consider this repayment for the guidance you provide?

The warning bells faded to silence. Yes, that was an acceptable reason for a meal together. She was not above being bribed with food.

I suppose that is fitting. You may take me out for dinner.

The diner on 2nd?

She dropped her phone onto the table, and it landed with a dull thud. Just like that, Lani's chest tightened again, this time for a different reason, and she struggled for breath. Her fingers curled into fists of their own accord, knuckles white as she fought for control of her emotions. She closed her eyes, but that proved to be a mistake as the image of August's broken body surfaced in her mind's eye. Every one of her muscles bunched up with tension.

That was the diner she, Luna and August had left from before the drunk driver had hit them.

Breathe. In. Out. In. Out. With a sheer force of will, she pushed the picture in her head away, searching for a more soothing visualization to help calm her down. Nathan's adoring face as he looked up at her from where he kneeled between her legs floated to the forefront. Her muscles loosened, but accompanying the relief was a large dose of guilt. With shaky hands, she reached back out to type a response, to call the whole thing off, but Luna's words resurfaced in a faint whisper.

"Being with someone doesn't invalidate your love for another person."

Forcing more air into her lungs, she resumed typing,

Let's go somewhere else. How about the pizzeria on Park St. in Little Rome?

Sounds good. Tomorrow at 7? I'll make reservations.

See you then.

The next two days became in a blur. She remembered to send Nathan more reading material, but with the number of client sessions she had, time passed with ease. Still, the best part was the message that came late Tuesday morning.

Luna's back. We're fine. We'll be okay.

Lani wanted to ask more but understanding that Jacob and Luna needed time to themselves to reconnect, she only expressed her joy in a subdued text back and refrained from calling to squeal over the phone. Still, it had her grinning until dinner with Nathan.

She entered the restaurant in a pair of skinny jeans, a light drop-shoulder black sweater and shiny but simple plain stilettos. When she spotted Nathan, her lips curved into a delicious smile. She was looking forward to this and hoped he was, too.

Instead, Lani found him staring at his phone with a frown, his brows drawn together.

"Is everything okay?"

Nathan looked up and put down the device. "Yeah. One of my business partners, Daniel, said he's throwing a party next week."

Lani tilted her head to one side. "Not a party person, I gather?"

"No, it's not that. I'm not sure why he is trying to persuade me to bring a date."

A small laugh spilled from her lips as she leaned closer. "Ah, it appears we seem to have similar problems."

"You mean Darryl?"

Lani nodded with a theatrical sigh. Of course, he would remember their first conversation at the bar. Darryl wasn't hiding his intentions, and Nathan was observant. "That dear boy needs to go look in the mirror."

She could see she had piqued his curiosity as he leaned in as well. With a teasing smile, she eased back in her chair. And when she saw the waiter approach, she gave Nathan a wink.

"Good evening, as requested, our pinot noir." He introduced the wine as he opened the bottle and poured a little for tasting.

Nathan gestured toward Lani. "Please, for the lady's approval."

Damn, he served well. Lani took the glass, inhaling the aroma before taking a sip, letting the liquid swirl around her mouth. When she swallowed and nodded, the waiter dipped his head and served them each a glass.

The waiter retreated afterward, allowing them time with their menus. Lani scanned the choices distributed between pizza and pasta. Silence settled as she contemplated, but when she looked up, she found Nathan studying her.

Another small smile graced her lips. "See something you like?"

"Yes." The answer came swift and sure. His steel grays darkened.

Oh my.

The waiter returned, oblivious to the tension building at the table at first. But the entire time they gave their orders, Nathan's gaze never left her, and the waiter had to clear his throat several times. Lani watched in amusement as the waiter retreated with haste before she returned her attentions to him.

"Darling, you're going to bore a hole into me," she chided.

And with that, Nathan cast his eyes downward. "Sorry."

"It's all right." She kept a giggle from spilling forth but smirked. "I think you just made the waiter a tad uncomfortable." Before Nathan could come up with any more protests, she folded her arms on the table and crossed her legs. "So what did you want to ask about?"

Rather than answering her question, Nathan brought his phone up, and after a few taps, turned it around to her. "This paragraph about the lifestyle, about the submissive not being passive. How realistic is it?"

Lani took his phone in hand and scanned the paragraph he'd indicated. Everything in her softened, and for a moment, she fought to not let tears spill.

"Very." Her voice was quiet. "But like every relationship, every D/s dynamic has their own rhythms. It's not black or white. Some subs are more passive, some choosing to be more active in their service. And Doms have their own preferences, too, and that is why finding the precise right pairing is rare and more difficult than most people think."

"You had someone."

Startled, Lani's eyes rounded into saucers and her breathing hitched. It took all her control to keep herself in her seat.

"I did." There was a slight quiver in her voice, but she kept her tone even. "He passed away three years ago. His name was August."

Nathan reached across the table, offering his hand, palm up. She stared at it before placing her much smaller one on top.

"I'm sorry for your loss." Nathan gave her a small squeeze, and for some odd reason, the simple gesture helped ease the pain in her heart.

"Thank you."

Chapter Fourteen

A quiet settled between them, but Nathan's warm touch kept her steady while waves of grief washed over her. The moment broke them apart only when the food came.

Lani cleared her throat and withdrew her hand. With her eyes misting over, she took the napkin in her lap and wiped the corners.

"The paragraph you showed me portrays a relationship that already has parameters and boundaries established, that the trust in each other has already been developed. It's different for each pairing, but with enough time, knowledge and communication, anyone can get there."

She found Nathan watching her once more.

"Lani, your food is getting cold." There was a gentleness in his voice that made her flash him a smile. They both understood her need for a distraction. Only at her first bite, though, did he start on his own meal.

They ate and sipped their wines in the same companionable silence, and bit by bit, the knots of tension eased within her until she felt she could breathe once more. She considered the man in front of her, who seemed to have an instinct to anticipate what she needed.

"You mentioned different styles," Nathan began as she finished the last of her dish. "What is yours like?"

If anything told her that this was more personal than Nathan had first let on, this did. Lani dabbed at her mouth with her napkin to hide her smile. But when she lowered it to speak, she gave her reply with all the seriousness the question deserved. "It depends on the dolly. I've been formally trained and am proficient with whips and other implements, but I'm not into pain play." And now she allowed herself to lean forward, touching her lips with steepled hands. "I do favor exerting control in so many other ways."

To her delight, Nathan swallowed hard. "How?" It came out as a hoarse whisper.

Luna's words echoed in her mind, soothing the guilt away. She could play, could tease, and it didn't lessen her memory of August.

"Darling, do you really want to find out in public?"

Their waiter, of course, chose this precise moment to return to clear their plates. Nathan cleared his throat again and shifted in his chair. Lani wondered what she would find if she could peek under the table.

"Would anyone like to see the dessert menu?"

Across from her, Nathan stiffened. She could prolong this bit, but for his behavior this evening, the boy deserved some reprieve. "Not tonight, thank you."

"Just the check please." The strain in his voice was audible.

"Certainly."

She was about to do this. Her heart pounded, but on the surface, she smoothed her expression into one of serenity. "Come over." She did not phrase it as a question.

Nathan nodded.

He settled the bill, and they both rose. Nathan offered his arm and Lani linked hers with his. They flagged a cab, and she gave the driver her address. As they sat side by side, she played her fingers over his thigh and under her touch, his muscles bunched and flexed in small twitches.

Lani leaned her head close and whispered in his ear. "This is for preemptively ordering the wine but giving me control over your choice of it." She studied him as the hints of comprehension crept into his expression and she grinned.

It didn't take long before the cab pulled up to her modest two-storied house at the end of a cul-de-sac. Or perhaps she was just having too much fun teasing him. As they left the car, Lani glimpsed Nathan adjusting himself again before exiting.

She led him up the landing and let them in. As soon as she closed the door, she grabbed his hand and tugged him toward her. Before he could react, she pressed her mouth against his. He groaned, and she devoured the sound as she threaded her fingers through his hair.

When he enveloped her in his arms, she tilted her head back to break the kiss but remained still close enough that her lips brushed against his as she spoke. "And that's for dealing with Bryan the other night. Your protective side is very sexy."

"I can get used to these rewards," he murmured, leaning forward to catch another kiss, only for her to hold two fingers up between them to stop him.

"Now now, a reward is not a reward if you also receive it for no reason." Her eyes lit up as she winked. "Besides, there are more conversations to be had."

Nathan sighed but nodded once, releasing his arms around her. "Yes, Ma'am."

Good boy.

She led him to the kitchen where she bustled to make herbal tea. "Have a seat." She gestured to the small table. "Would you like some tea, too?"

"Yes, thank you."

When she brought two mugs over, Lani decided that she rather enjoyed the sight of him sitting there.

"We alluded to this, danced around with our words before. But now let us speak plainly." Lani noted the way Nathan straightened to attention. "Do you want to take the next step and try submitting to me more formally in the bedroom?"

Nathan opened and closed his mouth once more. Lani understood being so direct might cause his discomfort, but she would have no misunderstanding between them.

"Have I been that obvious?"

Lani shook her head a little. "Only in that your questions were becoming more and more personal. This isn't the line of inquiry you would have taken had it been to understand The Playgrounds."

A look of guilt flashed across his face.

That would not do. "You're doing the right thing, Nathan. You should ask. It's the best way to learn, not just about the lifestyle but about yourself and if it's for you."

He nodded once.

"Now, back to my original question. Is this something you desire?"

"I'm...not sure."

Honesty. But she saw hesitation in his eyes, in how he held himself stiff, donning an invisible armor. She would crack those defenses he hid behind, strip him down to his bare essence.

"Would you like me to take the choice away from you?"

The next nod came much quicker. It was all the permission she needed.

"Give me a safeword."

"Willow."

Lani tilted her head to one side.

"There was this giant willow tree by the house I grew up in. I used to climb and hide in it when I was a kid." Nathan turned his gaze downward.

She swung around the table and tilted his chin up with two fingers. "Come along, then."

Certain he would follow, Lani spun on her heels and led the way upstairs, past closed doors that held her personal life's secrets. With each step, her confidence grew as her dominant side surfaced until they stepped into her master bedroom.

The king-sized bed took up most of the space in the middle, the headboard against one wall. Above it, three canvases stretched across the expanse, each a tasteful image of a body bound by rope. The model was unidentifiable, but only on closer look would one realize it was the same man in each of the black and white shots. She stopped by the side of the mattress and spun around, aware of his gaze upon those pictures.

A small voice whispered in her mind about the significance of even this simple gesture. It was the first time she had permitted another male in this room in three years. But it didn't feel wrong. So, Lani didn't let herself dwell on the implications, choosing instead to lose herself in the moment.

"Take your top off and kneel."

The man struggle with the command, conflict playing over his face. She gave him the time and space to come to terms with his own desires. Despite her commands, he would have to choose to submit with his actions, if not the words yet. She would not force him. When he bent his knees onto the hard floor before her at last, she touched his shoulder with featherlight caresses, trailing her fingers against his heated skin.

"You may not understand yet, but submission requires strength. Maybe not the kind you're used to, but it is *not* a weakness."

Taking her time to circle him, she traced along the curve of his neck, the taut muscles across his back. "In this space and for this time, you are mine and you will follow my orders. Submission will be rewarded, and disobedience will be punished, each according to the act's magnitude and at my discretion. But I will also make it clear what you did right and what you did wrong. Do you understand?"

"Yes, Ma'am."

She dipped her head in approval.

"You hesitated when I ask you to strip and kneel. Given your newness, I will let it go, but normally, that itself is a punishable offense." Lani returned to stand in front of him and tilted his chin upward so that she could look him in the eye, a smile playing on her lips.

"And my punishments are not of pain but of denial. I don't think you would like that much, would you?"

"No, Ma'am." The answer came quick enough. He was learning. There was a seriousness in which he took in her words, but there was also a glint in his eyes. "And Ma'am, what of rewards?"

Lani laughed at his boldness, the hint of playfulness in his tone. "Why, darling, we'll have to think of some suitable treats, won't we?" She bent forward to whisper in his ear. "And won't it be fun to find out?"

Not bothering to wait for an answer, she straightened and walked toward a chest of drawers leaning against another wall. It had been a while since she'd cracked open her personal collection, and she chose a pair of Velcro handcuffs, one of the simplest things she could start with. A man of Nathan's size and strength could break out of them without a problem, but it was the symbolism she sought.

"Come. Take off the rest of your clothes and sit on the bed." She held up the cuffs for him to see.

It was a pleasure to witness someone like him bend his will to her and move to her commands. As he unfolded himself, his steel grays met hers, even as he reached down to unbutton his pants, each gesture slow and deliberate. His gaze never broke hers as he slid the now offensive piece of clothing over his hips, freeing his already-erect cock. Oh, he was teasing her, and she approved.

He sat on the edge of her bed, and she grew hot at the sight.

Still clothed in contrast, she climbed on beside him, then shuffled until she kneeled behind him. She brushed her lips against his nape and giggled as his muscles bunched up again

"So tense." She kneaded his shoulders and worked her way down along his arms, over his biceps then drew his hands backward until his wrists lay crisscross against the small of his back. She pressed another kiss on his shoulder, then strapped the cuffs on.

His breathing grew more shallow as he tested his bonds. Lani grinned in delight as she slid off the bed until she stood before him, observing the way he wrestled with his own arousal. When she wrapped a hand around his erection, she felt it throb and heard the sharp intake of air above.

Lani took a step back, allowing her eyes to roam over his body in admiration. "Well, darling, let's play."

Chapter Fifteen

If Nathan had to take a long, hard look at the darkest recesses of his memories, he would have to admit that being handcuffed during sex was one of his fantasies. But all his imagined scenarios paled compared to the actual situation he found himself in right now.

Here he sat with a throbbing erect cock, waiting for the goddess before him to lead them to the next step. A part of him yearned to see her strip, to behold what lay beneath the sweater and jeans, but he waited with stoic patience instead. An instinct stilled his tongue.

"Tonight, we will explore the edges of how far you're willing to submit." Again, she brushed her fingers, featherlight, against his cock, that only made it twitch. "You may not come without my permission. You may not move or touch without my approval. Do you understand?" Her voice held an almost sing-along lilt that was near hypnotic.

He bobbed his head, holding himself as still as possible. Never mind that her maddening hands kept wandering across his body, exploring and teasing. It would be so easy to snap these cuffs and break free, but he knew crossing that line would end things — and he wanted to see where this would go.

Lani took one step closer, then threw a leg over his to straddle and settle onto his lap, the roughness of her jeans scraping against his skin. As she descended on his neck to kiss and nibble, he stifled a groan. With infinite slowness, she worked her way back up to place a light peck on the corner of his mouth before out of nowhere, she produced a strip of black silk. Her hazel eyes were the last thing he saw before the blindfold she tied around his head cut off his vision.

It wasn't so much that his other senses sharpened as he paid more attention to them, deprived of sight. Her breath caressed his skin, first in front, before she moved behind him. The weight on the mattress shifted and bare flesh pressed against his back as her lips brushed along the ridge of his ear.

"Tell me... What are you imagining in your head right now?" Lani whispered.

That was easy. "You topless. I can feel you pressed against me." He swallowed and took a risk with his next words. "I want to see you."

Her soft laugh tickled him. "Hm, in that case, why don't we make that your first reward?"

He groaned at the thought of needing to wait to be granted the sight of her, but his cock only pulsed, as if in agreement. Again, the weight behind him shifted and now a bare leg with silken smooth skin slid and straddled over him, contrasting the jeans. Molten heat pressed against his length. Shit, she was naked on his lap, and he could neither hold her nor content himself with the image of her nude body. The woman knew how to torture a man without inflicting a single ounce of pain.

Before he could finish the thought, the warmth that enveloped his shaft began to move up and down, coating him with slickness. One arm draped over him for balance, and a moan from her sent shivers down his spine. She was rubbing against him, using him for her pleasure. Next, she brushed her hand against his cock. Or he thought that was what it was, given the temperature and textural difference. But rather than holding his length, it seemed to bump against him instead in uneven touches. Her moans grew louder and her movements became faster, even as she squirmed on him. *Is she pleasuring herself?* In his mind's eye, he imagined her playing with her clit as she rubbed herself along his manhood.

Christ, he was going to come from that image alone.

She must have felt his body tighten in response. Lani slowed and pressed her chest closer. "Remember my standing command."

Fuck, why had he agreed to this?

Because you love this. She has given you the best lays of your life.

Traitorous voice.

"Yes, Ma'am," he managed through gritted teeth.

"Good." Lani exhaled and began moving again.

Behind the blindfold, Nathan closed his eyes, losing himself to the sensations—her wetness coating his cock, the sounds of her pleasure filling the air, the heat of her flesh against his. He curled his fingers into fists, digging the blunt nails into his palms, hoping to hold off his impending orgasm.

Her breathing grew more ragged, and he had to resist the temptation to thrust up, to grind harder against her to bring her over the edge. But he remembered her orders and held himself still. As her body trembled, he tilted forward. "Please, let me kiss you." His arms strained against the position the cuffs kept him in.

The arm on his shoulder moved with swiftness, and before he could guess its path, she fisted his hair and pulled his head back. Her lips descended on his with an almost-savage kiss. When her tongue tangled with his and stars filled his vision, she grinded and bucked against him. A fresh torrent of her juices soaked his lap, and he could only hope that she stayed pressed to him, even as he swallowed her screams of ecstasy.

At last, she slumped against him, great heaves shaking her shoulders as she rested her forehead against his shoulder. His cock throbbed against her, but despite the achy need that filled his body, he remained still, letting her take what time she needed for recovery. Nathan contented himself with basking in her heat and nuzzled her with the ridge of his nose.

With a shaky hand, she reached up and undid his blindfold, tossing the material somewhere on the bed out of his line of sight. He smiled at the sight of her, sweat drenched, glowing from her orgasm, and chanced pressing a kiss on the top of her head.

She looked up, her eyes fogged with a sexual haze. "Good job. You held still and didn't come."

"I tried." Despite the modesty, his smile broadened.

Lani chuckled in return and kissed him with much more gentleness this time. "You did well." She slid her hand between them and with slow care she scraped a nail along his length, drawing another harsh growl from him.

"Do you want to be inside?" she whispered. "To feel my pussy clenching and squeezing you? Do you want to thrust into me until I let you come?"

"Yeesss," he hissed, his hip almost bucking as her fingers played over the sensitive head. "Please. Christ, woman." He needed her.

She laughed softly at his desperate plea and ground herself against him, soliciting a moan from both of them. Her lips descended onto his bare shoulders once more with lazy licks and nibbles that did nothing to relieve his arousal.

"Tell me." She was moving against him again, grinding, rubbing herself against his shaft.

Nathan was pretty sure he couldn't handle another round of teasing like that, especially given that he could see the wanton expression on her face. But she must know by now that words were not his forte. Perhaps that was what she meant by pushing him to the edge of submission. It took a different kind of strength to act despite a weakness.

"You. I want to sheathe myself inside you — fuck you until I have you screaming beneath me. I want you to come on my cock, then I want to come inside you."

She had stilled as he talked, and now she smiled the most beautiful smile he had seen yet, pleasure shining in her eyes and pride on the curve of her lips. With deftness, she leaned in and ripped the Velcro off, freeing his hands. "You have free rein."

Yes!

With his newfound freedom, he cupped her ass, rubbing and kneading her cheeks as he lifted her almost without effort. With one thrust upward, he plunged into her, a growl rumbling in the back of his throat. There was no finesse, no slow build-up as he arched into her. It was his turn, and he sought his relief. As she spasmed around him with the first strokes, his logical brain switched off. All he wanted, all he needed was her.

"More," he grunted, and it became a chant in his head. *More of this. More of her.*

"That's it, darling. Take all of me," she cooed in his ear, her voice husky with clear want of him.

As she rode him, he grasped her ass tighter and moved her up and down, lifting her weight as though she were no heavier than a feather. As he furrowed his brows with concentration, his world narrowed to that intense sensation of his cock enveloped by her tight muscles. He feasted on her breast, capturing a nipple, which was hardened to a pebble, and sucked it hard. When she spasmed in response, almost milking him right then and there, he let go, then captured the other one, swirling his tongue around it.

Lani's stomach tightened seconds before she tossed her head backward, curls cascading down her back, squeezed her eyes shut and exploded around his cock. Nathan watched the sight in awe, but he could not stop thrusting into her until his every sense was overwhelmed and pushed him over the edge. With a roar, he pulled her hips tight against him and thrusted hard one last time to pour his seed into her.

His orgasm made his head light and the world spin. They both collapsed onto the bed, him still inside her, her resting her body along the length of him, their legs dangling off the side. Neither of them spoke, both trying to catch their breaths.

"Christ," Nathan muttered under his breath and rubbed his face with one hand.

Lani giggled and nuzzled his chest. To his surprise, she flexed her muscles, giving his cock another squeeze. He groaned, over-sensitive from his climax. But when she tried to rise, he wrapped his arms around her.

"Please."

"All right," she replied, relaxing against him once more. He stroked her hair, combing through the tangled curls, careful not to tug on any knots.

"Mm-m, that's nice." From her tone, she must be sleepy. He felt the same way.

"Let me take care of you." He reached for her hand and drew it up to kiss her knuckle.

"Permission granted," Lani murmured, her eyes already closing.

With more willpower than he'd thought he still possessed, Nathan lifted her off him, suppressing a groan. He rose from the bed and carried her to lay her down, then followed, scooping her into his arms.

She shifted, adjusting to cushion her head against his shoulder. "You did well, Nathan." She traced idle shapes along his chest, and he savored her touch on him, her softness flushed against his body.

"So do I get a treat?" He grinned with daring.

A small chuckle made her shake against him. "You already got your reward, but all right. I'll indulge you this one time. What would you like?"

Nathan considered, his hand caressing along her back. "Information. I want to know more about you."

She stilled beside him and when she looked up, her lips curved into a bittersweet smile as she reached up to trace his jawline with a finger. "Ah, Nathan."

He prepared for her to reject his request.

Lani sucked in a breath. Usually, she was so certain of herself, oozing confidence with every action, but Nathan could make out the conflict playing out inside her head, in the way her brows drew together, and she pursed her lips.

"Very well." Her poise and surety returned with those two words. "You may ask one question as your treat."

Her agreement surprised him. Nathan knew Lani was trying to not get too close, but he wanted to get to know her more. The risk had paid off. "What's your favorite ice-cream flavor?"

She pushed herself up, staring at him, her brows arched in apparent surprise. Good, he had caught her off guard. She had probably expected him to use the opportunity to find out something more personal, and he was going to respect her need for distance. Meanwhile, he would be patient.

"Butterscotch," she replied and giggled. "Yours?"

"Chocolate." He was a simple man, after all.

"Mm-m, I'll remember that." Lani lay back down and resettled in his arms. After a few minutes, her breathing evened out, and a quick glance downward proved she had fallen asleep.

Nathan closed his eyes, a sense of contentment settling deep within him. He listened to the rhythm of her beating heart and let it whisk him away to the land of dreams.

Chapter Sixteen

Are you going to The Playgrounds?

I believe so. Are you working there tonight?

Yes, but just to check on our equipment. Should I come find you after?

You may.

Friday night meant both regulars and tourists packed the club. But that wasn't why Lani was thrumming with joy. No. It had much more to do with the couple standing before her. Both Luna and Jacob glowed with renewed love for each other, and it made Lani grin ever wider to see it. Then there was also Nathan, hovering over her from behind like a bodyguard. That part amused her.

"I'm sorry," Luna started after their hug, but Lani waved her off.

"Lunch is on you next week, and I'm ordering the most expensive tea latte and an extra piece of cake."

Luna laughed. "Done. Lunch next week sounds wonderful."

Out of the corner of her eye, Lani glimpsed Bryan, and her body stiffened in alarm. The man moved through the crowds, a scowl on his face. She could only hope that most subs would have the good sense to avoid him tonight.

Her eyes met Jacob's, and he gave her a perceptible nod before his attention was taken away from needing to soothe Luna. Before they could converse, Jacob left, but not before jerking his head toward his sub. Lani understood what her friend meant. Distract and take care of her.

A hand startled her enough for her to glance back at Nathan, who remained as stoic as ever. But even in the dim lighting, she spied the concern etched on his face.

"I'm okay, but there may be trouble," Lani mouthed.

Nathan nodded in response and pivoted, his gaze tracking Jacob's path toward Bryan.

But Jacob could take care of himself. She needed to keep Luna occupied. Tugging at Luna's hand, she moved and half-turned to include Nathan into the conversation. "Sweetie, I'd like you to meet Nathan."

"Hello, Nathan," Luna greeted with a smile.

Lani struggled to suppress a giggle. Most people would not have spied the surprise that widened his eyes ever so slightly. But she was learning all Nathan's minute expressions and knew that her introducing him to her friends had caught him off guard. To his credit, he recovered fast enough to incline his head in acknowledgment.

Luna eyed her and raised a brow in question. The giggle broke out at that. "I'll tell you over lunch next week."

Then Lani noticed Luna's gaze straying again. *Crap.* "Luna?"

"I'll be right back, Lani!" Luna shouted over the noise as she left them to push through the crowd.

This was not good. Lani started to follow Luna, but the wall of people had already closed the path the sub had taken. She tried to see past the throng to spy where her friend had gone, but with her height, even with the heels she wore, it was impossible to catch a glimpse.

A warm hand grasped hers. On instinct, Lani was about to pull away when a familiar low voice murmured in her ear. "This way. Follow me."

Although Nathan was not as tall compared to Jacob or Darryl, the crowd parted for him, regardless. Perhaps it was his build or that brisk, no-nonsense posture he held. Or maybe it was the business-like expression that brooked no arguments. A moment of gratefulness welled in her and she made a mental note to reward him later, even as he led her toward the door and out to the parking lot.

They emerged out of the club, the last of the summer night heat blasting them. Under the twinkle of streetlights, Lani could just make out the figures by the cars, and when her eyes adjusted, they rounded with horror as the action unfolded in the distance, too far for either her or Nathan to do anything about it.

Bryan lunged. Jacob turned around. Lani's hands flew to cover her mouth as Luna threw herself in between the two men then collapsed on the ground.

"Luna!" Jacob's scream rang through the air in anguish and fear.

Oh God.

"Lani, go get Darryl *now*. Tell him to notify my team and call 9-1-1." Nathan's tone was commanding, but Lani recognized that his professional side had kicked in. With herculean effort to suppress the rising wave of terror inside her, she nodded and spun around to hurry back into the club, resisting the urge to freeze on the spot and curl up into a ball.

Lani burst into The Playgrounds and forced her way through once more. "Darryl," she half screamed, drawing his attention away from the current patrons he was talking to. Any thoughts of discretion fled her mind. Her chest heaved in big breaths. "Call 9-1-1 and security. Something happened outside. Luna's hurt."

She waited only as long as she was certain that Darryl had received her message before she hurried back out to the parking lot, her heart in her throat. Already, people streamed after her, curious about what was happening, but she didn't care.

As she approached, trembles made balancing on her heels more difficult than she ever remembered. Nathan had Bryan pinned down, his hands bound behind him. But it was Luna's still figure in Jacob's arms that shook her to the core. *Blood.* There was so much blood. Her mind superimposed August's broken body on top and she took one step backward, a strangled whine like that of a wounded animal emerging from her throat. No, she couldn't lose anyone again. She couldn't live through that.

"Lani. *Lani!*" Nathan's voice cut through her haze and her eyes snapped to meet his. Something about his steadiness stilled the gibbering horror within her. "Stay with us." His gaze strayed to behind her, where a small crowd was gathering. "Shit. Lani, I need you to watch this guy."

Bryan. Lani's expression hardened, and she nodded. Hatred and anger helped her focus, and she strode over until she stood next to the culprit's prone form. With a vicious need for revenge driving her, she placed one firm heel on his upper back close to his neck. "One wrong move and I swear..." Lani could hardly recognize her own menacing voice.

But the man had no regrets and only scowled at her. *Psychopath.* It didn't matter. There was nowhere for him to run now.

"That's it, Jacob. Keep her in recovery position," Nathan instructed, then rose to hold up his hands. "Give them space." He was pushing back the crowd single-handedly.

"Fuck." Darryl had arrived with the rest of his team close at his heels, and in the distance, the sound of sirens grew louder and louder as the emergency vehicles neared.

She watched the scene unfold as the paramedics rushed toward Luna. Every squirm beneath her made her press down harder, drawing grunts as responses. Lani had no problems crushing the worm, and she only grinded her heel down until a warm blanket and steady arms enveloped her.

"Come on, Lani. The cops have got this." Nathan's low voice slid in to reach her consciousness, and she allowed him to lead her away. He never stopped holding her, even when he tilted her face up toward him.

"Luna will be okay. She's alive," he told her.

It was what she needed to hear. Her entire body sagged with relief, and he tightened his embrace, holding her up.

"She's okay," Lani echoed, working her throat with the words then repeated the phrase, clinging to it like a lifeline. The image of August's still form receded from her mind.

"Yes." Nathan stroked her hair and kissed her temple.

"Nate!" A Latino woman approached. Though not in uniform, it was clear she was one of the detectives.

Nate. People called him Nate. Not knowing that detail until now annoyed her.

"Julia." Nathan did not relinquish his hold but turned toward her.

"What kind of mess have you landed yourself in this time?" The woman's discerning eyes moved from Nathan to Lani. She looked up and straightened, ready to meet any challenge this cop may have readied for her. Every part of her bristled at the tone the woman used with her sub.

Her sub.

She chalked that thought up to the shock of the situation and the adrenaline pumping through her system.

"Look. We're the closest thing to your witnesses here, besides the victim and her boyfriend. But can you cut us some slack and let us get to the hospital first?"

The detective hesitated, still looking back and forth between her and Nathan before, with a sigh, she nodded. "Want a lift there?"

"Yes, thank you." That came more easily as Lani recognized the allowance for what it was, banking on Nathan's goodwill with the force. And when Julia waited until the doctors had confirmed Luna was in stable condition before taking their statements, Lani's appreciation for both her and Nathan increased further.

After they gave the cops what they needed, Julia returned to the station, leaving her and Nathan alone at last, just hovering in the hospital hallway.

"I'm going to go check in on them." With a pat on his shoulder, Lani rose from the chair and opened the door to the temporary room they had Luna in. They were still keeping her in ICU because of the depth of the knife wound.

She stood next to Jacob but remained silent, giving him the time to compose himself first.

"She's stable for now, but she lost a lot of blood. We'll know for sure tomorrow." Jacob looked like hell as he clutched Luna's pale, limp hand, and her heart went out to him. Lani knew how it felt to lose someone, and she placed her palm on his shoulder.

The smell of the place threatened to overwhelm her, the beeping sound of machines scraping at her nerves. Lani had never been good with hospitals, but since that day August had died, she found even the thought of one intolerable.

Jacob brushed his free hand by the back of hers, and it was only then that she realized she had fisted Jacob's shirt, her knuckles white. "Go home and get some rest. I'll text you as soon as there's any change."

She opened her mouth to protest but exhaled a slow breath instead. It was useless to argue and even more futile to suggest Jacob do the same. Luna was his responsibility and his heart. It would take a team of men to wrestle him away from her in this moment. "All right."

As she closed the door behind her, Nathan stood and opened his arms without another word. Relieved, Lani stepped into his embrace, buried her face against his chest and let him comfort her with gentle stroking of her hair. "Thank you."

He nodded and she felt more than saw the movement above her.

"Lani?"

She looked up at the speaker before easing away. Nathan released his hold around her and remained where he was to give her room.

"Richard?" Another one of her clients. *Right.* He was a doctor at this hospital.

"Are you okay?" Richard, dressed in his scrubs, looked from Lani to Nathan then back but Lani didn't feel up to explaining that part, nor did the doctor inquire. She always appreciated his tactfulness, even though sometimes it impeded their counseling process.

Lani cleared her throat and stepped away from Nathan's arms, straightening. "I am. But my friend got hurt in an incident." She glanced at the door to Luna's room.

"Ah. The patient with the stab wound?"

She nodded, still not trusting her voice. Everything about this place, this situation, threw her off.

"It's my shift, anyway. I'll keep a good eye on her."

"Thanks." Then it was as if her brain restarted. "I know the hospital is always lacking space. Is there any way I can get my friend moved into a private room?" She lowered to a murmur. "I think if we try to pry her Dom away, we may be asking for trouble."

Richard nodded, his expression thoughtful. "Let me walk you to the reception and find someone to help you with the paperwork."

By the time all was said and done, the night had exhausted Lani and wrung her out emotionally. Once she finished setting everything in motion and was certain Luna had a nice room to move to, Lani looked up at Nathan. "Let's go home."

Again, Nathan dipped his head in acknowledgment then guided her out of the hospital, taking out his phone only to order a Lyft. As they stood there waiting, he wrapped one arm around her, pulling her close. Lani's shivers receded. She hadn't even realized she was shaking.

"They'll be okay. I'll check in with Julia in the morning."

"Thank you." Lani's eyes misted over, but she refused to shed the tears about to spill. "You didn't have to do any of this. You're not obligated just because…"

Nathan shook his head and gave her a tender smile that threatened to break down every defense she had erected around her heart over the years. "I wanted to."

The trip home was quiet and somber as Lani wrestled with her emotions and the swirl of confusion inside. Never had she felt so uncertain, but she knew part of it was because of how near death her friend had gotten and how much it had drenched up old memories and fears. When they arrived at her place, she shuffled in like a zombie before she remembered Nathan was still there.

One look at him, hovering at the threshold, unsure of his welcome, brought out the Domme in her. All night, he had been her rock, lifting the world from her shoulders in unwavering support. And now it was her turn to reassure him. How could she not accept his presence?

"Come in. Stay."

Chapter Seventeen

Nathan stayed the night—and the following three. After the first, it had become clear to both of them that she needed him there, especially when she woke up screaming as memories and nightmares blended into a disturbing cocktail in her sleep.

There was always so much blood when she dreamed.

In the early morning, as fingerlings of light filtered into her room, Lani bolted up, shaking in a cold sweat, and drew her knees to her chest.

Nathan sat up, already alert, and reached to rub her back, concern chasing the sleep from his eyes. "Another bad dream?"

She worked her throat, swallowing several times before nodding. The nightmares still rattled her, but they were getting less visceral as the immediacy of the incident faded. Now they consisted of vague waves of anger and grief rather than vivid imagery, producing unsettling dread instead of heart-pounding fear.

"Do you want me to get you a glass of water?"

Lani shook her head. "Hold me." Her voice was hoarse as she unwound herself, letting Nathan's arms surround her. She nudged him back, and they both lay down once more, her settling to rest one cheek against his shoulder.

The days were not so bad. Lani had Ophelia, her assistant, rescheduled some appointments, making time for Julia and her colleagues so that she could provide what information she had. Yesterday, it had been a relief for her to report to Jacob and Darryl that the cops thought it was a solid case against Bryan. *A small comfort in dark times.*

Exhausted, she let Nathan's warmth and quiet breathing lull her back to slumber before her phone buzzed, vibrating against the night table. She shifted in his arms and, as his hold loosened, she grabbed the device with one hand, rubbing her bleary eyes with her other.

It didn't take long for her vision to focus on the screen, and when she made out the words on it, her first genuine smile in days spread across her lips. "She's okay. She woke up. They're keeping her for a few more days for observation, but she should be able to go home soon."

Nathan smiled down at her and gave her a gentle squeeze.

With a soft sigh that released much of the tension in her body, she closed her eyes again.

"Do you want to visit them today?"

Lani shook her head, though she kept her eyelids shut. "They should have some time alone. Jacob will have an overwhelming need to reassure himself that

Luna's okay and still his." She giggled. "I'll let Luna deal with the consequences of her actions by herself."

When she looked up, Nathan was staring at her, his brow furrowing. "Is that just Jacob or part of being a Dom?"

Lani chuckled and reached up to trace his jawline with one finger. "Oh no, we're a possessive lot once we decide someone's ours."

A shiver coursed through his body at her touch, and it was Lani's turn to arch her eyebrow, but she kept quiet, studying all the micro-expressions on his face as he worked through his thoughts. It was a fascinating thing to watch.

"Should we celebrate, then? I can make some French toast and bring it back to bed."

"Yes, go ahead, but leave them in the kitchen. It's time for me to get up, anyway." Lani rose and gave him a light kiss. "Thank you." Then she walked, nude with hips swaying, into the bathroom, closing the door behind her.

In her temporary solitude, she wrapped a silk kimono-styled robe around herself and braced her hands against the cream-colored marble top of the vanity. She lifted her head to study the wreck of her reflection in the mirror. Red rimmed and puffy-eyed from the lack of sleep, Lani looked like she had been through hell herself. She had grappled with the thought of losing someone again for the last few days, but only now, when everything had turned out okay did she allow herself to feel the full range of her emotions.

Tears came rolling down her cheeks in big fat drops. It was close—too close—and she could not help but churn in her mind what would have happened if the knife had entered just an inch or two over, had pierced an organ. Her heart wouldn't survive if she had lost Luna as well, before her time. Unable to bear the sight of her own meltdown, she turned around, but rather than remaining standing, her knees gave out and she sank to the ground, sitting while leaning against the cabinet.

Her shoulders heaved with great racking sobs now that the floodgates were opened. A small whimper struggled to escape in the back of her throat as fear of what could have happened washed over her in crashing waves. There, on her bathroom floor, she came apart, collapsing into the raw pain that she had held at bay for years, that once more tore at her until she knew nothing else.

Caught up in the storm that battered her heart, she must have missed the knocks, looking up only when the door opened with slow reluctance. Nathan poked his head in, his expression drawn in worry and concern.

"Lani..."

He didn't need to see her this way, broken and still falling apart. Lani wiped her face and struggled for at least a veneer of serenity. The last thing she wanted was his pity. "Ah, you seem to have caught me..."

She never finished the sentence as he kneeled down in front and drew her into his arms in a tight embrace. "No, Lani. I get what it's like to lose people. Let it out. Let yourself feel it."

They stayed that way, him letting her cry it out until she had nothing left to shed and she leaned back at last. With gentle fingers, he brushed the last of her tears away. "You don't have to pretend to be okay—not with me. Vulnerability doesn't make you a lesser Domme."

A strangled laugh spilled from her lips, and she laid a hand on his cheek. "How did you suddenly get so wise in the ways of power exchange?"

Nathan grinned. "I have a brilliant teacher."

"Clever boy." She closed her eyes and took a deep, steady breath. The scent of cinnamon and nutmeg called to her, and when she looked at him again, she rewarded him with a smile, dropping her hand to his. "Well, shall we give these French toasts of yours a try before they get much colder?"

"I'd be honored for you to taste test them, Ma'am." He grinned and winked at her.

"Cheeky boy, too." She liked that he was relaxing around her enough to let playfulness slip through. Lani suspected it was a side of him very few got to see.

By the time they settled at her kitchen table, Lani had composed herself. She was still aware, but less concerned about her own fragility. The French toast was impeccable, and she entertained the idea of using Nathan to challenge Jacob to a cooking contest.

Toward the end of breakfast, Nathan's phone rang, and he glanced at it with a groan. "Remind me to shut that thing off," he mumbled with a sour expression as he picked up.

"Hey, Daniel." Nathan made another face at her, and she stifled a giggle. "Yes, I remember the party next week." A pause. "Wait, what? You need an answer *now*?" His brows drew together. "Well…"

"Put him on speaker," Lani ordered.

Hesitation and curiosity warred in his expression, but he did as she'd commanded and set the device down on the table.

"We would be happy to accept your invitation."

"Who is this?" The suspicion was clear in the voice over the line.

"Oh, my name is Lani, and I'll be Nathan's plus one."

There was another pause and Lani smirked as she sensed confusion on the other end. But she had to give credit at how fast Daniel recovered. "That's great. We'll see you two then."

"Till then."

When she looked up, her smirk grew wider at Nathan's stare at her, accompanied by a slack-jawed expression. It was a pleasure to catch him off guard. "Consider it another form of reward."

"Thank... thank you," he stammered.

Lani tilted her chin up. "You're welcome."

* * * *

Nathan knocked on the door, a bouquet in hand. After his tour, then later as a cop, he thought he'd be used to hospitals by now, but they still made him uneasy.

"Come in."

He let himself into the room and breathed a subtle sigh of relief to see Luna alone. From what he'd heard from Lani, Jacob had rarely left her side, and he wasn't sure how the man would feel about his presence. But he needed to take the risk.

Luna's eyes lit up in surprise and a smile spread across her lips. She was still pale but seemed in good spirits. "Nathan, right?"

"Yeah, how are you doing?" He coughed to clear his throat. "Oh, and these are for you."

"Thank you, they're beautiful, and I'm doing okay. Getting better every day." She gestured to an empty chair.

Nathan set the flowers down and eased himself into the seat.

"I heard I have you to thank for helping with…" Luna trailed off and waved at her lap.

"Just doing my job." He rubbed the back of his neck, his gaze straying away with uncertainty.

"How are things with Lani?"

He jerked his head up, then chuckled. "That obvious?"

Luna's lips curved into a small smile. "As much as I appreciate the visit, I know if I were you, I'd try to talk to one of Lani's friends, too, if I was trying to get on her good side."

"Sorry," he muttered, but Luna was already shaking her head.

"Don't be. So how are you two doing?"

"Okay, I think." Nathan paused. "This has shaken her a bit."

Luna's smile faltered and she knitted her brows together. "I'm sorry for worrying her." She exhaled. "I can see why."

"August?"

Startled, her gaze snapped up to him, her lips shaped into an O. "She told you?"

He nodded. "Not in so many words, but she mentioned him as someone she'd lost in the past. I figured this may have called up some painful memories."

Luna cast her glance into her lap, tilting her head forward. "It's not my place to tell you about him and Lani, but I can say that August was a close friend of mine. He helped me come to terms with being a submissive, and he was very dear to her, too." She swallowed hard, then winced as the movement must have tugged at her stitches. "We lost him in a car accident. He was driving when we got hit by a drunk driver."

God. At least on tour, they'd all known death was a risk. To lose someone out of nowhere like that... He couldn't imagine it. With a sigh, he slumped back in the chair and shook his head. "I don't know what I can do to help her." There. He'd said it. Despite his assertion in front of Lani, he worried he wasn't doing enough.

"Just be there for her, Nathan." The gentleness tinged with bittersweetness in Luna's voice made him look up. "It's always been my biggest regret about what happened. When August passed away, I got scared and hid instead of being there for her."

He opened his mouth to speak but couldn't find the right words, so inclined his head in acknowledgment.

"You're a good sub. It's clear to anyone you care for her, so let that be your north star."

It was different hearing it from someone other than Lani. Nathan shifted in his seat with unease.

"Ah, sorry. I thought..."

"We are trying things out. I...have very little experience in the area and Lani is helping me...explore." He left it at that.

Luna reached out and patted his hand. "I understand. It's not easy to come to terms with being a submissive, especially for a guy." She ducked her head to catch his straying gaze. "I'll tell you what. I'll make you the same offer August once made me. If you ever want to talk, my proverbial door will always be open. You can ask me anything."

Nathan stared at her, considering her open invitation. To accept was to take one more step toward acknowledging something he wasn't ready to admit to yet. But at least Luna would be another source of information, another perspective. It was what drove him to his answer.

"I'll remember that. Thank you."

Chapter Eighteen

"Part of your reward."

Lani led them through a door that had always been closed to Nathan before, and when they stepped in, he widened his eyes as he found himself in a walk-in closet larger than he could have ever imagined.

Do I think 'closet'? No, this is a room on its own.

"Come on."

As the initial shock wore off, Nathan began to discern how she organized her clothing. Along one side of the wall hung what must be her professional attire, full of suits, skirts and blouses. His mind drifted, wondering what she did for a living and why he'd never asked. But he had been trying to stay away from questions that seemed personal, as Lani felt to him still skittish about such details.

Next to those articles, there was a smattering of more casual clothing, some jeans, though only a few. It was, for sure, less than the row of formal dresses that filled the rest of that space. Then his gaze landed on the other side, and he sucked in a breath through his teeth.

Fetish-wear of every kind imaginable. Some items he recognized, but others he had never seen her in. As he spied latex material peeking out between a strappy thing and a full-length corseted dress, his cock stirred in his slacks, and he let out an audible groan.

Lani turned and raised a brow at him with a knowing smile but made no other comment. Instead, she laid a hand on the formal wear. "You may choose something for me from this rack."

Nathan cleared his throat. "Yes, Ma'am."

When Lani stepped away to take a seat at the vanity along the back wall, he walked up and sifted through the items with care. He curved his lips into a smile with fondness as he recognized the number he had met her in at the masquerade ball. But, roving onward, he zeroed in on a royal blue dress that was both demure and revealing. Lace covered the top part, transitioning to the opaque material at the breasts, cascading down to the thigh, where more lace would flare out to reach just above the knee.

On Lani, it would be breathtaking.

He felt too big and clumsy as he unhooked the hanger and lifted the dress up as if the slightest tug would tear a hole in the fabric. When he returned to Lani, he almost choked. She had stripped off the casual skirt and blouse she had worn, leaving on a matching set of laced bra and panties, then pulled on a pair of hose held up by a garter belt. As she watched him bring his choice over, she completed her braided updo, fastening a simple silver clip to hold it all up, nestled in her red curls.

"Excellent." She beamed and rose to take the dress from him. Without a single shred of self-consciousness, she slipped the outfit over her head and slid it down her body until the rest of the fabric settled in place.

"Now, do me up." Lani pivoted to face away from him. Upon closer inspection, Nathan spied the little pearl-like buttons that would pull the lace tight against her collar and chest. He leaned down, working each button, all the while wishing he were undoing them instead of doing them up. Maybe later, if he were lucky.

She took a spin, the material of the dress twirling around her. Without her heels, their height difference was even more pronounced as Nathan towered over her. But that mattered little, considering how she radiated power and confidence. "Almost, then we'll go." She patted his cheek and sauntered toward another door next to the vanity. Before she entered, she paused and threw him a glance of expectation over her shoulder.

He followed.

It was a smaller room, more like an actual closet, or that's what Nathan kept telling himself. From floor to ceiling, shoes of every conceivable form filled row after row. A few sat apart from others. Special ones, he guessed.

"You may pick out something to match." Lani gestured as she stood back.

Christ. This was a more daunting task than he had expected, although he was delighting in the exercise. In some ways, it was as if she were allowing him to make a claim on her by wearing his choices.

He curved his lips into a smile when he found a pair of blue suede Mary Janes with kitten heels and retrieved them for her. Okay, so having noticed her love for shoes, he had been studying the terminology, and tonight, it seemed to have paid off.

"Excellent." Lani took them from him and strapped them on. With her outfit completed, they stepped out of the maze of closet and dressing rooms. "Let's go party."

The drive was shorter than he expected as Lani lived in an adjacent neighborhood to Daniel and his wife. When they pulled up to a large house that sprawled across most of its lot, Nathan parked the car with a sigh.

"What's wrong?"

He forced a smile as he turned toward the passenger seat. "Nothing. Just Daniel's parties are..." He trailed off, searching for the right words to describe his unease. "They both came from money and want everyone to know about their..."

"Affluence?" Lani finished the sentence for him and patted his hand. "Remember the party we met at?" When Nathan nodded, she continued. "Don't worry. I'm used to running in such circles, even if they're not my preference. I guess they are not yours, too?"

Another weak smile. "He's a business partner."

Lani gave him a sympathetic squeeze. "I understand. Come on. And the signal is 'honey'. If either of us calls each other that, it means it's time to go."

The knot of anxiety that he didn't realize he had unwound itself, and he nodded. Turning his hand palm up to envelop hers, he offered a small smile. "Thank you."

It was like that, hand in hand, that they approached the grand entrance. Nathan reached over to ring the doorbell and no more than a minute passed before a woman with long blonde, straight hair and cherry-red lips opened the door.

"Nathan!" The woman spread her arms for a hug, and when Nathan obliged, swallowing another sigh, she gave him a light peck on both his cheeks. Was it his imagination that her hand slid a little lower than it should be, and the embrace was a wee bit too long to be decent?

"Janet, this is Lani. Lani, Janet."

"Oh, it's so nice to meet you. Daniel and I've been so curious who Nathan's plus one is. We were hoping he would bring someone. Parties are so much more fun that way." Excitement pitched Janet's voice even higher than normal.

Lani's smile appeared cooler than what Nathan was used to from her. That, he was pretty sure by now, was not his imagination.

"I'm glad I could accompany him to this one."

Well played. Not a single word of untruth. But it was time to intercept. Nathan held up a wine bag. "For the party."

"Aww, you didn't have to. Come in, come in."

They followed the hostess into the house, taking their shoes off in the foyer. It wasn't his first visit there, but it always struck him how staged everything seemed, as if it were a show home rather than a place where people lived. Even his own minimalist apartment looked more inhabited than this one.

Others were already there as they entered the main living room, mingling and chatting, holding glasses. Nathan scanned the area, looking for a familiar face. He was hoping he'd see Wilson there, at least.

"Can I get you something to drink? Wine? Red?"

"Sure, thanks."

"Lani?"

"Red for me as well, thank you."

As soon as Janet left, Lani turned toward Nathan and whispered in a low voice. "Fake much?"

He struggled to not burst out laughing and kept it down to a smirk instead. Lani was right, though, and he could definitely see Daniel as a shrink-wrapped plastic doll. Why hadn't he seen it before?

"Nathan! You made it!"

Daniel entered the room and strolled toward them with an arm around his wife. "I wasn't sure if you would bail again at the last minute." Before Nathan could reply, he turned to Lani. "And you must be Lani. Janet here is buzzing with excitement for me to meet you."

Only when Lani leaned closer to him did Nathan realize he had clenched his jaw and was grinding his teeth. It was odd. Daniel had never been this obnoxious at work.

"And you must be Daniel. Nathan has been telling me about you."

"Oh? All good things, I hope."

Lani only smiled.

A moment of awkwardness, one that Lani seemed to have no problems with. Daniel cleared his throat and looked at his wife.

"Whoops! Silly me, here we are chatting away and I'm just holding these." Janet passed the long-stemmed glasses over and they both murmured their thanks.

More silence settled as both Lani and Nathan took sips of their wine, although Lani held her most serene expression still. This entire conversation reminded him once more of a game of cat and mouse and, so far, Lani was winning. Then again, he was biased.

"So, how did you two meet?" Janet's gaze moved back and forth between them, with a little more scrutiny than Nathan liked.

He cursed inside, wishing the couple would just go socialize with other guests and leave them alone. No such luck.

"At a party, actually. A masquerade one." Lani's voice remained smooth and even.

Daniel's brows arched in surprise. "Weren't we contracted for security detail for one a while back?"

Nathan shrugged. "I was off duty by the time we talked." Technically.

"Why, you sly dog! I didn't know you had it in you." Daniel play punched him in the arm, but Nathan only kept his deadpan expression.

"Well, I think it's rather romantic — bodyguard style and all." Janet sighed.

Oh, the theatrics. Nathan wasn't sure if Janet or Daniel was worse.

"So, Lani, what do you do?"

"I run my own business," Lani replied. Nathan noted the way she again sidestepped from giving away any personal details, but this time, he did not mind. If he was to find out, he wanted it to be because she felt comfortable telling him, not because someone else asked.

"Ah, a woman after my heart! I always had great admiration for those who make their own way. Like this security firm we have…"

Christ, here it comes. It was one of Daniel's favorite topics, how he and Wilson had started the company from the ground up. Nathan couldn't deny that it was Daniel's connections from his family background that had brought in the contracts, but he always made it sound as though he had done all the work, when in fact it was Wilson with his expertise who had set up the well-oiled machine that their operation was today.

The droning continued until someone called out to the couple. Gratitude welled up within Nathan for whoever was the owner of that voice.

"Ah excuse us." With that, they sauntered off, leaving both of them slumping their shoulders in relief.

"I understand what you were trying to warn me about."

"Sorry," Nathan started, but Lani shook her head.

"I regret nothing. This is also part of a Dominant's job." She leaned closer to whisper in his ear. "That said, I can't wait to show you better parties in the future. Then maybe you'd get a chance to see that latex outfit you seemed to like so much in action."

Shit. She had noticed.

"Nate!"

He tensed his shoulders, then loosened them again when Wilson stepped into view.

"So you got roped into coming, too?" Wilson gave a weak grin and extended a hand toward Lani. "Ah, sorry about that. I'm Wilson."

"Lani." She took the hand and shook it with a more relaxed smile.

"Do you have any idea why Daniel's even throwing this party?" Nathan kept his voice low. He wanted to give Lani more context, but he needed to find out what Wilson knew more urgently.

"I was about to ask you the same thing."

Nathan frowned. "You told him about you leaving?"

"Yeah, and my offer to you. He didn't take it well at first, which was why I had the same question."

Both men furrowed their brows.

"Excuse me. Perhaps I can help?"

Wilson looked up at Nathan and, at his nod, spoke. "I'm moving away for family reasons and made an offer to sell my share of the company to Nate here."

When Lani turned her gaze toward Nathan, he shook his head. "I haven't given my answer yet."

"I told Wilson last week, and before I knew it, he started throwing this party together."

"Hmm, I see. Perhaps he is trying to create an opportunity for observing the interaction between you two, to see what has changed and if he or anyone else can persuade either of you otherwise, since Nathan hasn't given the final decision yet."

It made some sense. If so, he wasn't sure how much longer he wanted to be there.

A single loud ding interrupted their conversation. Wilson dug out his phone. "Ah, crap. It's the wife. The munchkin is having a meltdown and she needs me to come home. I'd better get going."

Wilson looked up and gave them a curt nod. "Sorry we can't chat more. It was nice meeting you, Lani."

"Likewise."

With that, he rushed off, leaving them alone. Lani moved to set her wineglass down. "Well, is there any reason we should be staying?"

Nathan grinned. "Let's head out, honey."

One last task. They made their way toward the host and hostess to say their goodbyes. Luckily, Janet and Daniel were both distracted enough that they let them go with only another snide comment about leaving so soon.

When they reached the foyer, Nathan retrieved their shoes, then kneeled down. Lani raised a brow at him.

With a smile on his lips, he prepared her heels before guiding each of her foot to the shoe. With each, he took his time to do the straps up before standing to put his own Oxfords on. A gesture of gratitude, among other things.

"Good boy," she murmured. "Let's go home and have a proper party of our own."

Chapter Nineteen

They sat once more at her kitchen table, steaming hot cups of tea in hand, but mirth was the last thing on Lani's lips as she regarded the developing sub in front of her. The entire event had been an educational experience. Despite the earlier promise of a party of their own, unspoken tension filled the drive home as Nathan fell silent, lost in his own thoughts.

"Tell me what's on your mind."

Nathan tightened his shoulders as if to brace himself and took a sip of his tea. Only when he set the mug down again, each movement slow and deliberate, did he speak. "I'm worried about Wilson and Daniel. And..." – he hesitated, then plunged on ahead – "I'm sorry you had to go through all that back there."

"Nathan, what did I say earlier?" A note of impatience crept into her voice as she leveled him with a stare.

"That it was part of the Dominant's job."

"To support the submissive in things they have to do…yes. Now, you would do well to remember that. I'm not in the habit of repeating myself." She studied him once more, the way he remained hunched over, almost as if he were trying to curl up around the mug of tea for comfort. That would not do. Daniel had shaken him worse than he would care to admit, and she was going to find out why.

"Come on." Lani rose, sliding her chair back.

Startled, Nathan blinked at her before following with slower movements, uncertainty written all over his face.

"We're going to play a game." When they reached the bedroom, she gestured toward the armchair in the corner. "Pull that up for me, then have a seat on the bed."

He did as she commanded, and Lani kept from smirking at the confusion in his expression. How long before he would ask?

She took her time to settle in the chair, crossing her legs in the dress he had chosen for her, its hem riding up to giving a teasing glimpse of the garter belt holding her stockings up. As she leaned back, she rested her arms on either side of the chair and tilted her chin up.

"Ma'am, if I may ask?"

Lani inclined her head. "You may."

"What game are we playing?" His voice held a tightness to it.

Ah-ha. At last. She allowed herself that small smirk now. "Strip questions. I will ask them, and for each answer I deem satisfactory, I will take off an item of clothing." She trailed her fingers over the lace that made up her bodice.

When his chest rose and fell as he sucked in a breath, Lani knew she had struck the right chord. She leaned to her left, propping her chin up on a crooked hand. "Ready for the first one?"

"Yes, Ma'am." His Adam's apple bobbed up and down as he swallowed, and she delighted in his reaction.

"What are your thoughts on Daniel?"

His eyebrows arched in surprise, but she kept her expression neutral.

"As a person? Or as a business partner?" he asked with slow caution.

"Let's start off easy. As a business partner."

He continued to hold his gaze on her as the minutes ticked by. She could almost see the gears turning in his head, sifting through words and information. That thoughtfulness was one of the many things she liked about him.

"I'll borrow what Wilson mentioned. Daniel can be charismatic when he wants something, but mostly he's after glory, which makes him too aggressive in trying to expand our business. The need to gloat drives him beyond reason." Nathan rubbed his face. "But I can't deny that his connections have kept us afloat. It's cutthroat out there, and Wilson had said more than once that he wasn't sure if we would have been able to get any contracts in the beginning if it hadn't been for Daniel. We're holding steady now, like we should be, but I'm not certain if some of our clients would stay on board if Daniel left."

It was more than Lani had asked for, but she knew he needed to unload his worries on someone and to give them a voice. The professional in her recognized it, but it was the Domme who had demanded her to take action. She nodded in acknowledgment, then stood and slipped the dress off to reward him for his forthcomingness.

As she sat back down, she heard more than saw the sharp intake of breath. Aware of her near nudity, left with only a matching set of panties and bra, stockings and garter belt, she recrossed her legs. "Next question. Thoughts on Daniel as a person?"

"He is not someone I would hang out with if I had a choice," Nathan replied with care.

Lani raised a brow and reached for her dress. She hadn't mentioned a penalty, but of course, there would be one.

"Okay, he's an arrogant prick." That came out much more rushed.

She smirked and eased backward in the chair once more. "Better. I'll let it go this time."

He sighed in relief and muttered something unintelligible under his breath.

"Hmm, what's that?"

She could see he wanted to brush it off by the way he looked down, but he stopped himself, swallowed and tilted his head back to meet her gaze once more. "Just that you'll be the death of me, with all due respect, Ma'am."

That made her laugh. She reached up and undid one of her earrings. Sass should so be met in kind. Setting the earring down, she leaned forward. "Do you feel he's a better man than you?"

"No, Ma'am." That answer came too quick.

"Really?"

"He may be successful in the conventional sense, but I recognize that only the privilege he was born with gives him that leverage."

Still skeptical, Lani undid the other earring then resettled, resting her chin on her hand once more. "Then how come you let him and his wife push you around?"

He gaped at her, opening and closing his mouth without uttering a single word. But he had to have realized she was leading up to this. Right?

When he did not answer after minutes had passed, she frowned. He hadn't known. How could a man so self-aware in some ways be so clueless in others?

"I..." He turned his gaze to the ground between them then shrugged his shoulders in helplessness.

"Try." This was an important breakthrough. "Speak what's on your mind right now."

"I want to say I don't let them, but this party proved otherwise, didn't it?" He gave her a bitter smile and shook his head. "I guess maybe I do it for the sake of harmony. If he wants to be the big man on campus but will keep bringing in the contracts, then letting him bullshit around is a small price to pay."

She leveled him with another hard stare. "You just mentioned earlier that you should hold steady, not be looking for new work. So why does that matter?"

A look of guilt passed over his features. "I also said that I'm not sure if clients wouldn't pull out if Daniel left." But he didn't sound convincing to her, not one bit.

"Are you so uncertain about the quality of service you provide that you think it will not stand on its own merit?" She had no desire to be cruel, but Nathan was acting like a puppy that had been beaten for so long that he was no longer aware he was walking around with his tail tucked between his legs.

Shock widened his eyes. "Of course not. The team is extremely good at what they do, and they're damn hard working."

Ah, there was that fierce pride she was looking for. She beamed at him, straightening her back with triumph as she saw realization light up his entire face. For that last answer, she reached behind, undid the clasp of her bra and let the item fall to the chair.

Once done, she stood up once more, hovering over him, though she didn't need to lean down much. "Now...are you going to push back the next time he tries to belittle you?"

"Yes, Ma'am."

She tilted his chin up with two fingers so that she could stare into those steel grays. "And are you going to let his horny little suburban housewife grope you whenever she wants?"

"No, Ma'am."

The answers came out stronger and more confident than she had heard from him all night. Lani smiled at that and closed the distance between them, brushing her lips against his. "Good boy. You may take off an item of your choice."

There was no pause of indecision this time as Nathan placed his hands on her hips and peeled her thong off beneath the suspender straps of her garter belt. With a mischievous spark in his eyes, he undid the snaps to pull the underwear off, then redid them.

"Cheeky boy." She stroked his hair with a chuckle, giving in to the moment. It covered her other urge, the one that wanted to tell him in no uncertain terms that he was hers and under no circumstances was another woman—or man—allowed to touch him without her permission. This was just a trial—her helping a friend and having some fun along the way. No need to get that serious. She wasn't ready for that...yet.

At least she wasn't too proud to admit that last part to herself.

Once she stepped out of her thong, she cast a glance downward. Sure enough, he had tented and didn't bother adjusting himself this time. He also couldn't seem to keep his hands off her as he returned to caress up along her legs to her calves through her stockings then to her hips, the calloused pads on his hands rough against her silken flesh. It made for a pleasant feeling, and she allowed it to continue until he trailed his fingers toward her now-bare mound.

A *tsk* sound escaped Lani's lips, and she grabbed his hand to hold it still, though she did not move it away. "Bold."

He grinned up at her, the earlier hesitation gone. "You like it better when I'm bold."

With a shake of her head in amusement, she slid her hands down his chest, scraping her nails over both of his nipples through his thin shirt. She held back a smug smile at the hiss he made in response.

"I think that deserves both a reward and a punishment." She took his hand and tugged him until he followed her.

Lani led them to one side of the room, then, without warning, spun him around and pushed him up against the wall. Under normal circumstances, she would have stood no chance against his strength, but she had caught him by surprise, and he wasn't unwilling. To close the gap in their height, she rose to the balls of her feet and fisted his hair to draw him in for an open-mouthed kiss.

Rather than lingering, she worked her way down, along his jawline and downward farther until his groans filled the air. When he pulled at her hip with a renewed urgency, she didn't stop him but nipped the crook of his neck. As he pressed close, his hard-on pushed with its own insistence against her, and she trailed her hands down his shirt and over his stomach to undo and push down his pants.

"Please," Nathan whispered, bowing his head.

"Ask me."

"Let me inside you. *Please*." The need in his voice was clear.

She pulled his face closer, resting his forehead against hers as she looked into his bright eyes, finding herself reflected in them. Lani breathed out the next two words. "Fuck me."

He wasted no time in sliding one hand down to her thigh then lifted that leg up to pin against his body. But given their height difference, even with her flexibility, it wasn't enough. With a groan, he reached out and did the same on the other side. With sheer strength, he picked her up and instinct drove her to wrap her legs around him.

Lani used his hold as leverage, and lining her opening up against his pulsing member, she lowered herself onto him, letting gravity pull her down. She let out a long moan as his cock pushed into her, stretching and filling her.

"Christ," he swore, his every muscle trembling. As she bottomed out, he spun them around until he was pressing her back against the wall.

The sudden coldness had her hiss in surprise, and she surged forward, only grinding harder against him, even as her inner muscles spasmed around his cock.

"That's it, darling. Take what you need," she crooned in his ear.

She could tell that what semblance of control he had was dissolving as each thrust grew deeper and more powerful until he was slamming into her. His pelvis rubbed against her clit, and she shuddered, growing closer and closer to her own orgasm, until she tilted her head back and parted her lips in a wordless cry as she climaxed hard on his cock. Her vision blurred and the world spun, but in this singular moment, she couldn't care less. All she could focus on was the pleasure he brought her.

He followed not long after, his strokes shortening until he'd buried himself deep within her, and with a growl, he came, every muscle in her embrace twitching from the exertion.

At last they both slumped against the wall, trying to catch their breath. She nuzzled his shoulder and dotted it with featherlight kisses. When his grip only tightened, she moaned against his bare skin, then smiled. "You can let go now, darling." Her voice was still hoarse.

He loosened his hold, and she slid off him with an audible groan. Cum trailed down her inner thighs toward her stockings, but she paid it no heed. Instead, she focused on steadying her wobbly legs until she looked up at him. "Sit on the bed."

He looked at her, puzzlement clear on his face, but she ignored it as she turned and, with more confidence in her stride than she felt, stepped into her bathroom to clean herself and retrieve a washcloth for him. On the way back, she stopped for something special.

When she returned, Nathan's chest was rising and falling in a regular rhythm while he kept his eyes closed. He opened them at her approach and smiled only for the expression to falter when he glimpsed the metal object in her hand.

With a smirk, she eased herself into the chair she had abandoned earlier and began running the warm cloth over his cock, cleaning it thoroughly. "I mentioned a punishment as well as reward. You didn't think I'd forgotten, did you?"

He swallowed hard, then his eyes widened into saucers as she held up the chastity cage.

"I did rather like your boldness and your honesty — but it's also important not to be too presumptuous. This will remind you of such for the next few days."

He made a sort of strangled sound, and she resisted the urge to giggle. "Any questions?"

He had quite a few once he found his voice, and she answered with all the patience she could muster as she waited for him to become flaccid once more. When he ran out of words, she took his cock in hand and fitted the cage around it, then locked it with a small key.

"I suggest you keep to looser-fitting pants the next little while. It'll come off when we meet again in two days." At his crestfallen look, she patted his cheek and softened. "If it gets to be too much, text me your safeword."

Nathan shifted in her bed, his focus traveling back and forth between her and his caged penis until she lifted the chain the key hung from and placed it around her neck. The key itself rested between her breasts.

"Remember… I'll be thinking of you, too, as I now hold the sole power to your pleasure."

His answering shiver was enough for her to know that she had made the right move.

Chapter Twenty

Damn that infernal cage.

Nathan wasn't sure how many times he had sworn out loud or in his head about the thing the last two days. At least it was coming off tonight. The thought gave him a bit of relief.

It wasn't even the peeing or the mild discomfort from wannabe morning wood that were the biggest issues, like he'd expected. It was the fact that wearing the device served the opposite purpose of encouraging chaste thoughts. Instead, he wanted to fuck Lani...constantly.

He sat on the edge of his bed and rubbed his face with a sigh. *No use dwelling.* With a slight groan, he tugged on his khakis, pulling them over his caged cock with care. He stood, grabbed his T-shirt and plodded to his washroom. Standing far enough from the vanity to see his crotch in the mirror's reflection, he tried to reassure himself that it was not obvious he was wearing an extra bulk under his pants. The day before, he had walked around, certain that everyone had noticed. Of course, no one had.

His first counseling session was going to be real fun today. With a growl, he pulled the simple black T-shirt on and made his way across the apartment. It was time to go, and he grabbed his wallet and keys before stalking out of the door, slamming it behind him. Sexual frustration was turning him into a gnarly man.

The drive was short, as this counselor was in one of the newer buildings downtown. As he parked and stepped out of the car, Nathan looked up at the state-of-the-art tower. With her office somewhere on the thirtieth floor, she must be fairly successful to afford such rent. Well, she'd better be as good as her reputation said she was, at what she cost.

When he was sure nobody was looking, he adjusted his pants again and cleared his throat before entering the building. More self-conscious than he was any other day, he glanced this way and that, noting various suits and more casually dressed people going about their business. Not a single person gave him a second glance, not even the three others who shared an elevator with him.

Once he arrived at the floor, he walked down the hall until he came upon a simple sign to his left, engraved on a metal plate. *Alana McMillan. Counselor.*

Well, here goes.

He pushed the door open and breathed a sigh of relief to see nobody in the small waiting area. Instead, a blonde woman sitting at behind a reception desk tilted her head up and gave him a friendly smile.

"Hi, I have an appointment for nine-thirty."

"Of course, one minute." She turned to check at her computer screen, then looked up at him. "Mr. Pelletier?"

"Yeah."

"Please, have a seat. Ms. McMillan will be with you soon."

He nodded and glanced at the upholstered wingbacks and loveseat positioned tastefully around the room. No cold bench for this upscale office. He spun around, wishing that he could adjust himself again but knew he wouldn't be able to get away with doing that without the receptionist seeing him.

With that thought, he crossed the small space to ease himself into a chair, sweeping his gaze across to pick up the little details. A framed piece of abstract art spanned most of one side, soothing colors aimed likely to relax her clients. Rather than the harsh fluorescent lights of most offices, wall-mounted ones provided a soft atmosphere. Spa-like music played in the background. On top of the coffee table, a few magazines were fanned out to entice the bored.

"Mr. Pelletier? This way please."

That was a shorter wait than he'd expected. Nathan stood and tugged his khakis down by the material at the thighs, missing his jeans already. But they would be too tight for what he was sporting underneath. With a nod toward the receptionist, he crossed the room and stepped through the door she held open for him.

Two steps—that was all he was capable of before everything, including his brains, grinded to a halt. Before him stood the one woman he'd least expected.

She had walked over to greet him, but now she stared at him wide-eyed, her hand paused in mid-extension for a shake.

The receptionist, seeming oblivious to the sudden tension, spoke. "Mr. Pelletier, Ms. McMillan."

Lani cleared her throat, dropped her hand to clasp the free one in front of her and nodded. "Thank you, Ophelia."

Nathan only felt a smidge of relief as Ophelia left and closed the door behind her.

Lani returned to their staring contest and for several breaths, neither of them spoke.

"Joseph?"

"Alana?"

They both started at once with the same note of incredulity in their voices.

He grimaced. "Nathan is my middle name. Joseph was my mom's favorite uncle until it came out that he was a con artist who was cheating the entire family out of their money for years."

"I see." She paused as if considering her next words before speaking again. "Lani is what I go by in the scene and with friends and clients that I've gotten to know and who know what I am. I use Alana, my legal name, professionally."

He knew she didn't owe him an explanation, but when she offered it nonetheless, he bowed his head deep in appreciation. Still, he was at a loss with what to do.

"Have a seat, Nathan." Lani seemed to recover first and gestured toward the couch by the coffee table while she lowered herself into a large wingback chair. It reminded him a little of the one she enjoyed sitting at in her bedroom. The thought brought his awareness back to his cock and the torture device enclosing it. That was when his eyes strayed until he realized what he was searching for.

There, dangling on a chain around her neck, a small metal key hung almost like a decorative piece of jewelry, resting against her breasts.

Ah, shit.

His cock twitched within the cage, and he sucked in a breath to calm his racing pulse.

Lani opened his file, and he watched with more nervousness than he had ever felt in his life. Now she knew everything — his failed marriage, his PTSD, all his little insecurities. It made for an unpleasant thought.

With a sigh, she closed the folder once more, then looked up at him. "Nathan, let me get straight to the point. I can help you as a Domme or as a counselor, but not both. Beyond even professional integrity, the two roles will sometimes be at odds with each other. But only you can make that choice."

He needed a counselor, but there were others he was sure he could go to. The bigger question — was he comfortable being with someone who knew his psychological profile with such intimacy? And given that the relationship was one already with a power imbalance, could he stand to trust her enough that she wouldn't use any of that information against him?

That vulnerability scared the shit out of him.

When he said nothing, Lani lifted the chain from her neck with a soft sigh and placed the key on the coffee table, pushing it toward him. "Let's call a break. I'd like you to take some time to think about it and consider which you prefer."

He looked up, pursing his lips into a thin line as Lani spoke with the most neutral expression he had ever seen on her. Even the mask she wore when they'd first met held more emotion than what she showed right now. It hurt.

Maybe a part of him was hoping she would make the choice for him, despite her earlier words. But he understood. Lani had drilled into him through readings and discussions how important willingness was in submission and what the dangers of being coerced into it could be. Still, something in him wished she would just claim him.

That yearning should have been enough of an answer for him, but he was a cautious man. So he reached across the table and took the key to the cage with a slow nod.

"May I continue to contact you?" He wasn't certain if he could stand not hearing her voice at all. *Shit. When did I become so attached to her? Why?*

Lani tilted her head and said naught as a clock nearby ticked the seconds away. Finally, she nodded. "You may. I know there will be questions as you process today, and I'll answer them to the best of my ability."

Her words were too formal. Nathan hated it, but he would take what he could get. He knew on a logical level that he needed distance to assess, but it didn't mean he enjoyed the idea. "Thank you."

"You're welcome."

He wanted to stay, but there was nothing more to discuss until he could sort this mess out. Bunching the key and chain in his hand, he rose. What could he say in farewell that would be appropriate for this situation?

She stood and gave him a bittersweet smile. "Goodbye, Nathan."

Why did that sound so damn final?

* * * *

She stared at the door that closed with a soft click as Nathan exited her office. Ophelia was going to wonder why the appointment had been so short, but Lani was grateful. It would give her time to compose herself until her next client.

In an uncharacteristic move, Lani fell back and slumped into her chair. It had taken everything in her to remain professional, to not cross the small distance between them, grab his shoulders and shake him, to not scream at the joke the universe had played on them. None of this was fair.

God, now she sounded like a petulant child throwing a tantrum.

A phone ringing startled her from her churning thoughts. It was her personal cell rather than the office line and she picked up without looking at the screen, functioning on autopilot.

"Hello?"

The only response was the sound of heavy breathing. Lani's eyes narrowed. These calls had started a few days before but were occurring with increasing frequency. She pulled the phone away from her ear to check her number. Blocked. Lani had half a mind to ask Nathan if there was any way to trace the caller, but given what had just happened…

About to hang up, she paused when a crackle from the other end of the line came through. That was new.

"Well, that was a short appointment. Client not your cup of tea, Ms. McMillan? Or can I call you Lani?"

Whoever was speaking was doing so over a voice modulator to disguise him or her. But the words alone were enough to chill her blood. This no longer was just some prankster who thought it funny to harass someone at random. This was a bonafide stalker.

Her first instinct was to run to the window, but given how high up her office was, there would be no way to make out anything. Instead, she walked across the space and opened the door to look into the waiting room, her phone still in held up to her ear. The voice had gone silent again.

No, no one was there besides the receptionist. Ophelia looked up, puzzlement on her face, but Lani just shook her head and retreated once more to the large desk that took up most of the other end of her office.

"Well, come now. It's no fun if you don't react."

Lani held herself in a stiff posture, and after a quick pause, hung up and tossed her phone onto the hard surface before resting her weight against the desk.

Her mind raced to figure out the next step but came up blank. She didn't feel comfortable going to Nathan. Jacob and Luna were in the process of recovering. For a moment, she considered Darryl, but shook her head. The last thing she needed was him freaking out. No, she would have to deal with this on her own. But how?

First, there was still the rest of the day to handle. Lani sat herself in her office chair and shut out her vision to focus on her breathing. *In. Out.* She sought with each breath to find her center, to shed worries outside her control for now. Bit by bit, she refocused until all that was left was the job she had to do.

Lani opened her eyes and retrieved the folder sitting at her desk. She had fifteen minutes to prepare, and she was going to use that to the fullest.

The day became a blur of discussions with clients, ranging from identity crises to broken marriages. The mental work was exhausting, and by the time her last appointment walked out of her office, Lani was not confident she had the capacity to even tackle the issue of her stalker.

She drove home, pulling into her garage with a sigh of relief. It was bad enough that on her way, she kept glancing at the rear-view mirror to make sure she wasn't being followed, but now she couldn't shake the idea that he or she may already know where she lived. Lani pushed her hair back with one hand. Damn it, the paranoia was getting to her.

Her gaze fell on the covered motorcycle gathering dust on the other side. It had been ages since she'd ridden, as if August's death in the car accident had emphasized how dangerous the roads were. But now, she wanted nothing more than to abandon all caution, to feel the powerful machine roar to life between her legs as the wind whipped around her.

Well, why the hell not? At least it would help her clear her head. What did she have to lose?

Chapter Twenty-One

A dam had broken after that. Lani had always kept her bike tuned and took it out for monthly rides around the neighborhood as part of its upkeep, but now she rode every night to de-stress.

Because she was stressed.

The calls continued, although the caller never spoke again. Not that she gave them a chance, as she ignored any coming in from a blocked number. Then they started diverting to her office.

The first time she noticed this, Ophelia was yelling into the phone. Fortunately, no client was in as Lani rushed out to see what was going on.

"Stop calling, you mouth-breathing creep!"

Ophelia slammed the receiver hard then jerked up to exchange wide-eyed stares with Lani.

"Sorry about that, Ms. McMillan." Ophelia's cheeks turned red in embarrassment.

Lani composed herself and shook her head. "That's all right. I trust you had good reason. Who was it?"

Flustered, Ophelia stared down at her phone then gave a sigh. "Probably some stupid teenage prankster. They've just been calling and breathing all heavy. It's disgusting."

In return, Lani suppressed a shudder. It was too much of a coincidence to not be the same caller — or perhaps it was her paranoia talking. Still... "I want you to start a log of when these come in. Write down the day, time and how long each one lasts. Oh, and also the number...if it's listed." Though Lani doubted they could trace the calls.

At least so far, that seemed to be all they were doing at the moment. Lani found no signs of them following her physically. She'd just contact the phone company and figure out a way to get those calls blocked.

Or so she kept telling herself. It still didn't keep her from looking over her shoulder when she walked down the street or help her sleep at night.

So when her mobile buzzed as she stepped through her house's front door, Lani almost jumped out of her own skin. As the phone continued to ring, she placed a hand on her chest, trying to calm her racing pulse before daring to take a peek at her screen. *Wait! Nathan?*

With a deep breath to steady herself, she picked up the device. "Hello."

"Hi, Lani." A pause. "How are you?"

There was so much awkwardness in those few words that a pang stabbed Lani's heart. It had been over a week since she had heard from him.

"I'm doing well, and you?"

"I'm good." He cleared his throat. "I was wondering... I mean..."

"What can I help you with, Nathan?"

"Ah, I have a kid on my team who's on The Playgrounds contract that got interested in the scene."

"Yes, I remember you mentioning him."

A sudden bang from somewhere in her backyard startled her enough that she almost dropped the phone. Her entire body stiffened, and her heart raced all over again.

"Yeah, well, he was asking..."

With her attention pulled away from what Nathan was saying, she made her way to the kitchen, one hesitant step after another. At least everything inside remained the same as when she'd left that morning. Relieved to discover she had drawn the venetian blinds earlier, she stepped up to it and peered through two slats. From what she could observe, nothing seemed out of place. So, what was that bang? Perhaps it had come from the neighbors'? Or something on the other side of her hedges? She let her gaze travel beyond the yard and spied the top of a white van stopping in front of the neighboring garage. It had been hanging around these parts for a few days now, and this was not the first time Lani had seen it in the alley. Maybe it was the elderly lady next door getting some repairs done on her house and the sound was just that old van's engine. Lani must believe that, or she was going to drive herself insane.

Only then did she realize Nathan had stopped speaking on the other end of the line and she made a small "Mm-hmm."

"Lani, are you okay?"

Realizing that she had missed most of what he said, she flushed in embarrassment. This was not like her. "Yes. My apologies, I got distracted for a moment." Why was her voice still shaky?

"Jasper mentioned he didn't want to hang out at The Playgrounds since he's not ready yet and it's too close to work, but he was wondering if there was anywhere he could go to talk to people firsthand."

Lani swallowed the disappointment that welled up in her throat. He was calling because someone else was asking. "I'd be happy to answer any questions he may have if you pass on my contact information."

"Oh. Well..." Nathan trailed off again and Lani could envision him rubbing the back of his head. "I think he was thinking more about somewhere online besides Reddit."

It took her a moment to hypothesize the reason for his hesitation. Was it possible that he didn't want to share her? Now Lani smiled to herself, only to give out a small yelp when another loud clang pierced the air like someone had knocked a garbage can over.

"Lani? You sure you're okay? Do you need me to come over?"

She could make out the concern even over the phone and forced false confidence into her reply. "I'm fine."

"All right." His tone told her he didn't believe her for a second, but she knew he would respect her intent.

"Is there anything else?" She sounded more curt than she intended to be.

"No. I mean..." Nathan muttered something intelligible under his breath. "I wanted to see how you were doing."

A pause again, but Lani sensed there was more so kept silent.

"I missed you."

Ah, the dear boy. Lani knew how much it took for a man like Nathan to admit such things. Her heart ached, and she wondered when had he embedded himself so deeply into it?

"Have you given further thought to your decision?" This time, she gentled her tone.

"I haven't stopped thinking about it, but I don't feel any closer to clarity." She could hear the low growl sitting in the back of his throat.

"If there's anyone you feel comfortable confiding in, I think it would be wise to do so. And if you want to speak with another pro-kink counselor, I can recommend someone for you."

"Maybe. There might be a person, but I'll let you know if I need that referral."

Over the line, Lani picked up the ring of a different phone.

"Oh crap. That must be Wilson."

"Are you buying his shares?"

"No, but I wanted to work through what it would look like if I did. He offered to come over tonight."

Lani nodded before she realized he couldn't see. "That's smart. Get what you need." There was no sting in her words.

"Thanks. Talk to you later?"

"Yes. Don't keep your friend waiting."

"Have a good night." Nathan hung up and silence settled in once more.

With a soft sigh, Lani set her phone down on the kitchen table. Perhaps it was time for another ride.

* * * *

"Lani!" Luna grinned from ear to ear as she opened the door, then stepped back to let her into the apartment. This weekend had given Lani a chance to visit her recovering friend at last.

Despite her still healing, Luna glowed with a pure happiness that Lani hadn't seen from her for a long time. It made her respond in kind, such that she beamed with pleasure. "How are you doing, sweetie?"

"Bouncing off the walls when she should be resting." Jacob came up from behind, a scowl on his face.

"I'm fine. I'm taking my naps."

"You should rest more." Jacob sighed and shook his head. "She's turning into a brat since I can't give her a good spanking while she's recovering."

"Am not!" Luna's cheeks turned into a lovely shade of red.

Lani laughed. "Before you guys get more into it, let me put these down." She held up the box of baked goods from Luna's favorite bakery and watched the girl's grin widened farther.

"I'll make some tea," Luna offered.

"You'll do no such thing. You pick your pastry, then sit your butt back down." There was a hint of a growl in Jacob's voice, and Lani was certain that this was an exchange they had daily...perhaps even hourly.

Luna sighed and threw Lani an apologetic look. "Yes, Jacob." She grabbed an apple turnover and sat on one of her stools.

Despite the bravado, Lani noticed Luna was favoring one side, her movements careful. Jacob was right in trying to rein in Luna's overactive ways.

"Does it still hurt?" Lani gentled her voice.

"It's more of an ache now. The stitches are out but the wound is a bit tight."

Jacob returned to join them with a teapot and three cups. About to reply, Lani stiffened when her phone made a loud *ding* in her purse. Her hand trembled as she reached for the bag.

"You okay, Lani?" Luna laid a hand on her shoulder.

"Of course!" Lani mustered a smile, but even she knew it fell flat when she glanced at the screen to see that the call was from a blocked number. Again. She hit the hang-up button.

Jacob raised a brow at her as he poured the tea out for them, and in return, Lani shrugged. "Not important." It wasn't a lie, but she found herself reluctant to tell the couple about the situation. They had enough to worry about on their own plate.

Luna looked as though she wanted to ask more, so Lani only gave her a brighter smile. "So how's it been with the overbearing grouch here?"

"Pest." Jacob glared while Luna coughed.

"Now, we are all aware that you barely left her side to even take a shower or eat while Luna was out, so I fairly certain I'm close to the truth."

"Wait! You didn't? But that was days." Luna gaped at Jacob.

"I—"

"Nope, I had to bring him changes of clothes. He was developing a particular smell by the end there. I'm pretty sure if you hadn't woken up when you did, the nurses would have kicked him out."

For a moment, everything felt so normal again that Lani reveled in teasing Jacob, so much that she failed to dodge his pinch.

"Ouch!" She rubbed the sore spot.

"Well, I'm not staying here to put up with this," Jacob grumbled, and picked up his keys. "I'm heading out for a grocery run."

Luna pouted, but Jacob only shook his head. "You do realize this is so that you can't follow and insist on carrying a bag."

"Damn. Foiled!"

"You girls have fun. I'll be back."

The two of them waved as Jacob left the apartment before Luna let out a sigh of relief.

"That bad?" Lani returned her focus to Luna, who nodded with a weak smile.

"Well, it's understandable. He almost lost you."

"I know. But still…" Luna trailed off, then gestured to her body. "How am I going to rebuild my strength if he insists on doing everything for me?"

Lani shook her head. "Give it a few more weeks. Let him fuss for a little longer. It'd be a kindness."

"A kindness to let him do it all?" Surprise tinged Luna's voice.

"Yes. Jacob's more shaken than he lets on. There's nothing worse for a Dominant than feeling a loss of control, especially with their sub's wellbeing. Right now, he's trying to reassure himself that he isn't as helpless as he was while you were out in the hospital."

Luna lapsed into silence, furrowing her forehead in apparent thought.

But Lani's own words, spoken out loud struck a sudden chord within. Was that why she was so off balance, because she felt just as helpless as she waited for Nathan's decision?

"I'll try," Luna said at last then leaned forward. "So, how's Nathan? He seemed nice."

Surprised by the switch in topic, Lani tried to keep her expression neutral, shrugging as she projected nonchalance. "We're on a break right now. It was a trial, anyway. He's not sure if he's ready to submit yet."

"Wait! What? But why?" Luna's jaw dropped.

"Something happened. It's not anything I can talk about. I gave him a choice on whether he wants to continue exploring his submissive side with me."

Luna's eyes grew round and Lani wondered if her friend knew how she looked at the moment.

"You made him the same offer Jacob gave me all those years ago."

"Not exactly. I'm not offering him a contract of any sort."

"Why not?"

Lani stared at Luna, words failing her. If Nathan continued with her, would it lead to a contract? For the first time since August's passing, the answer wasn't an outright no. It would be one thing if he turned his back on the scene. But if he stayed while submitting to someone else? At the latter thought, the dull ache of missing his presence flared to life. He was hers. She wanted him to be hers.

When had that happened?

Something must have shown on her face as Luna reached across to cover her hand in hers, giving it a light squeeze. "August wouldn't have liked the idea of you being alone forever. He would want someone to serve and take care of you."

Lani swallowed hard to hold back the tears that threatened to well up in her eyes. She wasn't sure if she succeeded.

"You know" — Luna's voice grew quieter — "sometimes I go to August's grave and talk to him there. It helps me sort out my thoughts."

"I do that, too." Lani's smile was bittersweet.

"Maybe it's time to pay him another visit?"

"Yeah." It would help clear her head, both about Nathan and her other situation — or so she hoped.

Chapter Twenty-Two

Unease for another person was not something Nathan was used to feeling for a while now. At first, he chalked his relentless pacing to the two big decisions before him — whether to buy out Wilson's share and how to continue forward with Lani. Every time he thought he was close to a decision on one or the other issue, doubts would assail him and make him unsure of his choice.

But no, it wasn't either of those that made anxiety well up in him in those quiet moments. It was the call with Lani a few days ago. Something was off. He had never known her to be so distracted and jumpy. It took everything in him to not rush over and check that she was okay. He knew she wouldn't appreciate it, especially when she told him in no uncertain terms that she was fine.

So instead, here he was, doing the next best thing he could think of.

"So, enough about this damn wound. How have you been, Nathan?" Luna set down the chocolate almond croissant he had brought over as a thank you—or a bribe, as she referred to it.

"Okay." He cast his glance toward the glass of water he was nursing then put it down. "I've been better."

"Lani mentioned you guys are on a break."

Startled, Nathan snapped up his focus to stare at her, only for Luna to shake her head and chuckle. "After what feels like a near-death experience, I've learned that time is precious and it's best to get straight to the point."

Perhaps it was a lesson he would do well to learn, too. "Did she say anything else?"

"Only that the choice to continue was yours, but no. Most Dominants are private about this stuff. Or rather, she respects your privacy, knowing you're starting out."

He studied the sub in front of him and found no trace of guile in her expression. Besides Lani, Luna was the only other person who knew about his experiment with submissiveness, although there was that one introduction at The Playgrounds. Well, Lani had said to talk to someone, and Luna was as close to a confidante as he could get at the moment.

"I was in line for counseling services. It turns out the referral from my psychologist was to Lani."

Luna sucked in a breath, her eyes rounding like saucers. "Oh my." Somewhere a clock ticked the seconds away, and it took several more moments before she shook her head again. "How did you find out?"

"When I walked into her office." He struggled to maintain a neutral expression in the face of her incredulity.

"That's...quite the sucker punch."

"I know." He summoned his courage. If Luna could help him, she needed all the information. "Lani asked me to choose — to continue with her as a submissive or as her client."

"And she can't do both for you because of professional ethics." She nodded to herself. "No wonder she offered you the choice." She leaned forward, her eyes meeting his. "You haven't decided yet, have you?"

Now it was Nathan's turn to shake his head. "Every time I'm close to a decision, I start second-guessing myself."

"And is that because of Lani or because of the D/s part?"

Her question made him pause, and he gave it due consideration before replying. "The latter. But the two are the same."

"Are they?" Luna tilted her head. "I would challenge that. Because one is about her and the other is about you. If you are certain that you have feelings for Lani, then this isn't about whether you want to be with her, is it? Maybe it's more about if you are ready to be a sub."

He stared at her, his brain still processing his words.

Luna leaned forward and grinned up at him. "Because face it, you can't imagine submitting to anyone else, can you?"

The idea made bile rise in the back of his throat, and his stomach performed a sickening flip-flop.

His expression must have said it all, as she eased away with a satisfied nod. "So if it's submission that's making you hesitate, let's talk about that. Why are you so uncertain about it?"

He opened his mouth, then closed it again. Doubts had been circling his mind like pesky flies, but he always failed to give them full shape. Now, confronted with the question, he was caught off guard and had no ready reply.

"Because I am?" It was a poor answer, and he shrugged in helplessness. "Because for a guy, to not lead is to be weak. Because we are supposed to be dominant in the bedroom. Because…" Now he faltered and had to pause to compose himself. "Because I'm being asked to take charge in my career, and if I can't do that in a relationship, what qualifies me to become a leader of an entire company?"

"Hmm-m." Luna clucked her tongue. "Well, regardless of what society says, we both know Lani prefers to be the dominant one in the bed, and frankly, society has no business in your bedroom, so that point is moot." She took her croissant and waved it in front of him. "How do you define submission?"

"To follow someone's lead and trust they have your wellbeing and best interests in mind."

"And what do you bring to the table?"

"To serve, to protect, to take care of that person and put their needs above yours." The words came with a kind of confidence that surprised even him. But he had been doing his readings, and a lot of thinking.

"You were a cop before, right?" Luna's voice softened.

"Yeah, and the army before that."

"Is submitting to Lani so different from those identities you've had before?"

It was the same line of reasoning Lani had set him on before. The two were peas in a pod, despite one being a Domme, the other a sub.

"Not in the way you put it," he admitted.

"I doubt anyone out there regards someone with any of those jobs as being weak." Luna bit into the croissant, grinning in triumph.

No, of course not. Most saw both careers as heroic, macho even. That the same dynamic was seen as soft in other applications seemed a little absurd.

Luna swallowed her bite and set the plate down. "So for the third point, did those jobs make you submissive in other aspects of your life or with other people?"

Now that was a new tangent that made him blink. "No. But that's work."

"So what gave you the idea that submitting to one person in the bedroom or even beyond that would change who you are or how you interact with others?"

"Because..." He trailed off, having no suitable response to the question. Because, at the heart of it all, it wouldn't change anything else if he didn't want it to. That was the actual answer. Hadn't Lani tried to encourage him to stop taking shit from Daniel and his wife just a short while ago? It wasn't as though she was asking him to be submissive to everyone and everything, either.

Luna shook her head. "I struggled with that at first. After I signed the contract with Jacob for training, I thought that was it, that it was my identity going forward. But Jacob helped me see that it's just one part of me, not the whole. It didn't mean I was any less a feminist, that I couldn't take charge at the workplace or that"—she chuckled—"I can't boss my friends around."

It was as if another puzzle piece fell into place, but Nathan wasn't ready to admit to the clarity yet.

"If this doesn't work out, I'll lose more than just a sexual partner. I'll lose a friend, a mentor in the scene and the chance at a damn good counselor." The excuse came out as a pathetic mumble, and he rubbed the back of neck.

"And if you choose the other route, what do you lose?" Luna asked in return.

The best sex of his life? A potential actual compatible partner? At one time, he was sure that was Stacey, but now he could see that they had grown apart rather than together. His ex-wife had wanted him to take control of everything. It wasn't a duty he desired, not in a relationship.

But it didn't mean he trusted just anyone with it.

He only trusted Lani.

The conclusion rocked the core of his being enough that he slumped against the couch with a loud exhale.

"You okay?"

Nathan nodded and gave her a weak smile. "How did you know so much about this stuff?"

"Years to process and reflect. Besides, I had wonderful mentors and a Dom who challenges me to find the answers that sit well with me." She glanced down at her abdominal. "I made mistakes, too. Mistakes that almost cost too much. I got lucky."

His gaze followed hers, then sat up once more. "There's one more thing."

Luna blinked at him.

"You saw Lani recently, right?"

She nodded, wariness now tensing her body.

"Did she seem off to you?"

"What do you mean?" But something in her tone told Nathan that he didn't have to explain very much, so he plunged on ahead.

"When I was on the phone with her a few days ago, she seemed distracted, jumpy." He furrowed his brow. "The Lani I know wouldn't have missed an entire part of a conversation. She's too damn good of a listener for that."

Luna chewed her lower lip, then nodded as if she decided herself. "She had a moment when she was here last. I swear she jumped out of her own skin when her phone rang, but when I asked, she brushed it off."

Shit, it wasn't just him being a worrier. He needed to find out what was going on, despite her reassurances.

"You don't think she's in trouble, is she?" Worry drew Luna's lips downward.

"I'm not sure. I'll call her." Not that it had done much good the last time. "Or I'll go check in on her tomorrow?"

Luna nodded. "Ring her now and invite her out for lunch tomorrow. Best of both worlds."

"Thanks, Luna."

"She's one of my closest friends. Take care of her, Nathan."

"I will." He had much to discuss with her, and as her sub, it would give him the right to ask her to share with him what was wrong. He would protect her.

Nathan didn't stay long after. Luna had almost pushed him out of her apartment, insisting that he contact Lani as soon as possible. But he knew it was best to wait for the end of her workday. Besides, he also had to drop by the office for some paperwork, and for the rest of the afternoon, he threw himself into the tasks of running a security company, reviewing the existing contracts, the jobs coming up and the personnel schedules for each. It helped keep his anxiety down.

At five p.m., he left work, slid into his car for privacy and grabbed his phone, not bothering to even wait to go home first. As he dialed Lani, his leg shook in nervousness, but when no one picked up and it went to voicemail on the other end, he stared at his screen in disappointment. Perhaps she had a late client? He would try again when he got in.

As soon as he crossed the threshold into his own apartment, he called once more. No answer. Rinse. Repeat. Still, he never ended up reaching Lani that night.

Chapter Twenty-Three

Another tiring day. Lani found it difficult to be energized by her work like before. The calls never stopped, despite her having a few numbers blocked already. Ophelia kept up with the log, but they continued to increase in frequency, both to the office and to her personal cell.

If she was to take a hard look in the mirror, Lani would have to admit that she was turning into a nervous wreck.

She rode every evening after work but went out less and less. It had gotten so bad that people had texted, asking about her whereabouts. The previous evening, Darryl's incoming text had startled her so much that she had dropped her glass of warm milk on the floor.

Peeved at herself, Lani had spent the rest of the night scrubbing her soiled rug.

All day, Luna's words bounced around in her head. Her gaze kept wandering toward the picture frame sitting on her office desk, holding a photo of August. In it, he held the camera's attention with an intense stare, one she remembered well from the height of their play sessions.

She missed him so damn much, even after all these years and despite the short time they'd had together as a couple.

That evening, as she pulled on her riding leathers and threw a leg over the saddle, her survival instincts and fear warred with the stubbornness of not letting the culprit behind the phone calls scare her into hiding. But as the engine roared to life, the fears in her heart eased and she made a quick decision to throw caution in the wind, changing her original route to one that would lead her to the cemetery.

It was quiet when she rode into the parking lot, populated by only two cars, while a white maintenance van pulled into a stall in the far corner and idled there. Lani turned off the motorcycle, flipped the kickstand down with her heel and lifted her helmet from her head, shaking her curls loose.

She should have stopped for some flowers. With a sigh, she dismounted from her bike and with a measured pace, made her way to August's grave.

There it was, a simple, elegant tombstone with his name and dates. Lani kneeled down and traced the cursive A with a bittersweet smile on her lips. "Hello, my dearest."

A cool evening breeze tousled her hair, and she shut her vision out, imagining it to be August's fingers running through it. It was a silly fantasy, but the thought gave her a sense of comfort. As she opened her eyes once more, she sat back on her heels and regarded the stone that represented the life that had passed.

"I miss you." Lani swallowed the lump in her throat. "Then again, I guess you knew that, considering how often I say it." Her voice wavered, taking on a more plaintive quality. "It's been hard, and I miss the way you would lift my world. You know, when we were together you made everything just a little easier—like that cup of tea you would have waiting for me."

She drew air into her lungs and squared her shoulders. "Luna told me to talk to you about my problems. I guess you've become quite the listener for both of us. Then again, you always were." She was straying from the topic, as if she could avoid giving them shape. No, no more stalling.

"I met someone, August. I hadn't meant to, didn't think I was ready. But somehow one scene led to another then it wasn't just all play anymore." She chuckled, remembering the tightness in Nathan's voice, the heated glances, the barely restrained strength with which he held her when she finally gave him permission. *More*. She wanted more of him.

"He's new, though, and at a crossroads. He needs to decide for himself if he can let go of everything he's been taught about what he ought to be and embrace what he really is. I can't make that decision for him, as much as I want to."

Lani reached over and caressed the top of the gravestone. "You'd like him. He's so different from you—but serving comes natural to him." She exhaled and shook her head. "I don't know if I'm ready to move on yet, either, to be honest. In some ways, I never will be. When… When you left, you took a piece of me away with you, permanently." A single tear rolled down her cheek. "But Luna said you wouldn't want me to be alone forever, and I think I might be ready to let someone else in. Is it odd for your Domme to be kneeling before you, seeking some sign that you would be okay for me to take another?" Her voice broke as more tears fell and she hunched over, resting her forehead against the cool stone.

"Please, August…"

Her shoulders shook as she cried with sobs that racked her entire body, releasing all the stress that had been building up for days. It was a cathartic experience as she let all her emotions, all her doubts run free at last.

"Lani?"

She was so consumed by the swirl of conflicting thoughts that she almost missed the voice at first calling her name and didn't react until they repeated it again while a large hand covered one shoulder. Startled, she straightened to rise and turn around.

Lani never got the chance.

A hand clamped right over her face, and the texture of a rough rag rubbed against her skin. The scent of sweet alcohol filled her nostrils as she tried to scream, but the sound came out muffled and she wasn't sure if anyone would even be close enough to hear her.

She thrashed like a wild beast as another arm wrapped around the trunk of her body and hauled her up from her kneeling position. Whoever he was, he was tall enough that in their grappling, he lifted her until she was left kicking her legs in the air. When he set her down again, self-defense training took over, and she scraped the side of one biker-boot-clad foot down her assailant's shin, ending with a hard stomp on his toes.

The man grunted in her ear. "Bitch!"

It should have worked, but he was wearing steel-toed boots, too, and the pain along the front of the leg alone wasn't enough to loosen his grip. Unlike in the movies, the rag did not render her immediately unconscious, but rather, heaviness seeped into her limbs and the world spun. Fighting grew harder and harder until she had no choice but to slump against the man behind her.

Another hand, covered in a thick leather glove, brushed her hair back. "Ah, there we go. That's better," the guy murmured in her ear, then shifted to sling one of her arms over his shoulder.

No! Her heart hammered, and she screamed in her head, but her body refused to obey her commands. Terror threatened to overwhelm her, but in a last moment of clarity, she dug into her pocket and dropped her wallet, disguising the gesture as a last attempt at struggling. It worked. Her assailant mistook her efforts as resistance and rather than spotting what she'd dropped, he focused on securing his grip.

There was no care or gentleness in the way he handled her. Without ceremony, he opened the back door of the white van she had glimpsed earlier and dumped her in. Lani winced as she landed on her side but was too helpless to resist as he zip-tied her hands behind her back and her feet together. Trussed up like a pig, she squirmed to get a better look at her assailant, only to realize that he was wearing a respirator mask that covered the lower half of his face and a ball cap that kept the rest of it shadowed. He bent forward, patting her down, and confiscated her phone and keys. Groggy as she was, she lacked the strength to push him away.

Before she could even utter a word of protest, he shut the doors and darkness engulfed her.

Lani struggled to sit up straight, but the effects of what must have been chloroform were still impeding her command of her muscles and being hogtied made the task almost impossible. As the vehicle moved, she tried to keep track of the route in her head, but after the eighth turn, she gave up.

Her brain pushed against the disorientation, striving for enough clarity to process what had happened. At least all that paranoia that had her questioning her sanity these few days had proven to be valid. There was that.

So next was trying to figure out who the culprit was and their motivation. For that, she had too little to go on, but if he was also the caller, fear and intimidation was definitely a part of his goal.

As the van made another turn, Lani braced herself as best she could from being tossed about again, indignant about the number of bruises she was gaining from this process alone. The anger helped sharpen her focus and gave her the push she needed to break through the mental fog.

It was hard to keep track of time in the windowless back carriage of the van. At some point, the vehicle came to a full stop, and she heard sounds just outside, but no one opened the door, and before long, they were moving to God-knew-where. Several bumps on the road jostled her around, then everything came to a halt. Lani's heart raced once more, but she pushed herself up with renewed effort until she was upright at last. With grace and poise, she composed herself to sit in the most prim position possible. She would not let him win by stripping her of her dignity.

"Rise and shine, sweetheart." The guy had exchanged his respirator mask for a ski one that covered everything except his eyes and mouth. But there was no mistaking the crazed light in those black orbs, nor the cruel sneer that twisted his lips. There would be no mercy coming from him. This was not some business-like kidnapping for ransom. He was out to hurt her. Somehow, for reasons she had yet to fathom, this was personal. Lani racked her brains, trying to figure out who would hate her that much. The only name that came up was Bryan, and this man did not have the same build or voice.

"I'll stay awake, thank you." Lani tilted her chin up in defiance, knowing that wherever he had taken her, there would be no use screaming. They would be isolated or else he would have gagged her, just like how he had picked the one place where there were the least number of eyewitnesses possible to kidnap her.

Her composure threw him off as his sneer faltered. Muttering under his breath, he drew his switchblade and advanced toward her. Although fear threatened to make her curl up into a ball, she kept the serene mask as her expression.

He muttered something under his breath and sliced the zip tie that held her feet together. With a threatening growl in his throat, he grabbed her arm hard enough to leave another bruise and hauled her out of the van then held the blade up to her. "March." The threat was clear.

Having regained some muscle control over the course of the ride, Lani focused on putting one foot in front of the other, letting him lead her while trying to take stock of where she was. It looked like the warehouse district and, judging from the broken windows and worn walls looming before them, her kidnapper had chosen an abandoned building as her holding spot. Any other businesses still in operation would be spaced far enough away that no one would look too closely at any activity going on here.

Damn it.

He led her into what looked like a two-part office, past the front and through another door to the rear office with old furniture that the previous tenant must have left behind. Lani spun around to face him, only for him to shove her backward hard until she fell onto a large wooden chair. For the next few minutes, they wrestled, but he overpowered her, enough to tie her securely to it.

This was rather unbecoming of a Domme, and she glowered at him.

He stared at her for a moment then turned around, leaving the room. He didn't go far before returning to the front office. Separated only by a windowed wall, she could catch glimpses of her kidnapper as he took off his mask and pulled out a cell.

"Hey, it's me. Yeah, I have her." A pause. "No, not yet. Let him sweat a bit first." There was another moment of silence before he spoke up again, and this time, he answered in a louder voice. "No. Remember our deal. I call the shots, and I want to see him suffer."

Him. Suffer. It hit her then. This wasn't about her at all. There was only one man she could think of that her kidnapper might be referring to.

Nathan.

Chapter Twenty-Four

In some ways, waiting was the hardest part. As she sat, tied up, she contended with trying to pick up sounds that would give her hints to what her kidnapper had planned. Sometimes, she heard some good-humored whistling and clanging. Chains? Tools? She wasn't certain. But the worst was the periods of silence. As time stretched on, Lani noticed her own discomfort, from the rough rope that chafed at her skin to the way the hard seat dug into her ass. She flexed the muscles in her limbs to keep circulation going, but soon thirst and hunger pangs distracted her too much to continue. She regretted not eating dinner before her visit to the cemetery.

The room was sparse. Besides the chair she sat in, a wooden desk that had seen better days stood to one side, worn and scratched. An unpleasant scent permeated the air, and it took a second for Lani to figure out what it was. Beneath an exposed pipe running along the ceiling close to the wall, an old, stained mattress lay on the floor. She suspected that someone might have dragged it in from the dump.

The only solid thing in the room was the door with a shiny deadbolt that locked from the outside. Her captor must have made sure of that.

"All right, sweetheart, let's get you settled in for the night."

He returned, still sporting a ski mask.

"I have a name, you know." Lani leveled him a glare.

"Right, right. Lani? Or do you prefer Alana?"

Fear slithered down her spine, yet she refused to show any outward signs of it. "Ms. McMillan," she replied with a curt nod.

"Sassy. Maybe I should stick to 'bitch' instead," he retorted with a chuckle. He crouched down before her. "Now, I'm going to untie you and trust that you will do as I say. If you are good, I won't tie you up to the chair and may even let you sleep on that mattress tonight."

Bile rose in the back of her throat.

"What do you want?" She had her suspicions. Still, since he was in a talking mood, it was an opportunity.

He laughed and grabbed her chin between his fingers. "Nothing from you except a bit of suffering...a little pain."

She resisted the urge to spit in his face but wrenched her head away from his grip instead. Her kidnapper only chuckled and patted her hair. "Blame it on dating the wrong guy."

Well, that just about confirmed it.

"He took everything from me—my job, my life. Even my wife took the kids and left me."

How? Someone he'd gotten convicted in the past?

"Anyhow, come on."

Her bonds loosened, she rubbed her wrists to get the blood flowing once more. When he stepped back in front, her eyes widened as he waved the barrel of a sidearm in her face. "Move."

He guided her out of the door to the other side of the windowed partition where she had seen him spend most of his time so far. As they passed by, she glimpsed tools of various sorts—hammers, pliers and the likes. A sledgehammer leaned against one corner. Perhaps she should use that on him when she had a chance. The thought gave her a tiny shot of satisfaction, but right now, it was more of a fantasy. Lani kept her eye out for anything that would assist in an escape but spotted nothing.

"In here." He shoved her into an adjoining small room, and she startled in surprise at the sight of a clean washroom she found herself in. Unfortunately, it was windowless. She cursed in her head.

"Do your business and knock when you're done." He closed the door behind her, opting to remain outside.

Gratefulness welled up in her for this moment of privacy. At least so far, he had shown no interest in her sexually. In a situation like this, it was an actual possibility.

She relieved her bladder, took a quick drink from the basin then took stock of what she had in her pockets. A small, grim smile graced her lips as she found several hairpins. In her younger days, she had picked up lock-picking as a skill after one too many incidents of losing keys to handcuffs. Never did she dream it would come in handy for other reasons.

She just had to hope that he cuffed her instead of tying her up again.

Lani squared her shoulders and knocked on the door.

"Let's go."

She followed his directions while she seethed with rage inside. But now that she had a rough course of action, Lani knew she had to bide her time.

As luck would have it, he settled her on the mattress and grabbed a decent length of chain he must have looped around the pipe above earlier, cuffing her hands to it with standard handcuffs. She had limited range and could not turn in her sleep, but it was much better than when she had been in the chair. He set down a bucket down next to her, a sneer once more peeking through the opening of the ski mask. "For if you need to go at night. Not that one more piss on that thing would make a difference."

She said nothing.

"Sweet dreams!"

Then he left, not even bothering to switch off the single glaring overhead lamp.

Lani sat there in stony silence, straining to pick up any sounds of movement. When she caught him staring at her through the window, she made herself lie down and feign sleep. She swore she would not vomit from the putrid smell.

Her heart thumped in her ears, and she forced herself through breathing exercises that kept her muscles as relaxed as possible. More time passed and Lani resisted the urge to open her eyes until she caught the first snores drifting in from the next room over.

It was now or never. She counted in her head, hoping she had waited long enough for him to be in a deep sleep. This was her one chance, and she knew if she screwed this up, her life would be in a whole new level of danger. Yet, she refused to just sit there and wait for a rescue, not when she had a shot.

With her limited range, Lani wiggled until she pushed herself up. She looked over the window, glimpsing the man with his mask off, head against the glass pane. Reassured he was still asleep, she rose to her feet. So far, so good. If he stirred now, she could claim that she was taking a piss. Meanwhile, she twisted to dig into her pocket and drew out two bobby pins.

The cuffs were the straightforward part, and she sighed in relief when they came off with a soft click. It was fortunate that she had kept herself flexible with various exercises over the years. In the distance, a particular loud snort almost caused Lani to jump out of her skin and she cast a nervous glance in her kidnapper's direction, only to exhale a silent breath. *He's just shifting in his sleep.*

Next was the scarier part. Lani removed her heavy boots and with them in hand, shuffled across the floor in her socks. Crouching down, she worked on the deadbolt lock. That was harder. The tumblers remaining elusive in the beginning, and she paused often as she heard signs of stirring. If he woke up now, he would be able to see that she had escaped the chains. With her heart hammering in her chest, she continued, her mouth set to a grim line as she kept working until the first pin clicked. She grinned with triumph.

Progress sped up after that, and with a final click, she felt the deadbolt give way. Lani winced as the lock made more sounds, and she froze as the door creaked open.

Another loud snort and a shift. He was sleeping in an old armchair with half the stuffing sticking out. Light from the room she was in spilled into the darkness and she swallowed her fear, pushing forward, her boots in hand, then turned to close the door behind her.

She wanted to curl up in the corner, to hide. Instead, she forced her body to move and, keeping a low crouch, she crept along the wall. As she passed by the table, she grabbed a hammer, testing its weight.

If she got past this next exit, she would have made it. She reached for the knob, almost tasting her freedom.

Arms encircled her midsection and yanked her away without a word. Lani screamed and kicked her legs, throwing her boots back. He grunted in her ear. Encouraged, she gripped the hammer tighter and tried to hit her assailant. But with the awkward angle, it was no use. Rather, he caught her by the wrist and squeezed until he forced her to drop the makeshift weapon with a cry of pain.

She kept screaming, fighting, scratching like a wildcat — anything to keep him from gaining control. He yelled at her, and though she had trouble discerning what he said, she knew she was tiring. In the end, he pinned her arms to her body with a bear hug and carried her back into the room she had just escaped from.

He threw her onto the mattress, and when she tried to rise, he punched her in the face, stunning her. She lay there for a moment, dazed enough for him to cuff her once more to the damn chain, this time shortening it so that she dangled, her toes dragging on the floor.

"All right, bitch. No more Mr. Nice Guy."

Now she shivered as she watched him stomp his way to the other room, returning, with all things, the sledgehammer. Cold sweat trickled down her back as she eyed the tool, then at him as he brought in a video camera on a tripod next.

It took a second for her mind to catch up to the fact that she could recognize him without the mask. *Renard Dickson*. She had seen him on the news. Pieces fell into place. Nathan must have been his arresting officer at the time.

He glared at her, and with his entire face exposed, she could study the rugged visage, scarred in more ways than one. Time in jail had not been kind to Renard, but even his long shaggy hair did nothing to hide the crazed light in his eyes.

When he stepped closer, Lani couldn't suppress the whimper that escaped. He peered at her and kneeled down, running a hand down a leather-clad leg.

"Now you've done it, you little bitch," he cooed at her. "Naughty girls like you deserve a bit of punishment. And I do so wish I could enjoy your boyfriend's anguish when he sees this. Alas, I'll have to settle for imagining it." With that, he hoisted her leg up and cuffed it to a vertical pipe running down the wall. It connected to the one that ran above her head. Pipes and chains. She was developing a special hatred for them.

Renard took a step back and started the camera. Lani glimpsed the little red light showing that it was recording. Her body trembled as she struggled, but bound as she was, she only ended up wiggling like a fish on a hook.

He grabbed the sledgehammer and inched closer, dragging the thing along the floor with the screeching of metal scraping against concrete. Lani wanted to close her eyes, but she could only stare with growing horror.

"Smile for the camera, bitch." He hoisted the hammer up over his shoulder. "Tell him your name. Tell him something to prove you are you."

In a last act of defiance, she kept her mouth shut.

"Tell him," he screeched in her face.

"I… I am Lani McMillan, and I'm a Domme." She was strength. She knew the ways of pain and pleasure. She would cling to that.

He grinned, his lips twisted with sadistic glee. "Good girl. We'll only do one then." With that, he brought the hammer down.

Lani howled as blinding agony radiated from her limb and tore through her consciousness until it consumed her. *Broken*. In a small remaining rational part of her mind, she knew he had broken or even shattered something. But all she wanted was for the pain to stop, for all of it to go away. A bad dream. It had to be a nightmare. Her screams continued to pierce the air, but through the haze of red that coated her vision, she heard Renard's voice. He was speaking to someone else.

"You know who I am and what I'm capable of. This is just the beginning. And it's all happening because of you, Nathan Pelletier. This is all *your* fault."

It wouldn't stop. There was no relief. Then, at last, it became too much and by some modicum of mercy, the darkness took her away.

Chapter Twenty-Five

By morning, Nathan was trying to hold back the rising dread that threatened to overwhelm him. Lani hadn't returned his texts or picked up when he'd tried to call. Part of him reasoned that perhaps she was busy. Or maybe she was even playing with another, as much as he hated that idea. But gut instincts, combined with the earlier conversation with Luna, told him something was wrong.

And that was why, after he downed his cup of coffee to clear his head, the first thing he did was to call into work to say he wasn't coming in. With his calendar cleared, he got into his car to make his way to Lani's office. The devil's advocate in him tried to tell him he had no right intruding on her everyday life, that he was being paranoid and stalker-like, but the prevailing thought that Lani was in some kind of trouble spurred his actions on.

He struggled to not break into a run and hoped that when he arrived, she would be there with a raised brow and hands on her hips. Hell, he'd take anger and incredulity over the idea of her not being there. And he would accept any punishment she wanted to dole out, as long as she was okay.

As soon as the elevator reached her floor, Nathan walked a brisk pace down until he reached the door. Without breaking his stride, he opened it and entered.

It was the same receptionist, except she was all too preoccupied on the phone. Ophelia... That was the name Lani had used.

"No, how would I know who last saw her? Look... She didn't come in today and she hasn't called. That is not like her. She had clients this morning and she would never just ditch them." She fell silent then spoke again, her voice rising in volume. "What do you mean I have to wait twenty-four hours to report? This is ridiculous! Let me talk to your superior. What? No! Fine!" The blonde slammed the phone down, then looked up, startled. "Mr. Pelletier!"

Damn it. Damn it. Damn it.

He crossed the room with purposeful strides. "What happened?"

Frazzled, Ophelia flapped her hands in the air, then grabbed the mouse, clicking this way and that. "Ah, I don't have you in for today. Is there —?"

"I don't have an appointment."

"Apologies. Unfortunately, Ms. McMillan is not available for any unscheduled —"

"I'm not here for a session. Where's Lani?"

Ophelia gaped at him before she narrowed her eyes in suspicion. She stiffened and drew herself to up to sit taller. "Mr. Pelletier, Ms. McMillan is unavailable at the moment, and if you would like to book something with her, I would be happy to schedule you in. Otherwise, I have to ask you to leave."

Shit. Only then did Nathan realize the many ways she could interpret his insistent questioning. "Look." He rubbed the back of his neck and softened his tone. "Lani and I are…friends. The last time we talked, she sounded jumpy, and I'm worried about her. If there's something going on, please let me help."

At the dubious look Ophelia continued to give him, he raced on ahead. "I know people on the force. Here." He dug out his phone and pulled up his text messages to her, scrolling to the last response. Luckily, it was just a wish good night, nothing kinky or romantic. "See?"

She was wavering, her shoulders relaxing. It was obvious Ophelia knew something, and he needed her to trust him, so he tried another tack. "Do you know Luna Weir or her partner, Jacob?"

Her eyes lit up. "Mr. Dakota?"

Nathan nodded. "They can vouch for me."

It was what she needed to hear. Ophelia's ramrod straight posture crumbled. "Ms. McMillan was supposed to come in, but she hasn't been in the office. I've canceled all her morning appointments but haven't been able to reach her." Her hands fluttered about with renewed nervousness. Her voice wavered as if on the verge of tears. "I'm so worried. First the prank calls, now this?"

Nathan froze. "What calls?"

"Here." Ophelia reached for a pad of paper and handed it to him.

Christ. It was a call log—date time, duration, comments about noises made on the other end of the line. Nathan's blood ran cold. And they had increased in frequency.

"Whoever's been calling never says anything. We've gotten some numbers blocked, but it seems they keep switching phone numbers or something." She paled and wrapped her arms around herself as she spoke. "I think Ms. McMillan has been getting these on her personal cell, too. And she has been growing more frazzled and stressed the last few days."

It fit the rest of disparate pieces of information he had gathered—the way Lani had yelped in surprise when she was on the phone with him, what Luna mentioned about her reaction to her phone ringing.

Damn it.

"Please, the police won't listen. They told me they can't do anything unless it's been twenty-four hours. But you know Ms. McMillan is not like this."

Nathan nodded. The blanket of calm that descended on him was more because of his past training both in the military and as a cop rather than a reflection of how he truly felt. There would be time for panic and self-blame later. Right now, he needed to find Lani.

"I'll talk to my friends on the force. Do you have any idea where Lani might have gone last night?"

Ophelia paused. "She mentioned a few times that she's been riding her motorbike again after work."

Bike? The image of Lani in leathers surfaced in his mind, but he shook his head, suppressing a growl at himself. It was completely inappropriate.

"Okay. You have my number on file, right?"

Ophelia nodded.

"Call me if anything comes up." At her nod, he turned to leave.

"Where are you going?"

"I'm going to go talk to a few more people and see if I can track down where Lani's last known location is."

He didn't wait for an answer. Instead, he let himself out, striding with purpose back toward his car.

As soon as he got in the vehicle, he took out his phone. There was little doubt who he would call first, and he thumbed through until he found her number.

It rang once, twice. He tried to wait with more patience than he had the capacity for at the moment. Just as he was about to hang up, the ring tone stopped, and Luna picked up. "Nathan?" She sounded hoarse.

"Sorry... Did I wake you?"

A male voice muttered in the background. Luna pulled away to let the other know it was him before she spoke again. "It's okay. We're just waking up. Jacob took the day off. What's up?"

"When was the last time you heard from Lani?"

"Hold on. Let me put you on speaker." There was a shuffle, a pause and a murmur before more ambient noise came over the line.

"Morning, Jacob. Sorry for the interruption."

"No worries. I texted with Lani yesterday. What's going on?" Jacob sounded a little more alert than Luna, but not by much.

"About what time?"

"Hold on, let me check." After a moment, Jacob spoke again. "Around two in the afternoon. Nathan, explain."

"I've been trying to reach her since last night. I just checked her office and her receptionist said she never came in and never called to say she wasn't."

In the background, Luna gasped.

"I think you'd better come over." Jacob's voice held a commanding tone that brooked no arguments. Nathan recognized the dominance. "I'll call Darryl in the meantime and check on whether he saw her at The Playgrounds last night."

He found himself nodding before he realized they couldn't see his response. "I'll be right there."

It took all his willpower to focus on the drive and keep his mind from wandering. The morning rush hour slowed traffic enough that it made him growl with impatience, and by the time he had arrived at Luna's, his restlessness was showing with how he tapped his feet whenever there was a still moment.

When Jacob opened the door, he grunted in greeting, his manners forgotten.

"Darryl's on his way over. Take a seat."

Nathan nodded, forcing himself to move rather than complain about having to wait yet again. When he was a rookie, impatience had often been one of his biggest flaws and the first thing Julia had trained out of him. He'd thought he was beyond that now, but perhaps because it was Lani who was in trouble.

Without a word, Luna set a mug of tea in front of him, and he bowed his head in thanks. He sat but remained stoic, his back straight, posture stiff until Darryl walked through the same door he just had a few minutes before.

As soon as everyone settled in their own seat, Jacob nodded toward Nathan. "Take us through what's going on."

Later, Nathan would examine why he didn't change under Jacob's command. The man had the presence of a leader, and Nathan slid into the role of reporting to a superior, no different from when he served in the army.

"After I left here yesterday, I thought I'd call her after work and waited until five p.m. She didn't pick up, so I tried calling again later. I tried a third time around eight and when no one answered, I sent her a text. This morning, I drove to her office, only to find out she never went in." He tilted his chin up, challenging each of them to question his behavior.

"What made you think she was in trouble?" That came from Darryl, but there was no accusation in his tone.

"It has to do with what you asked me about yesterday, isn't it?" Luna murmured. Jacob and Darryl turned their attention toward her, even as Nathan nodded.

Luna looked up at her Dom. "Remember how she seemed distracted and jumpy when her phone buzzed?"

"I found out from Ophelia that someone's been prank-calling Lani both in her office and on her personal cell the last week and a bit. And now with her missing…" Nathan trailed off and swallowed hard, curling his hands into fists to keep from wanting to punch something in frustration.

"Well, shit," Darryl muttered under his breath.

"Ophelia said Lani had been taking trips on her motorbike after work. Would any of you have any idea where she might have ridden to?" It was a long shot, but it was all he had.

Jacob raised a brow and cast a glance over at Darryl who shook his head. "She wasn't at The Playgrounds last night. I didn't even know she was riding again."

Surprised, Nathan looked at Jacob for an explanation.

"She stopped after the car accident. I think the roads spooked her." Jacob didn't elaborate, but he knew enough that he could surmise the incident the Dom mentioned.

"Oh my God...August!" Luna shot up, then winced as the gesture pulled at her wound.

"What is it, Luna?" Jacob laid a hand on her shoulder.

"We talked about visiting August to clear our heads. Maybe that's where Lani went?"

A cemetery. Great. But Nathan had to admit, if there was ever a place for a kidnapping, it would be the perfect location, given the time of day it may have happened.

Fuck. Was he really thinking that somebody kidnapped her already? Julia had warned him about jumping to conclusions. And why would anyone want to kidnap Lani?

Realizing all eyes were on him once more, he nodded and rose from his seat. "It's as good a place as any to check. I'll head there now."

"You'll need someone to show you where the grave is. I'll come with you." Darryl was already grabbing his jacket, and Nathan grunted in gratitude.

"Keep us posted." Jacob wrapped his arm around a pale Luna as he spoke.

"I will." Nathan turned toward Darryl. "Let's go. We can take my car."

With grim faces, the two men headed out.

Chapter Twenty-Six

Darryl swore as they pulled into the parking lot and Nathan's stomach sank.

"That's Lani's bike."

He parked the car and fell back against his seat, rubbing his hand over his face, searching his mind for a reason, any reason she would have left her motorcycle behind. Would it be possible that it had broken down, and she called a cab? That rang false for Nathan, but he understood the need to not jump to conclusions.

"Now what?" Darryl turned to him, worry creasing his forehead.

"We search. Ask around." Nathan looked out of the window, up at the storm clouds hovering over the gray skies, then out toward where stones dotted the rolling hills a short distance away. "Show me where August's grave is."

"Yeah, sure." The other man got out of the car and waited until Nathan locked up before trekking up the path. They kept their eyes open, scanning for any signs of struggle. It didn't help that it had rained overnight, washing out any clues she may have left.

"There." Darryl slowed as he pointed to the simple tombstone that stood among the others.

Not for the first time, Nathan wondered what kind of man he had been that he continued to hold such a prominent place in Lani's heart. But before his thoughts could wander down that path, his foot nudged against something loose. He bent down and picked up the item with a half-crumpled napkin from his pocket.

The wallet was still soaked from the previous night, but Nathan's hands shook as he opened it. There it was, Lani's photo from her driver's license, staring right back at him. There may be a sound explanation that she left her bike here, but there was no good reason she would have dropped her wallet. She was too careful for that to happen.

"Fuck." He spat the word out with all the viciousness and anger boiling within him. Someone had taken her...may have hurt her. Red coated his vision.

"What is it?" Darryl's voice jolted him out of the fury that threatened to eclipse all reason. Nathan drew air deep into his lungs and exhaled as he held the wallet out for him to inspect.

"Well, shit."

Nathan nodded. Darryl's own swearing kept him from being sucked into a vortex of rage. Numbness settled in his bones instead. He cleared his throat, but his voice sounded dead, even to his own ears. "I think we have enough proof now that the cops won't turn us away. Let me make a call."

It took only fifteen minutes later before police swarmed the place, and they roped off certain areas as forensics got to work. Nathan had surrendered the evidence he found and was leaning against the trunk of his car with Darryl when his old partner and mentor, Julia, walked over with her hands in her pockets.

He looked up, hope in his eyes.

"Nate." A note of warning crept in her tone, and she brushed her hair back. As she neared, she drew out a notebook.

"Anything, Detective?" It was Darryl who asked, but Nathan already had an inkling of her answer.

"It's too early to tell. If you don't mind, I have a few questions for each of you." Julia paused, waiting.

It took a second or so for Darryl to register her meaning, and when he did, he nodded and walked farther away.

"All right, Nate." Julia tucked the notebook into her pocket, signaling she was going off record. "What's this woman to you?"

Nathan opened his mouth then closed it again. How could he even begin to explain their complicated relationship?

Julia sighed and shook her head. But it appeared that his silence was enough of an answer — or she knew him too well. "How public were you guys?"

That was a much easier question. "A few of her friends know" — he nodded toward Darryl — "and Lani came with me to one of Daniel's parties. We weren't official, but we haven't been sneaking around, either. But, ah" — Nathan cleared his throat — "we've been on a bit of a break."

He didn't like the way Julia's lips tightened into a terse line. It was never a good sign.

"This may be unrelated, but on a hunch, I just called Dickson's PO. He missed his check-in."

What? He clenched his fists and blood roar in his ears. If someone had kidnapped Lani because of him…

"Nate, stay with me. I need you to keep your head on this one. She needs you."

He blinked and found Julia's hand on his shoulder, steadying him. "Yeah, I'm here." The words came out rough, but Julia nodded in satisfaction and leaned back, breaking her grip.

"Give me a list of people, Nate—friends, family, coworkers, anyone else I should talk to and any potential suspects."

"Ophelia…"

"Right, you mentioned her on the phone. I have my partner over there interviewing her already and getting her logs."

She had always been efficient. "Thanks."

"Excuse me, Detective Martinez?"

Nathan and Julia looked up at the approaching uniformed cop at the same time. It wasn't anyone he recognized. Then again, he had been off the force for a while now.

"What is it?" Julia half-turned.

The younger man hesitated, casting a glance toward Nathan.

"He's fine. Spit it out."

It was a significant mark of trust from Julia, considering he could be a suspect. He shot her a grateful look.

"The place had surveillance on the parking lot. The director just handed the tape over, and we sent it to the techs in the lab."

"Thank you, Kumar. Keep me posted if they discover anything."

The officer nodded at both of them then walked away.

As Nathan eased backward to rest his weight against the car, he rubbed his face again.

Julia ducked her head to catch his eyes. "Hey, we'll find her. You know the first seventy-two hours is the most crucial, so go get me the names."

"Yes, ma'am," Nathan muttered, but how he wished the woman he was saying it to right now was one with flaming red curls instead.

The rest of the early afternoon went by in a blur. Darryl gave his statement and Nathan texted Julia the list — a pitifully small list that Darryl ended up adding to. It hit him then just how little he knew about Lani. Oh, he knew *her* but not about her life, and while he'd always thought that he was giving her space before, he resolved that when they got her back, he would fix that. He would earn the right to learn about her, all of her. As her sub, he could do no less... *if* she would allow him to serve her.

Both men remained silent as Nathan drove Darryl to his place. As they pulled up in front of the apartment building where the bartender lived, Darryl turned to Nathan.

"I'll let Jacob and Luna know. Call any of us if you have any updates."

Nathan nodded, still numb.

With a sigh, Darryl patted him on the shoulder. "We'll get her back." There was a firmness to his voice, full of conviction.

"How?" Nathan whispered.

"How what?"

"How can you be so sure?" Memories surfaced. Past seventy-two hours, it would not just be about finding

Lani. It may be about recovering a body. His stomach churned, queasy with that thought.

"I have to believe that. I refuse to think otherwise. Besides, I know a man who will move heaven and earth to save his lover when I see one, and I have faith in your abilities."

Unbidden, tears threatened to choke him. Nathan swallowed hard, his throat growing scratchy. "Thanks, man."

Darryl patted him on the shoulder. "Now, go find our Domme and bring her home."

"I will."

Words were easy. Once Darryl left, Nathan sat in his car, staring off into space, unsure what his next step would be. He wasn't a cop anymore. He couldn't join in on the investigation but could only wait to hear from Julia.

His phone rang. Nathan muttered a curse as he pulled the device out and saw it to be the office's number.

"Nathan here."

"Hey, boss, can you come in for a few minutes? There's something you need to see." Jasper's concern was coming through, loud and clear. Great… This was the last thing he needed.

"Jasper, just spit it out."

"I can't." He lowered his tone to a whisper. "I don't trust the phones, and besides, I want you to hear this first."

Damn these security techs and their paranoia. It was what made guys like Jasper so good at their jobs, but their overboard tinfoil hat tendencies would be the death of him one day.

"Fine, I'm on my way."

No sooner did he hang up than his phone rang again, this time with a number that filled him with equal parts dread and hope. He stilled his trembling hands then brought it to his ears.

"Nathan."

"Mr. Pelletier. Oh, thank God." Ophelia's voice quivered and he could picture her close to tears. "A package just came in from a courier. It's addressed to you."

Okay, more dread than hope.

"Are the cops still there?"

"No, they left about an hour ago."

"Okay, I'm on my way." Nathan hung up and called Jasper back. Fortunately, the boy picked right up right away rather than trying his patience.

"What's up, boss?"

"Something came up. I'll text you the address. Meet me there instead."

"Will do."

With some luck on his side, perhaps he could take care of both things at the same time—or so he told himself, borrowing a bit of Darryl's optimism. Still, he had a feeling in the pit of his stomach that a package addressed to him and sent to Lani's office could only mean one thing.

On the way, questions persisted in his mind. Who was the kidnapper? How had they found out about their relationship? How did they know that Lani's receptionist could reach him? All that implied that they had done their homework, which meant stalking. And that meant the phone calls were only the tip of the iceberg. Someone had been following him and Lani around.

Still, how had they gathered so much intel in such a short time?

He saw Jasper standing on the sidewalk in front of the building as he pulled into a parking spot that had opened up on the street. Another piece of blessed luck. He would need more of that to find Lani.

"Okay, what's going on?" Nathan struggled to keep the note of impatience out of his voice

Jasper leaned in toward him and kept his volume low. "Have you heard of a guy named Renard Dickson? He's a convicted felon who was released a few weeks back? It was on the news."

Nathan's blood ran cold, and he stiffened, rooted on the spot. "What about him?" He tried to keep a neutral expression.

"I saw him on the security footage at The Playgrounds. It doesn't look good, boss." Jasper's pale complexion tinged a little green as he took a steadying breath. "There's more. I was wondering what a guy like him was doing there, so I did a facial recognition search through the other tapes. It looked as though he was looking for someone and was sneaking around, asking questions of various people."

Shit. All of this was too much of a coincidence. The clues were all pointing toward Renard, but how would he have figured out that The Playgrounds was a place to look for him—or Lani, for that matter?

"You'd better come with me." Nathan willed his body to move, and when he started again, his pace sped enough that Jasper had to jog a few steps to keep up with him.

"What's going on, boss?"

"This is personal, so I'm trusting you."

On the way up, he filled Jasper in, keeping it as brief as possible. Nathan was hoping he wouldn't need to involve The Playgrounds or the company, but at this rate, he would have to tell Julia, too, and if the cops would be questioning Jasper, he deserved to be given the full picture. The boy's eyes grew rounder and rounder, but he kept his mouth shut the entire time, taking in the story.

They walked down the hall together, and when Nathan opened the door to Lani's office, Ophelia shot right up from her seat. Her features were puffy, and she looked even more frazzled than she had that morning.

"For you." Ophelia held out the world's most inconspicuous brown envelope with a printed label.

He stared at it, his pulse roaring in his ears, and took it in hand.

Chapter Twenty-Seven

For the rest of the night and into early morning, Lani slid in and out of consciousness, and when she was awake, she struggled to not get sick all over herself. At least even when she tried to hurl, there was nothing left in her stomach to regurgitate. Small comforts...sort of.

She avoided looking at her leg, unsure of how bad the damage was. At this stage, she didn't want to find out.

He kept her chained up in the same position, and her body ached without proper support. At first she didn't notice in her lucid moments, the pain of her injury eclipsing the discomfort and tingling from her rest of muscles, but as time passed and she adjusted, she noted the feeling, or lack of, in her other extremities. Unconsciousness became more preferable.

Her eyelids were drooping once more when the rattling of chains broke through her haze. Before her brain could process what was going on, the cuff holding her broken leg fell away and the limb dropped from where it had been pinned. A fresh bout of sharp pain lanced her mind, but all she managed was a whimper.

Then the chain above her head slackened, and she landed in a heap of awkward angles. A new scream tore from her throat as agony burned her from the inside out.

He ignored her, coming around instead to unlock the other set of cuffs. Distracted as she was, she only put up token resistance as he wrestled her out of her leather jacket with the pocket of remaining bobby pins. Her cries subsided once more into whimpers and yelps as he maneuvered her like a rag doll.

"Oh, shut up, bitch." That was all the warning she got before he doused her with a bucket of water. The cold shocked her into silence.

"Better," he muttered more to himself then took out his gun again. "Now, I'm going to give you one chance to go do your business. You better not fuck it up."

Lani stared at him, blinking without comprehension before she realized he intended for her to walk. *Is he nuts?* Actually, she did already know the answer, didn't she? With all the remaining shreds of dignity she could muster, she propped herself up and, using the wall and the very pipe he had chained her to before, pulled herself to a standing position, all the while grunting in pain.

At least he let her continue to brace against the walls for balance as she hobbled toward the washroom. Only when the door closed did she venture a look at the damage done to her body.

He had broken her leg in a bad way. Her stomach churned, and she retched into the washbasin.

There was nothing she could use to dry off. Her hair plastered against her cheeks, she began shivering and rubbed her arms, desperate to warm up. No luck. The soaked thin blouse she wore hindered her efforts rather than helped. Perhaps this was another form of torture Renard had in mind.

She had to get out of there. But how? She drew a blank.

A loud pounding startled her, and she stiffened.

"You better be fucking done in there."

Unwilling to chance provoking him again, Lani hastened to open the door to find the gun pointed at her once more.

"Back to your room."

They fell into silence now and he guided her return to the mattress, chaining her up like the way he had the first time. Lani felt an absurd sense of gratefulness and checked herself for any signs of developing any positive emotional response toward Renard himself. Nope, she still hated him and wanted to stab him with her heels.

Satisfied that he had cowed her into obedience and that she would not attempt another escape, he smirked and walked away, whistling. One day, soon, she was going to wipe that smug smile off his face. For now, she settled down and curled up as much as her broken leg allowed to conserve what body heat remained.

Lani wasn't sure how long it was before the sound of a new voice talking to her captor woke her up. Hopeful at first, she pushed herself to sit upright until she registered what the conversation was. She lay back down and feigned sleep.

"What the hell were you thinking?"

"Why, so nice of you to visit!"

"Cut the bullshit, Renard. What the fuck? We agreed to a kidnapping and a ransom—not fucking break her legs."

"Now, now. I only did one. Besides, she tried to escape. What was I to do?"

"I don't know! Tie her up better? *You're* the kidnapper!" The new speaker sounded familiar. Lani struggled to match a face to it in her head.

"*Tsk, tsk*, Daniel. You should be well aware by now that you're every bit an accomplice as well. If I go down, you'd go down, too."

"Shut up, and don't use my name," Daniel hissed. "Wait! Can she hear us?"

"*Pfft*, she's probably passed out from the pain again. Bitch sure sleeps a lot."

Lani swallowed her indignation and remained still while her mind spun at the revelation. *Daniel? As in Nathan's partner from the security firm?* Yes, the voice matched the face she recalled. But why? She shuddered. There was only one reason. This was some tactic to scare Nathan off from buying Wilson's shares.

"At least did you ask for the amount I told you to?"

"Yes, yes—and a little more." A pause, then Renard guffawed. "Stop worrying so much. It's not more than what that stinking ex-cop can afford. Now run along. I'm a busy man."

"No way. Someone's got to make sure you don't kill the poor woman."

Renard laughed again. "Well, you should have thought of that sooner, before you came to me."

Lani heard a lower muttering but couldn't quite pick up Daniel's response.

"Hey, hey, I'm joking. Whatever floats your boat. Make yourself at home."

Lani could only hope that Daniel could keep Renard in check, even if it meant escape would be that much harder.

* * * *

Part of him didn't want to open the envelope, but Nathan had no choice. With two pairs of eyes on him, he stiffened, his movements jerky as he broke the seal and withdrew the contents.

It was what he expected, a typed ransom note and instructions for dropping the money off the next day at noon. There was no mention of Lani, only that further directions would be given upon receiving the payment. His eyes widened at the amount. It was about what his savings, including what he had set aside to buy the shares from Wilson were, then some. But how? How would he know? Coincidence?

Bastard.

"What's that?" Ophelia pointed at the USB stick that fell onto the counter, drawing his attention away from the note.

It was as if something died in his stomach. Whatever was on that small inconspicuous device, it wasn't anything he ever wanted to see. His breathing grew shorter, and his heart hammered against his chest as Ophelia took the thing and plugged it into her computer.

"Wait," Jasper called out, but Ophelia was already opening the file from the screen that popped up.

There was Renard, grinning at the camera before backing up to reveal Lani. He had her chained up, one leg up, cuffed to a pipe on the wall. Nathan didn't want to see more, but he couldn't tear his eyes away. Cold sweat broke out and beaded on his forehead as he struggled for air, but he kept his gaze on Lani, watching her, defiant till the end as the son of a bitch screamed in her face. Even in that moment, she was the most beautiful thing he had ever seen.

The horror accumulated as he watched Renard lift the sledgehammer. Then he brought it down. A sharp pain stabbed at his chest, and his entire body seized.

He broke her leg. Christ, he broke her leg. Her screams would haunt him for the rest of his life.

Beside him, Ophelia's cry eclipsed Renard's next words, although his taunt was clear in his smirk. Nathan barely noticed, though, and instead, clawed at the collar of his shirt, struggling for a breath that seemed to elude him.

A panic attack. He recognized that was what was happening in the logical part of his brain, but he couldn't find the center he needed to start the mindfulness exercises he used to leverage it all the time.

"Boss. Boss!" Jasper reached for him.

Ophelia got to him first, chucking a stapler at him. "You! It's all your fault! He hurt her because of *you*," she shrieked, hysterical. Then she was right next to him and raining down slaps and punches. They did little, and he stood there, accepting the blows, lost in his own personal hell.

"Stop." More yelling. "Stop!" Jasper raised his voice.

Nathan wasn't sure what happened, but the screaming and hitting came to a halt, then Jasper was guiding him to a chair. "Sit."

Jasper taking over was enough to snap him out of it. Hand on his chest, he withdrew and focused on himself to find his way back.

A low murmur. Jasper talking in soothing tones to Ophelia. A clacking of the keyboard. Those sounds pulled him out of his head.

"Got it!" Jasper stood up in triumph.

It took a few attempts for Nathan to get his vocal chords working again. "What do you have?"

"Their location. This guy was an idiot and didn't strip the GPS coordinates for the video file." Jasper handed him a sticky note where he had scribbled the address down.

Location. They knew where he was holding Lani. He grunted and rose in one swift motion. "Thanks. I owe you, Jasper." Then he turned to Ophelia, who sat in the chair, trembling. "I'm sorry. I'm not sure what I can say, but I'm going to go get her back. *Now.*"

He had to do this…or die trying.

"Boss, wait!"

He didn't. Instead, he left the office at a brisk pace and drew out his phone.

"Julia."

"Nathan. We have an APB out for the white van the techs spotted from the CCTV in the parking lot. We think he may have stopped to switch plates, though, but we'll keep looking."

He shook his head and cut right in. "I have their location. It is Renard."

"What? How?"

"Ransom note got sent to Lani's office and had a video. My tech was with me and pulled it from the file."

"Okay, text it to me, and we'll meet you there."

"No."

"What?"

"We do this my way or I'm going alone."

"Nathan, don't be an idiot." Julia's frustration was coming through loud and clear.

"No. I know how this plays out. It's too risky for Lani. I get her out first. Then you guys can take him down." Nathan exited the building and walked the short distance to his car, ignoring the parking ticket clipped beneath his wipers.

"I can just get the address out of your tech." It was a last-ditch attempt to talk him out of his plan, and they both knew it.

"Sure. But I'm already on my way, and with the head start, I'll be inside before you guys arrive."

Julia lapsed into a string of Spanish swear words, too fast for him to follow, but he was certain there were a few creative choice phrases in there for him. Meanwhile, he started the car and began driving. There was one stop he had to make first, not that he was going to tell her.

Nathan tried another tact. "Julia, please. I need to keep Lani safe."

"What is she to you, Nathan?"

This time, the answer was easy enough. "Everything. She's everything."

The sigh that came over the phone in response was not what he expected, but hope brightened his countenance as he recognized it as a sign of Julia giving in.

"Fine, what's the plan?"

Nathan grinned, but there was no mirth in his smile.

Chapter Twenty-Eight

They met in silence down the street from the abandoned warehouse where he knew Renard was holding Lani. It took all his willpower to not storm in straight away, but it had been part of the deal he had struck with Julia to keep the rest of the force from surrounding the place with sirens and megaphones.

Nathan did not want to get into a hostage situation. Renard was never kind to his hostages.

Then again, he hadn't been kind to Lani already.

The darker side of him imagined how satisfying it would be to connect his fist to the bastard's face. He wasn't on the force anymore. He didn't have to uphold any ideals.

"Nathan...you listening?"

"Yeah."

Julia tapped her ear. "Can you hear me?"

He nodded. They had tucked a hidden earpiece and mic on him so they could monitor his situation. Julia had also given him a bulletproof vest to wear beneath his jacket. The familiar weight was a comfort.

"Okay, remember. Get in, get out. No heroics. Don't do more. Renard will be angry since he's not expecting you, so don't rile him up. You've got your reasons straight in your head?"

"Yeah. I'm not leaving Lani in his hands for one second longer."

Julia nodded. "That's good. But don't forget he's doing this because he wants to see you suffer. So expect this to not go the way you planned."

His face hardened, and he set his lips into a thin line. "I know. Get in, get her freed and us safe, then signal for you to come in."

"Good — and be careful."

Nathan gave her another curt nod.

"Boss!"

Nathan started in surprise as Jasper ran out of an unmarked car that pulled up next to them. A younger cop emerged from the driver's side and bobbed his head at Julia. That must be her partner.

"Boss." Jasper called for his attention again, and he turned toward the boy.

"What are you doing here?"

Now Jasper looked at him with a sheepish smile on his face. "I figured after the way you stormed out that you were going to try something crazy. When I heard the cop over there" — Jasper jerked his thumb toward Julia's partner — "talking about some reckless plan, I guessed you were going through with it." As if realizing he was babbling, Jasper paused, inhaled and handed him a small black bag. "I got these for you from the office. I signed them out all proper, too. Figured you can do the explaining after."

Nathan took it and peered inside, revealing a baton, a taser gun and a belt with holsters for both. He could almost hug the boy. Instead, he tilted his head back up. "Thanks. That's two I owe you."

Jasper shrugged and scratched his cheek. "Don't worry about it."

He was buckling everything on when Jasper spoke again.

"Boss, how dangerous is this?"

Nathan finished with the buckle and reached up to place a hand on Jasper's shoulder, catching his eye. "I won't lie and say this isn't an enormous risk. If I'm lucky, I'll come walking out with Lani and the money. If not—" He suppressed a shudder before continuing. "If not, then I want you to call up Wilson, his direct line—just Wilson—and tell him he needs to look for another buyer."

Jasper's eyes widened, then he shook his head. "Wait! This makes little sense. Why are you bringing the cash if this is a rescue mission?"

There wasn't time for an explanation, but Nathan knew he owed Jasper. And if he came out of this, he wanted to groom the boy for a bigger role. Throughout this crisis, Jasper had shown an astonishing mix of levelheadedness, quickness and smarts that boded well for his career.

"Because since Renard showed his face, it means he doesn't expect to come out of this intact. It's personal. He wants to see me suffer, even at the cost of his own freedom. But the fact he also asked for money may still mean there's a slim chance that he thinks he can make it out of this somehow. I can't discount that option if there's a possibility he will trade Lani back for it."

"But if the cops don't get him…"

"She's worth it."

Jasper's mouth snapped shut.

"I've got to go."

With that, he ducked back into his own car and drove alone to the warehouse, stopping just outside the property's boundary. As he emerged from the vehicle, he grabbed the duffel bag full of cash. The bank had taken longer than he had wanted, but the cops had helped smooth out the process. It was fortunate that he had already liquidated most of his funds earlier to prepare for buying the company shares. Again, he gritted his teeth at the thought. Something didn't sit right with him, like he was missing part of the picture.

As his gaze fell on the van, his heart did a flip and landed with a thud. If he had any lingering doubts, they dissipated as the van's presence confirmed they were there.

His feet stilled, rooting him to the spot even as his body stiffened. His heartbeat thundered in his ear, and when a car drove by, he clutched at his chest. In his mind's eye, he saw the police swarming the place, the shouting, the chaos then the first gunshot. The imaginary sound made him duck and cover his head.

No, not now! Not when Lani needed him. He *would* push past this.

Focus on breathing. In. Out. In. Out. It's a flashback. It's not real. He wrenched his gaze away from the van and up toward the gray clouds just breaking apart, racing across the sky, and he began bringing awareness back to his physical body. He wiggled his toes, flexed his feet, working up one part at a time. Bit by bit, the panic receded.

He would hold it together for Lani's sake.

With practiced stealth, Nathan let himself into the building. Most of the warehouse was a single large, cavernous space, but a long platform ran along the left side, comprising several smaller offices. The last rays of the afternoon sun filtered through the broken windowpanes on the other wall, casting odd shadows across the concrete floor.

One room near the back was lit by more artificial light. *There.*

He took care to walk beneath the platform, toward the stairs where Renard would least likely spot him before he was ready. Part of him wished for a gun, but he touched the baton on his side, right next to the taser, and thanked Jasper once more in his head.

As he neared, he could make out some emphatic muttering. Nathan froze. Of its own accord, his dominant hand itched for the weapons under his jacket, but he let out a silent breath instead, shifting the weight of the duffel bag in his grip. It was now or never. Steeling his nerves, he stepped out from beneath the platform to take the stairs. From this point on, there would be no more cover. He was exposed.

"Renard!" His voice bounced off the walls in odd echoes.

"The fuck?" That, Nathan recognized, was from Renard.

Closer now, he also caught a panicked whisper from an accomplice, but before he progressed farther to investigate, Renard emerged from the lit room and crossed the platform, waving what Nathan was pretty sure was a real sidearm in one hand.

"You have some guts, Pelletier."

Nathan took the last steps up and held up the duffel bag, his free hand up in the air. "I have what you asked for."

"You're shit at following instructions."

"I'm not leaving her in your hands a minute longer than I have to," Nathan shot back.

Renard stopped ten paces away from him and pointed the gun in his direction. The smile he sported sent unease coursing down Nathan's spine. One word came to mind…manic.

"How did you find this place, anyway?"

Nathan swept his gaze across, trying to see if Lani was being kept in that same room Renard had emerged from but no such luck.

"Hey, I asked you a question."

No reason not to answer, although the memory of what he saw made bile rise in the back of his throat. "The video."

Renard cackled. "That was damn good, wasn't it? Some of my best work, if I say so myself."

He clenched his fist, his knuckles turning white. "Where is she?" The words rumbled like thunder.

"Pretty demanding for the guy with the gun pointed at him." Renard smirked. "You know, I have to say, your woman's got sass and guts. If she hadn't tried to escape, though, I wouldn't have had to break her leg."

Fierce pride beat in Nathan's chest, and he straightened.

"Then again, what did she call herself? A Domme? Hmm, does this make you her bitch?" He leaned forward, malice gleaming in his eyes. "Tell me, does she peg you with a strap-on and fuck you till you cry?"

It was clear that Renard had a certain image of what submitting to a Dominant meant, but what was odd was how the accusations slid off Nathan with no effect. Instead, he leveled Renard with an expectant stare, not bothering to even dignify the comments with a retort. He served. It was none of anyone else's business, and he couldn't care less about how other people viewed it.

Silence prevailed, and Renard barked out another laugh. "Okay, okay. Stay here."

As Renard turned, Nathan resisted the urge to rush up and subdue him. Part of him reveled at the thought of a struggle, of wrapping his hands around scrawny neck and squeezing the life out of the bastard, or to just crack his head with a whack of his baton. But he remembered that there was at least one more person there besides Lani, and it would put her in too much danger. So he only remained rooted to the spot.

"Hey, slut, your sissy is here to get you. Consider yourself lucky." Nathan knew Renard had spoken with a boisterous tone on purpose. He wanted him to hear every bit of humiliation he could dish out.

What he didn't expect was the momentary silence followed by a loud slap and an emphatic "Bitch!"

Nathan surged forward before he knew what his body was doing. But before he reached the room, Renard emerged once more, this time dragging Lani by her tangle of red curls. She trailed behind the best she could, hobbling and avoiding putting weight on the broken leg while bent over. Renard was still muttering under his breath and wiping his face.

"Let. Her. Go." It took Nathan every bit of control to enunciate through his rage.

Renard only grinned at him and released his grip, thrusting Lani to the concrete before them. She gave a loud cry and crumpled into a heap on the floor.

Again, Nathan tried to move closer, taking another step forward, but Renard waved the gun at him. "Nuh-uh-uh-uh-uh. Back."

By then, Lani had propped herself up, composing herself. She tossed her hair backward and tilted her chin up, revealing several ugly bruises blossoming across her face. A trickle of blood trailed down one corner of her mouth, fresh from where Renard must have slapped her just now. Yet, despite every line in her body radiating pain, her gaze searched then held his. There was no doubt, no fear, only a fierceness and pride that he associated with her. Lani curved her lips into a small, tight smile. "Hello, darling."

Chapter Twenty-Nine

"Ma'am, sorry I'm late."

Lani's smile widened and an odd sense of happiness shot through him. With those few words, he had righted their relationship, and everything fell into balance within him, quieting his doubts. His focus sharpened.

"Nonetheless, you're here, so we can discuss your actions further once we are gone." How Lani managed such a regal nod in the state she was in, Nathan wasn't sure.

"Of course, Ma'am."

Renard cackled at the exchange and looked down at Lani. "Don't know why you got so worked up—just calling a spade a spade or a sissy when I see one...*Ma'am*." He mimicked the title with a little jeering laugh, rolling his eyes, then turned toward Nathan, holding the gun up. "You've seen her. Now"—he brought the weapon to rest the muzzle against Lani's temple—"the money."

"Okay. Okay." Nathan raised his arm again. "I'm going to walk over to give you what you asked for and help Lani up. Deal?"

"Open the bag first. Show me the cash is not some fake shit."

Nathan unzipped the pack and lifted it up to show him. There was no padding with paper. Every single bill was the real thing.

"Yeah, yeah okay, hurry up." Renard jerked his head in one direction.

Good. It would put him in his proximity, but he could protect Lani better that way. Renard was overconfident with the gun in his hand. Maybe he could use that.

"No heroics."

Julia's words came echoing back, and Nathan sighed inwardly. Getting Lani away and safe was the priority, no matter how much he wanted to beat the ever-loving daylights out of the little worm.

Fine.

He zipped up the bag and crossed the distance at a slow, steady pace, careful to not provoke with any sudden movements. Nathan wasn't sure how trigger-happy Renard was and didn't want to find out.

"You took everything from me that day when you arrested me. All I was trying to do was make some cash, get my family out of the ghetto and get my daughter a better education. They left, though. They didn't even wait a week after they incarcerated me. Then my crew, my friends, every one of them… Oh, of course, they have their excuses, but I know."

Nathan listened to the ramblings but remained silent. Renard may have claimed to have robbed banks for the money for his family, but he remembered interviewing the hostages and how they had trembled in fear as they'd recalled the cruel ways Renard had treated them. As soon as he was close enough, he dropped the duffel bag at Renard's feet and crouched down next to Lani. "Ma'am, can you walk if you lean on me?" He trailed his hand downward to pull his jacket back just a smidgen, revealing the weapons beneath to her alone.

Lani's eyes widened, and she gave him a quick nod. "Sure."

Relieved that she got the message, Nathan looped her arm around his neck and wrapped one of his own around her waist. "I'm sorry," he whispered, knowing how much this was going to jostle and aggravate her broken leg.

"Let's go." Lani gritted her teeth.

He nodded and hoisted her up, cringing at the groan that Lani bit back. Once they found their balance, he dropped his hold from Lani's abdomen and led them away. With their backs toward Renard, Nathan grabbed the handle of the taser with his free hand. He glanced down at Lani and saw her dip her head downward in acknowledgment.

Renard's laughter rang from behind them. "You didn't think I was—"

He never finished the sentence. Nathan spun around as Lani slipped from his side and he fired his weapon right into Renard's chest.

There was a split second where Renard stared down at himself, disbelief written on his face before Nathan pulled the trigger.

Renard's features twisted into a mix of horror and pain as his entire body convulsed. Although only seconds passed, Nathan watched for an eternity as

Lani's tormentor spasmed, then collapsed onto the floor.

"You okay?" Nathan glanced over at Lani, then sighed in relief when she nodded. Then he realized Renard has become deathly still. "Shit."

"What's wrong?" Lani didn't get up, but she straightened to gain a better look at Renard's prone form.

"A taser shouldn't render anyone unconscious, unless…" He drew his baton and inched closer, then took the precaution of kicking the gun away before bending down to check Renard's pulse. *Still alive.*

"Well, I'm pretty sure he's been snorting something half the time he was here," Lani replied in a dry tone.

"Ah." That would do it. Nathan re-holstered the stick, grabbed the bag of cash, and rose to his feet with a smile of relief. "Let's go home."

"Not so fast."

Nathan heard the telltale sounds of a handgun's hammer being pulled back as another man walked out of the room. Clad in an expensive suit and a ski mask, he made a sharp contrast against the crazed Renard. Even the hand that held the gun was covered with a fancy leather glove.

"Oh, stop it, Daniel. I know it's you," Lani called out from behind.

"Well, fuck." Daniel ripped the mask off his face. "At least I don't have to wear the damn thing anymore."

Nathan stared at his partner, shock freezing him on the spot. He had suspected that someone had been feeding Renard information, but never had he thought it would be Daniel.

Although Daniel kept his eye on Nathan, he moved to nudge Renard's still form then rolled his eyes. "Good help is sure is hard to find these days. He had just one simple task, and he couldn't even get that right."

"Why?" The question came out as a bare whisper, but his mind was already emerging from the fog to assemble the pieces. The ransom amount would render him almost cashless. Daniel didn't want him buying Wilson's shares.

"You think I will let you run the company as majority shareholder? That should be me, not you. Who was there from the beginning? Who brought in the contracts? That was all me. You're just some low-life who couldn't make it as a cop. Can't even cut it as a man, it seems."

"I don't know. From over here, Nathan looks about ten times the man you are," Lani shot back. "I mean, the last time we were over, your wife had to grope what's mine to get her kicks. What does that say about you?"

Despite the situation, Nathan felt his lips tug into a smirk on their own.

"Shut up, bitch." Daniel shifted his aim to point the gun at Lani, although she was farther from him.

Without another thought, Nathan slid with practiced movement to impose himself between the weapon and Lani's form. "No, Daniel. You know this is over."

"Oh? From my perspective, I seem to hold all the cards. You drop the money, walk away and swear you will turn down Wilson's deal. In fact, I want you to resign from the company. Do that or I shoot you both and make it look like Renard here did it. Hell, I can even say to the cops that I found you guys and tased Renard, but it was too late to save you two. I'd come out smelling a hero. Either way, I walk out of here."

Nathan was about to point out that the police had the place surrounded, but Julia's voice came over the earbud.

"Don't tell him. Remember, everyone acts differently when backed into a corner. Leave him to us. We've got every exit covered. Focus on getting out."

"Okay." Nathan held up both hands again. "We'll take the deal. I'll give Wilson a ring and resign tomorrow."

"Good. Smart move. Now throw the pack over."

Nathan glanced at the duffel bag in hand. "Why, Daniel? I can understand Renard, but you don't need the money."

Daniel shrugged. "Let's just say it's a little insurance."

"Fine." Nathan tossed the cash over, then keeping his hands up still, inched backward until he stood beside Lani, who had grown quiet again, watching their exchange with questions on her face. As Daniel kneeled down to grab the bag, Nathan crouched down, too. But when he lifted Lani up in a bridal carry, he whispered in her ear. "Julia."

Lani made no outward sign that she heard him. *Good.* He knew he could trust her to not give anything away.

"We're leaving," Nathan called out and walked with Lani back along the platform toward the stairs. Daniel waved the gun in a shoo-ing motion, then kept it trained on them again, following their retreat.

"Stairs. I'll go slow," Nathan murmured, more for Julia's benefit than Lani's. The next few minutes became an agonizing walk. He had to be careful to not sprint for the exit and aggravate her injuries further or seem too hurried. Yet, he feared Daniel would change his mind or that some cop would become too eager and rush in before they could cross the finish line to safety. A thousand little things could go south.

"Steady, darling." Lani placed a hand on his chest, over his heart. The gesture alone calmed him enough to help him maintain his cool as he crossed the rest of the floor toward the door he had come in, even as he sensed Daniel following behind, a distance away.

"On your word." Julia sounded terse, despite the distorting through the earpiece.

They hovered at the exit and Nathan half-turned to glance over his shoulder at Daniel. Pity welled up within him, for while the man was still smug in his countenance, Nathan knew that this was the end for him — not that this could finish any other way.

He looked down at the woman in his arms. She had become his north star, and if pressed for answers, he wouldn't have been able to tell how that was all possible in such a short time. Still, the smile she returned to him, full of encouragement and trust, was enough for him.

"You know," Nathan began in a soft voice thick with melancholy, as he gazed back at Daniel, "it doesn't matter what you think of me, because I've found the thing in life worth fighting for, the one person in my life worth bending my knee to. What do you have, Daniel? What purpose do you choose to serve?"

His ex-partner only raised a brow at him and laughed, shaking his head, but Nathan could see it now. A man like Daniel would never understand.

"Goodbye, Daniel." With almost a sigh of reluctance, he breathed out his next word. "*Now*."

Behind him, the door burst open and cops streamed in, their guns pointing at Daniel. But Nathan only turned his back toward the scene, gazing down at Lani as he walked her away. Neither of them needed to see how it played out. For them, it was done.

"I'm proud of you." She reached up to cup his cheek.

"You ordered me to not let him walk all over me anymore," he replied with a wry smile on his lips. She laughed, the sound chasing away all his worries.

"I did, and you pulled that off wonderfully."

"Does that mean I get a reward?" For the first time in the last few days, Nathan allowed himself to sound hopeful.

"Hmm-m, depends. What would you like?"

The answer came easy enough. "An ice-cream date."

Shock was evident in the way Lani's eyes widened and how her lips formed a small O. An urge to kiss her shot through him but he refrained, waiting for permission. And so, it was almost a surprise when Lani fisted his hair to pull him closer. She pressed her lips against his in a fierce kiss and he returned it as if he were suffocating before and she was the very air he needed to save himself.

Lani tugged him backward after someone cleared their throat behind them, reining both their passions in. But she kept him near as she spoke, her words featherlight against his lips. "You may take me out on that ice-cream date."

And that was the best news he'd heard all day.

Chapter Thirty

Lani glared at the pesky evil that her flight of stairs had become. With her broken leg in a cast, she'd had to resort to crutches to get around, which meant in the past few weeks, she rarely went upstairs. She missed her closet and collection of shoes, not that she could put on heels at the moment. Uncharacteristic of her, she muttered another curse under her breath. It was becoming a habit as a byproduct of her inconvenienced body.

And she was lucky it was just an inconvenience. Lani knew that had Nathan not found her as fast as he did, there would have been a chance that it would be too late for the break to mend straight, and it would have left her with a limp for life, at least. Nathan had filled in the blanks, told her the video Renard had sent of his little torture session was what had led him to find her location, thanks to Jasper. As soon as Lani was out of the hospital, she had called the very flustered but polite boy, who had then made inquiries about

Ophelia's wellbeing. That was very interesting and worth pursuing when things calmed down.

However, right now they were both swamped — her with medical appointments, Nathan with dealing with the fallout of Daniel's involvement and arrest at the company and both of them with the case itself. Wilson had offered to stay on to see them over this crisis, an offer Nathan had been all too happy to accept, but with his wife due soon, they were all running out of time.

Problems for another day. In this moment, she wanted to figure out how to retrieve a warmer sweater in her bedroom without help. Since Renard had left her in wet clothes for hours, she had never stopped craving warm fuzzy coverings, as if she could never quite get rid of the cold in her bones. Lani knew it was psychosomatic, caused by the trauma of the kidnapping. Lots of things were. But it would take time before they would heal, more than even her broken leg required.

The doorbell buzzed and Lani almost jumped out of her skin, her heart racing before she took a deep breath to calm it. Her friends, those in the know, had been doing their best to not surprise her, but she remained easy to startle at any ringing. *Another scar.*

"I've got it." Nathan's heavy footsteps echoed in her hall before he stepped into view. Before he passed her, he placed a hand on her shoulder, ensuring he was making eye contact. "You okay?"

Lani mustered up her most brilliant smile. "Of course, darling. Now don't keep our guests waiting."

Nathan dipped his head. "Yes, Ma'am." But his knowing eyes told her everything, even as he dropped his hand and moved toward the door. He understood trauma, understood the hundreds of little ways it affected someone. He also knew that sometimes calling it out would just make it worse, and that she needed her sparkly glass armor, as fragile as it may be. Thank God for that.

"Nathan!" Luna's familiar voice echoed down the hall and curious. Lani pulled away from the foot of the stairs to hobble over to the front entrance.

"Hi, Lani." Jacob stepped in behind Luna. No 'pest', no teasing, just a serious worry that made Lani sigh. It was the first time they had seen each other outside of the hospital since the ordeal, but did he have to be such a worrywart? They required some levity.

"I'm surprised you let Luna out of the apartment."

Jacob glowered. "If I had left her at home, she would tire herself out cleaning or wear a track on the floors."

Luna blushed but tried to stifle a giggle, too. Lani winked at her.

"I'll go put on some tea," Nathan offered, but looked at Lani, awaiting her permission. Only when she nodded did he leave for the kitchen.

"Looks like training is going well," Jacob murmured.

Lani's gaze followed Nathan's steps as he walked away. "He hardly needs any in the little things. I'm not sure how I got so lucky."

"I know what you mean."

When Lani returned her attention to Jacob, he was no longer watching Nathan but had wrapped an arm around Luna instead and pulled her to him, kissing her on the top of her head. The sub's cheeks only grew redder, and she buried her face against his side.

Lani smiled at that and, leaning on one crutch, motioned them to follow her. "Come on. The tea will get cold."

They walked in on Nathan, who was pulling mugs out of the cupboard. Luna surged past both Doms. "Let me help with that."

About to join the two, she stopped when Jacob placed a warm hand on her shoulder. She looked up. Funny how he towered over her, but never did he make her feel unsafe or uncomfortable around him. Sometimes it took conscious willpower to remember that not everyone was out to hurt her.

"Lani, I'm sorry."

"For what?" She couldn't fathom what the man had to apologize for.

"I was so preoccupied with seeing to Luna's health that I missed all the signs that you were in trouble. I should have been there for you more — should have been a better friend. Maybe then you wouldn't have…"

Her eyes widened in astonishment, and it took a full five seconds before she laughed.

"What?" he grumbled.

"Jacob, you could've helped only if I had let you — and I wasn't letting anyone help."

"Lani—"

"No more of this. Don't you dare go around carrying that guilt. I already have a sub wallowing in it so much that it'll take a good whipping to get it out of him. I don't need you going down the same path. The only ones who are guilty are Renard and Daniel." When Jacob hesitated still, Lani sighed. "Come on. Now give me a hug."

"That I can do." Jacob smiled at that and wrapped his arms around her, careful to not throw her balance off.

"Tea's ready." Luna set the last mug down and Nathan returned to help her into a chair. Lani would never admit to anyone that she ached from propping herself up on crutches all day. An unintended small sigh of relief escaped her lips as she settled and Nathan set those blasted walking aids aside, though he kept them within her reach. He knew without her saying a word just how important her independence was to her.

The rest of them gathered around and sat with their tea. They had visited when she was at the hospital, so the tears that they had all needed to shed were long gone. Nevertheless, emotions filled the silence. At last, Luna broke it by reaching for Lani's hand. "How are you doing?"

"Better." Lani gave her friend a genuine smile, then began chuckling. "I guess this is a bit of a role reversal."

It took the others a moment before laughter followed hers. They all understood gallows humor, having been through their own respective hells. It hadn't been long since it had been Lani visiting Luna with her stab wound.

"Well, to the villains in our lives. May they all rot in their jail cells." Lani held up her mug of tea.

"I could drink to that." Jacob clinked his cup with hers, and Luna and Nathan joined in.

Soon, they lapsed into small talk, catching up on where everyone was with work, or in Luna's and Lani's cases, when the return-to-work dates were. They talked about their next visit to The Playgrounds and other things they could look forward to once they healed. The normalcy soothed her soul more than she expected, and she made a mental note to invite more people over.

"Speaking of The Playgrounds, how's the company?" Luna asked Nathan, leaning in closer. Both she and Jacob knew the full story at this point.

"Funny thing." Nathan rubbed the back of his neck. "Daniel never bothered to involve himself in the day-to-day operations, so the disruption felt pretty minimal. It's more on the client side where we had to smooth things over, and Wilson staying on for a little longer helped with that." He dropped his hand and shrugged. "I guess, like Lani said, our work spoke for itself. We may have lost a few, but we've retained most of the contracts."

"So, what happens to the shares now?"

Nathan frowned. "Technically, Daniel can keep them, even in prison, but because we're a security company, if convicted, we would have grounds to remove him, based on our shareholder agreement. His lawyers may try to fight us tooth and nail on it, but if he ends up with a criminal record, they won't have a leg to stand on."

"I hope everything gets tied up soon," Jacob muttered, his countenance darkening. Lani wasn't sure if he meant with Daniel or Bryan. Perhaps both.

"Meanwhile, I'm testing some new equipment here," Nathan offered. At that, Jacob perked up in interest, much to both her and Luna's chagrin. But even Lani couldn't deny that the tech items that Nathan was working on around her house were sensible things she should have had installed a while ago, given that she lived alone. When he had proposed the additional measures, she'd had no reason to disagree.

"Oh?"

"Yeah, I was just putting up a new motion detection light. This one has a wider angle and range than most, and you can calibrate how long you want the LED to be on."

"Really? Show me?"

Nathan looked at Lani once more, and with a small laugh, she nodded her consent again. "You boys have fun."

And like children full of excitement about a new toy, both men left. Lani was still looking at her back door closing when Luna spoke.

"So, when's he moving in?"

Startled by the sudden switch in topic, Lani stared at Luna wide-eyed before shaking her head. "When are you moving in with Jacob?"

Luna mirrored her movements, giving her head a shake, too. "I asked first."

"When did you become so pushy, dolly?"

The sub grinned. "When I learned I need to do a better job standing up for myself, even with other Dominants."

Lani smiled at that, then exhaled. "Very well. To answer your question, we've got a few steps before we get to that. We haven't discussed a formal contract yet."

Now Luna's face lit up with alarm. "Why not?"

A small frown tugged unbidden at the corner of her lips. "I need to verify that our new closeness is not a product of two people who just went through a traumatic experience together. I want to make sure we will endure."

Luna's groan of frustration was the last reaction she expected. Lani arched her brow in question.

"I probably shouldn't be saying this, but hell, you need to hear it." Luna composed herself, folding one arm over another. "Nathan came to me for a chat right before you—" She struggled for the right words and Lani waited with as much patience as she could muster. "Before the bastard took you. It's how we were able to start piecing together that you might be in trouble. But the other reason he wanted to talk was to work through what serving meant to him." Luna grabbed Lani's hand once more and gave it a squeeze. "There was never any doubt in his head that he wanted you. He just had to figure out whether he was ready to serve. And by the time he was leaving my apartment, he was preparing to offer himself to you — as a sub...to his Domme."

Oh. Lani stared at Luna like a deer caught in the headlights. Her skin flushed, and a warmth coursed through her body, something she had missed so much.

Luna sat back, a satisfied, smug smile on her face. "What did you say to me all those years ago? Oh, yes. *'Don't let your fear of getting hurt stop you from what could be the most amazing experience of your life. The future's unknown. The risk is worth it.'*"

She had quoted the advice from the past her almost exactly. Lani recognized the words as the ones she had offered to Luna after August's death. Back then, they had been the push Luna had needed to take her first contract with Jacob. And now, perhaps, they were the push Lani herself needed. She turned her gaze toward the window where, on the other side, Nathan was explaining the light module to Jacob.

"You're right. He's worth it."

Chapter Thirty-One

A cast was damn hard to accessorize with—in particular for a Domme. Not that it stopped Lani from dressing up to the nines for her first night back at The Playgrounds. Rather than the corset and latex pants, however, she opted for a softer look with a white baby doll and matching lacy booty-short panties. And instead of her signature heels, she wore a pair of deep red flats with peep toes. It matched her bright nail color and the burgundy toenail polish.

She sat on the same bar chair as the one from over a month ago, drinking her cranberry lychee cocktail when Darryl returned, a towel slung over his shoulder like usual. In some ways, Lani was learning to appreciate the bartender's consistent presence there as an anchor to normalcy during her recovery phase.

"You know, I've been thinking that I should name that seat you're in 'the Blessed'."

Lani could almost hear the capitalization in his voice and tilted her head to one side. "How so?"

"Well, it seems to be where people are hooking up for more permanent arrangements — first Tara and Declan, and now you and Nathan."

Oh, that smug grin on his face. Lani decided then she had to take him down a notch or two.

"Technically, Nathan and I hooked up before we met here, and he was aware I was a Domme."

"What?" Darryl's jaws dropped and Lani smirked in return.

"Yes. I believe I still have your mask at my place." With impeccable timing, Nathan approached the bar and positioned himself to stand beside Lani, just a little behind to her right.

Lani's smirk bloomed into a pleased smile as she reached up with one hand to cup Nathan's face. The light touch was all Nathan needed to bend down so than she could place a small peck on his cheek. "Hello, darling. All done working for the night?"

"Yes, Ma'am." Nathan's eyes shone with appreciation as he made no pretense to hide his studying of her outfit. She didn't mind. It delighted her to arouse him with visual treats.

"Wait! Her mask?" Bewilderment still tinged Darryl's tone.

Lani laughed as she shifted back to the bar. "We met at a masquerade party. He was part of security, and I was a guest." She turned a little to level Nathan with a fond look. "I remember someone being rather bold in their approach."

"Well, there was something about you, right from the beginning." Nathan gave a small, almost sheepish smile that lightened his serious work expression.

Darryl eyed the two of them, then sighed. "It still doesn't invalidate my theory. Maybe I'll call it the

Hook-Up Chair." He passed a hand, open-palmed, in the air as if he was painting a sign with it. Nathan shook his head in response while Lani laughed again.

It felt good to laugh. After all the questions she had received that night, asking about where she had been and what had happened to her leg, she needed a distraction. While she appreciated everyone's concerns, she found answering everyone exhausting, given that she couldn't share much detail while the case was being prepared for trial.

The silly grin Darryl gave her, however, drew Lani back to the present, and her appreciation for him grew all the more. He had sensed that levity was in order and provided just that. His knack for reading moods and needs made him a good bartender and an even better Dom, if only he could find the right submissive for himself. Perhaps it was another project for her when things settled. It would be, at least, a sweet revenge after all the years he had bugged her about finding a sub. But Lani knew what the real deal was. Darryl still held a torch for Cassie, a switch who had used to be their friend until August's death. The girl had since then rejected all of them, despite their efforts to reach out, and she'd spiraled downward on a path of self-destruction. It was hard for all of them to watch.

"Here." Darryl tossed Nathan a bottle of water, which he caught with one hand.

"Thanks. How's the night down here?"

"Quiet on the home front. Or at least busy but quiet. Mostly regulars. Some tourists milling around, but I don't think any of them will be any trouble. Up there?" Darryl cast a glance over his shoulder toward the stairs.

Nathan shrugged, serious once more. "Most of the rooms are empty. Dungeon's busier, but we have a full complement of monitors, so should be fine. Jasper just wanted to do his routine check on the equipment tonight."

Lani smiled at the rapport the two men had built over such a short time. Nathan often commented on how important Darryl was, both as part of keeping peace at the club and as a friend, so he'd made a point of always touching base with him whenever he dropped by The Playgrounds, for work or otherwise.

"So, what are you guys up to tonight?" Darryl leaned over the bar, bracing his hands along the edge.

Nathan pursed his lips, then sighed, rubbing the back of his neck. "Well, I thought we were going on that ice-cream date Lani promised. But I'm not sure with that outfit…"

Laughter bubbled in her again and mischief made her smile wide. "My dear boy, that's what large coats are for! In fact, we should head out now before the place closes."

His reaction brought her further delight. Nathan wasn't the most expressive man in the world, but she had learned to read his micro-expressions with ease. The slight widening of eyes, the slow flush that crept up the back of his neck, the minute tensing of his biceps and shoulders all told her what he thought of the idea.

Darryl, on the other hand, barked out a jovial laugh. "I'm not certain whether to envy or pity you, man. You sure know how to pick them. Lani here is the master at teasing. So good luck to you."

Straightening her back, Lani beamed, then turned her chair around to grab her things. Ah, Nathan. She couldn't tell if he was trying to stifle a groan or to prevent a blush from blossoming. Either way, the poor boy looked like he had swallowed something down the wrong side of his throat. It was the reaction she was looking for. Pleased, she hummed to herself as she put on and secured her coat, then slid off her seat with the support of the crutches.

It took a few steps and a glance backward before she realized Nathan was still rooted to his spot. "Coming, darling?" she asked and chuckled as her man shook his stupor off, gave Darryl a last look, then hurried to catch up to her. Together, they made their way out, and Lani tried her best to not curse her awkwardness with crutches for the n-th time. It was impossible to affect a sexy walk.

Nathan helped her into his car. Once in, Lani loosened the belt, enough for the outer layer to fall open and reveal her almost-bare shoulders and hints of cleavage.

He gripped the steering wheel tighter, knuckles turning white before he apparently remembered he still had to start the vehicle. Once done, he pulled out of the parking spot, but with the insides of the carriage illuminated by the lot's bright lights, he kept stealing glances toward her.

"Eyes on the road. That's your challenge for the evening."

Lani thought she heard a responding, whispered "shit," but wasn't sure. Either way, she sat back and relaxed into her seat as she guided him with directions to the specific ice-cream shop she had in mind. For the rest of the trip, she alternated between trailing her fingers along the plunging V neckline her parted coat made and skimming them across his thigh. When a bump on the road rocked her hand to brush against his crotch, Nathan let out an audible groan.

"Steady," she murmured.

Upon arrival, he pulled into a spot on the street to park, and with a sigh, slumped into the driver's seat, sinking into it with the least grace she had ever seen from him.

"Are you all right?" Lani asked.

"That was…a tougher drive than I thought possible." Even as he spoke, his gaze gravitated toward her cleavage and remained glued to her curves as she shook with stifled giggles.

"Well, let's test and see how far your control goes tonight, shall we?" She adjusted her coat, pulling it back up. Lani knew he needed his focus for what she had planned next, and it would be unfair to tease him further…for now.

He swallowed hard, fingers curling into fists. "Yes, Ma'am."

Oh, the dear boy.

He came around to help her out of the car, but rather than walk the small distance to the ice-cream shop, she led them down along the boardwalk, enjoying the breeze coming off the water, chilly as it may be. The seasons were changing and as Lani lifted her face to the night sky, she realized it was time for her to change, too, to step into the next journey in her life, if Nathan would join her.

"Ma'am?"

"Lani," she corrected him, shifting their dynamics, then turned to ease herself down onto one bench before patting the spot next to her. "Come sit with me?" Again, a request, not an order.

When Nathan, with puzzlement still wrinkling his forehead, sat down beside her, she slipped her hand into her coat's inner pocket and drew out a tri-folded package of papers and a velvet jewelry box, larger than one that would contain a single ring.

"For you to consider." She handed him the sheets of paper first and tried her best to not hold her breath.

He could walk away. He could laugh in her face. He could ask for more time to think about it. They hadn't discussed a formal contract before, so this would be an utter surprise for him. It wasn't how she imagined she would have approached this, but Luna's words still haunted her, and she knew she had to do this. To drag it on any longer would be to turn her back on all the lessons she'd learned after all she had been through. If she didn't take that leap of faith, it would leave her with nothing but regrets.

Nathan unfolded the document and skimmed it before returning to the first page to read in more detail. His hands trembled as he lowered them and stared at her. "This is…" His voice choked with emotion.

She felt the same way, but she steadied herself with another draw of air into her lungs. "Yes, a service contract. I'd like to know your thoughts. I had guessed at the parameters that would suit you, but we can discuss further if there are any clauses you'd want to put in." She kept her tone neutral, business-like.

Instead of answering her, he returned his gaze to the document again then stroked the paper with a delicate touch. The reaction piqued her curiosity, and she leaned in a little closer. "Nathan?"

About to say more, to suggest he might choose to think it over and they could continue on the promised date, she almost fell back in surprise when he straightened and turned to face her in full.

"Ma'am, may I borrow a pen? I'm afraid I don't have one on me at the moment."

The smile that blossomed unbidden made her cheeks hurt. "Of course." From the same pocket, she drew out a pen, offered it to him and watched as he shifted to place the last page on his lap, adding his signature below hers.

"Take this." Now her voice held the ring of command as she assumed her role as his Dominant in full.

He took the box with care and, at her nod, opened it. His chest rose and fell with a sharp intake of breath that he let out at a more controlled pace.

It was a set. A dog tag on a long silver chain took up most of the room in the container, but rather than letters or numbers, Lani had it engraved with her clan badge, a hand holding a sword emerging from a piece of braided rope, encircled with a belt. The motto *Miseris succurrere disco* or *I learn to succor the unfortunate* curved within the belt itself. For more formal occasions, Lani included a tie pin with a variation of the same image, the sword acting as the arm of the pin. The jewelry paid homage to their bond, to his past and to his role as her protector while respecting his need for privacy on certain aspects of their relationship.

"Ma'am?" His voice wavered, then he cleared his throat. "Would you do me the honor?"

"I wouldn't have it any other way." She lifted the chain from the box and settled it around his neck, even as he ducked his head for her. The dog tag settled on his torso, glimmering in the evening light.

She wanted to take him home. Hell, she wanted to just take him. But it was part of a Dominant's job to maintain control so that their submissive could lose theirs. And he was hers now. Truly hers, completely and utterly to protect, cherish and...tease...

"Well then, I do believe celebratory ice cream is in order."

His answering grin was more than enough for her.

Epilogue

In a most cliche move, Lani pulled off her helmet and shook her curls loose as she strolled into Nathan's office. Being able to ride again months after had been exhilarating and called for some impromptu celebrating.

"Ms. McMillan!"

Lani turned to see Jasper scrambling up and out of his desk to greet her. The boy had never gotten used to calling her by her first name, and she had given up trying to correct him.

"Jasper, how are you?"

He stopped a few paces before her and gave her a shy smile. "I'm good. Keeping busy." He cast his gaze downward. "What brings you to these parts? Are you looking for the boss?"

"Yes, is he around?"

"Yeah, he's in his office. Just returned from a big meeting." Jasper gestured with his thumb behind him toward the room in the back with the door ajar, then stood aside to let her through.

"Thank you." She breezed past him with a jaunty wave and waltzed her way in.

Nathan looked up from what he was reading, surprise widening his reddened eyes. All work and no play had made her sub into a tired, stressed-out boy, and she was there to remedy that.

"Lani?" He set the papers aside and rose to greet her, stepping away from his desk.

Oh, he cut a handsome figure in his dark suit and black tie. Lani couldn't help but grin, spotting the glint of the clip she had given him. *Mine.* She leaned against the door, closing it with her back and snuck a hand up to click the lock in place without looking.

Nathan frowned as he approached her. "Did I forget something? Are you okay?"

Rather than answer, Lani pushed off from the wall to stand straight and twined his tie around her hand, using it as leverage to pull him down to her level. As he bent over, she pressed her lips against his, featherlight. Before he could lean in and deepen the contact, she drew back, far enough to lift the key hanging from inside her jacket out into his field of vision.

Nathan sucked in a breath and bit his lower lip hard as he glanced at the functional bauble. Her own gaze traveled downward, and she trailed her free hand down the same path to brush against his crotch where she knew his cock would be caged. After all, she was the one who had locked the chastity cage herself two days before.

"Come here." Lani pulled him closer, and when he allowed himself to be moved, she spun them around and pushed him against the door. With more haste than she'd intended, she pulled his shirt out of his pants and began undoing his belt.

"They'll hear," he hissed in an urgent whisper.

"Well, that'll depend on how quiet you can be." She unbuttoned his slacks, tugging them past his hips to reveal the cage and his cock within.

With a wicked grin, she pressed a hard kiss that left them both breathless while she slid her hand into his. When she broke contact, she raised it to position his palm to cover his own mouth. "Remember... No coming until I allow it."

Still meeting his gaze with hers, she sank with tantalizing slowness to her knees and without taking the chain off her neck, she inserted the key and unlocked the cage.

He groaned as the metal fell down with a clatter on the ground and she stroked his cock, massaging with a gentle touch. It only took a fleeting moment before it hardened in her hand. Lani noted the way his muscles seem to tremble as if he was struggling to hold himself up.

"Now, darling, remember... It's up to you."

It was another form of control and one so much harder to submit to since it required abstinence from willpower alone. Nevertheless, Lani was confident of Nathan's abilities and besides, success and failure would both lead to fun—just different kinds for her. While holding his length in her hand, she followed up with a slow lick along the underside of his shaft. His muffled groan urged her further and, still keeping eye contact, she swirled her tongue around the tip of his cock.

"Fuck." Nathan leaned back, only to bang his head harder against the door than he'd intended. "Shit."

He may have dampened his swearing, but Lani picked up the word nonetheless and had to giggle, the sound vibrating against his shaft, enough to make it twitch in her grip. From the corner of her eye, she saw Nathan almost stuff his fist in his mouth.

More. She wanted to push him to the brink.

She wrapped her lips around the head, already shiny from her efforts, and swept along the underside with the tip of her tongue. His muscles bunched and his face flushed a lovely red. The control she had over his arousal thrilled her and sent heat straight to her core.

He was struggling, his breathing growing more ragged, his chest heaving great breaths, the hand not busy keeping himself quiet clenched tight into a fist. But it was the way his darkened steel grays filled with unbridled lust that drove her on as she sank her lips down along his cock and back up again, establishing a slow and steady rhythm—but not enough, never enough to make him come.

"Lan— Ma'am," Nathan corrected himself before she could reprimand him. The low timber of his voice held a growl that added to its savage quality. It almost made her forgive the slip up...almost.

She danced her slender fingers up along his inner thighs before they both froze at a sudden knock.

"Hey, Nathan, I got those expense reports you asked for." It was not from someone Lani recognized, but she grinned regardless.

Ah, the perfect punishment had arrived. As Nathan pulled his hand away and cleared his throat to answer, Lani hollowed her cheeks, sucking hard and felt him swell against her in return. He choked on his words, and they tumbled from his lips garbled, along with a groan.

"Nathan, you okay?"

"Yeah. Just in the middle of something. I'll come out and pick them up later."

Lani wondered if Nathan realized he came off gruff and snappy as if to compensate for his desperation.

"No problem." Footsteps faded and Lani eased off, grinning up at him with all the satisfaction of a cat who had caught a mouse. He exhaled a long breath.

She replaced her lips with her fingers, wrapping them around his length, pumping nice and slow while she rose from her knees. "Now, shall I give you a break and get you to put yourself back in that cage?"

Nathan's eyes widened in alarm, and he stared at her, his mouth opening and closing before his expression shifted to one of agony when he realized it wasn't just a teasing question.

"No, please." It came out much like a horrified gasp. "Please, finish me." He reached out now, sliding his hands down the side of her hips. It was a bold move for him to touch her, but she had issued no command prohibiting him from it before. Besides, she liked his boldness. "Let me please you."

Lani smiled, softening for a moment as she cupped his cheek with one hand. "You already do." When his lips descended on hers with a more tender kiss than she expected, she sighed and melted against his body. "Free rein."

That was all he needed. Nathan slid his palms along the smooth worn leather of her motorcycle tights, only to come to a stop in front where he busied himself undoing them. Amused by his urgent movements, Lani watched and giggled as he succeeded at last with a groan of relief.

"Ah, fuck," he whispered again as he pulled her pants down, his gaze riveted to the black thong that covered her mound. With a trembling hand, he pushed aside the flimsy, already-soaked material and slid a finger along her slit.

She tensed in response and let out a soft sigh of pure pleasure as he worked his fingers deeper into her. Lani leaned forward, nibbling up his neck in encouragement, while returning to re-establish the rhythm. She slid her hand up and down along his cock, smoothing the pad of her thumb around the head on every stroke. "That's it, Nathan. Show me how much you want me."

To her surprise, Nathan eased back instead to catch her gaze. The naked hunger she saw stole her breath away, but it was the glimmer of mischief in his eyes that provoked her curiosity. Before she could ask, he began walking her backward until she bumped against the edge of his desk. She placed a hand behind to steady herself and dislodged a pile of paper that came fluttering down to the floor into a disheveled mess.

It jolted them from their make-out session, and Lani stared at the ground, only to glance at Nathan after and see him do the same. Their eyes met. With an almost animalistic growl, he moved past her to sweep more papers away until the desk cleared with enough space. When he returned to slide his palms along her hips, his intentions became apparent.

And that would just not do.

She covered his large hands with her smaller ones and shook her head. Dismay clouded his face, overshadowing his lust until she spoke again. "Lie on the desk, facing me."

As Lani sidestepped to give him room, he complied with eagerness until he was lying flat on his back, his feet dangling off the side, his cock at attention. Meanwhile, she bent over to undo her boots, easing them off before shrugging off her pants. When she straightened once more, she shivered with delight at the sight of him still waiting for her. Lani swayed her hips and repositioned herself between his legs. Tempted as she was to continue with her earlier oral administrations and edge him further, she gifted him instead with what she knew he wanted. With deft hands, she climbed on to straddle over him, holding herself above. She rocked to and fro, rubbing her warm slit over the tip of his shaft, her juices already coating it generously.

Thank God his desk was an oversized, sturdy thing. Maybe a little showy for both their tastes since he'd had to assume Daniel's office, but for now, it'd do.

"Tell me, darling, how many times have you dreamed of this, craved this, while wearing that cage? How often did you imagine thrusting into me, fucking me however you wanted as your reward?"

"Yes. Always. All the time." He reached up to cup her breasts, groaning in frustration as the layers of clothing got in the way.

Lani bent over with a grin. "Good answer." And with that, she locked her lips with his and plunged down, letting him enter her with a single long, hard stroke. With both of their moans muffled by the kiss, she rode him with abandon. He gripped her hips as he thrust upward, urging her on, and soon, they were moving as one, pushing each other headlong toward their mutual undoing.

She allowed Nathan to control their pace, and euphoria clouded her mind, silencing all thoughts as his warmth seeped through hers, the way his shaft was pistoning in and out, driving her to higher heights, spreading her wider in the position even as his pelvis rubbed against the bundle of sensitive nerves her clit had become. Then her world narrowed to the physical sensations alone as the tingle that started below spread through her entire body, pleasure racing through her blood until her orgasm consumed her in one explosive rush.

And still he kept going below her. Lani bit her lips as she rode through the prolonged climax, barely registering her sub below her through her haze.

"Ma'am, please," he whispered, agony and ecstasy mingling in his voice. His features twisted in an effort to hold back his own orgasm.

Oh, shit. Lani shuddered above him, her body still spasming from the slower descent from her peak. But she braced herself for the next command she would issue. "Come."

Digging his fingers into her hips, Nathan pulled her down hard against him, burying himself into her to the hilt with one deep stroke. He came within her with a harsh growl, pouring his seed inside. It was enough to trigger her own once more, and she came again, this time, letting the climax sweep her away, body and soul.

Lani rested against Nathan, her cheek pressed against his chest as they both caught their breath.

"Well then, I suppose I should get back to my office," she murmured, but made no move to withdraw when his arms only tightened around her. She propped her chin up to meet his gaze. "Darling, I have a client soon. I'll see you at home tonight."

With a sigh and a frown that announced his reluctance clearly, Nathan relinquished his hold on her and handed her a tissue box instead. It took a while for both of them to clean up, but she caught him stealing glances at her more than once or twice.

"Christ, you're gorgeous." He embraced around her from behind as she was doing her buckle. "Mine."

Lani chuckled and turned in his arms to kiss him. "Yes, just as you are mine. Be good, and I'll see you tonight."

Nathan perked up and grinned. "Maybe in that new baby doll you were texting me about?"

She laughed and marveled at how easy the sound came to her, despite both of them still being haunted by shadows of their past. "You're insatiable, darling...but perhaps."

His grin, like a little boy on Christmas morning, made her smile all the harder. She only wondered if the smile would remain there once he realized that the office outside had grown deathly quiet.

* * * *

Nathan swore as he pulled up into the driveway. *Late again.* Running the company alone now that Wilson had left was keeping him working almost constantly. It was something he had to fix soon if he didn't want to travel down the same path as his previous marriage. Perhaps a new partner was in order, and he had some ideas who to ask, given the men he had met since he'd discovered the local scene.

She was sitting on the porch when he made his way up the stairs, a blanket around her shoulders, staring up at the stars with a mug of tea in her hand.

"I'm sorry," he mumbled.

Lani's gaze up at him was not what he expected. There was no anger, no accusation, just a quiet stillness he had come to know as a side of her that few others saw.

"Sit with me." She patted the spot next to her, and the knot in his stomach tightened as he braced himself for a talk.

Instead, as soon as he eased down, she curled up closer against him, resting her head against his shoulder and tension eased from her body. Together, they relaxed in silence, listening to the occasional sound the suburbs offered — a car passing by, the low murmur of conversation drifting from a nearby house, a dog barking.

He wrapped an arm around Lani, looking down at the woman he had chosen to serve with concern. "Are you okay?"

"Sometimes when I close my eyes, I can hear that sledgehammer scraping against the cement or my clothes would feel freezing cold."

His heart stung with guilt. She continued to be in pain because of him. But no matter how many times he tried to bring it up, she refused to see him as the cause of her persistent suffering. He only pulled her closer and placed a light kiss on her forehead, choking down the apology he wanted to give her.

"But want to know a little secret?"

The strength in her hazel eyes took his breath away. "Sure."

"I think about what happened after. I heard your voice back there. At first, I thought I was hallucinating, but when I picked up your conversation with him, I knew then that you were already mine." The small smile that played over her lips summoned his own unbidden one.

"I was yours long before that. It just took me a little longer than it should have to figure that out." Nathan shrugged. He didn't mind admitting to these things.

In return, she snuggled closer to him and nuzzled along his neck. "I'd rather you take your time to be sure than to rush headlong into something you're not ready for."

He considered her words, rolling them in his head. "And you? I know before me…" He trailed off, almost afraid of the answer if not for the trust he held in her. Their relationship demanded nothing less.

"August will always have a place in my heart. But that doesn't mean there's no room for another. If anything, he was the one who taught me the need to live in the now, and the now tells me there is this man I should be with, should take care of." She trailed her fingers along his cheek as she whispered, tracing the contours of his face.

He caught her hand and kissed each fingertip with more fervor than he thought he was capable of.

The kiss she gifted him with in return spoke of all he needed to know of her heart, and the next words he uttered became a promise and a reminder for both of them.

"To us in the now."

Want to see more from this author?
Here's a taster for you to enjoy!

Some Like it Haunted:
The Fae Effect
P. Stormcrow

Excerpt

The old-style English pub was the little university town's best kept secret, and tonight, it was filled with sexy witches, grotesque murderers, charming devils and not-so-innocent angels. After all, it was the Saturday night before Halloween, when most parties were taking place. No one wanted to risk a 'hangover Monday' in the middle of midterm season.

In contrast, Keenan, a grad student in the Department of Computer Science, and three of her friends, all in normal attire, sat at a round table in the back, observing the revelry with amused smiles.

"Is that one of the jock babies over there in a chugging contest?" Keenan whispered to Aisha, the raven-haired woman beside her.

It was what Keenan and her fellow grad school friends called the group of undergrad jocks they'd had to teach this year. The university had admitted most of them based more on their athletic merit than their academic abilities, and it showed in their reluctance to learn.

"Oof. Yeah. I think you're right. Aren't you TA-ing his class this semester?"

Keenan winced as the third-year frat boy by the bar slammed his pint glass onto the bartop, threw his head back and howled—never mind that it was rather appropriate, considering he was dressed like a werewolf in a flannel shirt. "I'm not looking forward to marking whatever he ends up handing in on Monday."

"Forget about that," Dale waved at the two women for attention and leaned forward, his eyes flashing with excitement. His freckles were growing more prominent with the flushing of his normally pale cheeks. "Tell us, Kee… What do you have planned for your Halloween episode?"

Keenan grinned. She wasn't too proud to admit that she loved talking about her passion project. It had turned into a full side gig. She even had fans! "Well, a couple of weeks ago, I was covering this urban legend about peeling an apple at midnight. I figured I could air that one on the channel tomorrow."

"An apple?" Aisha shivered and wrapped her arms around herself.

"Yeah, there's an urban legend that says if you peel an apple in front of a mirror at midnight, you'll see an image of the one you'll marry one day. And every time the peel breaks, a scar will appear on their face and you would have cursed your future spouse with that scar."

Aisha gasped, her eyes round with fear.

At her friend's look, Keenan laughed and patted her back. "Relax. I did not see my future husband and there were no scars. It's just a myth, obviously."

"Luckily. I still think you're crazy, doing what you do." Aisha pursed her lips and shook her head.

"But brave." Jonathan pushed his glasses up the ridge of his nose then grabbed the pitcher sitting right next to a bowl of peanuts to refill everyone's glasses. "Besides, all this stuff has no basis in science. I think what Kee's doing with her YouTube channel, debunking these myths and legends, is doing the world a service."

"Here's to scientific inquiry." Keenan lifted her beer.

"Hear, hear!" Her three friends mirrored her gesture and they all took long, satisfying gulps from their respective pints.

"That said, I think you should do something different on Halloween. I mean…it being *that* time of the year." Dale was often her source of inspiration for her episodes.

"What do you suggest?" Keenan tucked a stray red curl back behind her ear then folded her arms on the table.

"Local rumor has it that the hill behind the old Donovan property is a fairy mound. You know what they say…"

"That they're really fairy forts and, on All Hallows Eve, you can see fairies dancing there?" A familiar thrum of excitement coursed through Keenan's body. Dale was on to something.

"I dare you, Keenan O'Brien, to spend Halloween night at the fairy mound." Dale smirked.

Ah, he planned this all along. The sneaky bastard!

To be fair, however, Keenan had already been planning in her head what to pack before he'd even dared her. *I'll need to shoot on my phone to livestream, so that means an extra battery pack. And a sleeping bag. Oh, and I better tweet out an announcement. It'll be touch and go with such short notice.*

"Earth to Keenan." Jonathan waved a hand in front of her face.

"She's off in planning land. You can see it in her eyes." Aisha's voice drifted back to her attention.

Her friends knew her too well. "I'm here. I'm here!"

"So, you going to do it?" Dale asked, affecting his most innocent smile.

Ha! If he's innocent, then fairies are real.

"You knew I was going to do it as soon as you opened your mouth." Keenan mock-glared at him but failed to hold it for long.

Dale only widened his grin as Aisha stared at the two of them and sighed. "Just be careful, Kee. Sleeping alone outside is not safe, no matter which way you look at it."

"Aisha has a point. I'll be up all night anyway, the way my block parties. Why don't you check in with me?" Jonathan offered.

Before Keenan could respond, Aisha clapped her hands together and spoke again. "That's a splendid idea. She can call in every hour, and if she misses a call, it means something's gone pear-shaped and you can call for help."

Keenan almost choked, and her face heated from the alcohol. "Every three hours."

"Two," Aisha shot back while Dale tried to stifle his laugh, and Jonathan watched with an arched brow.

"Fine, *Mom*," Keenan groaned with exaggerated exasperation. With that, Dale burst into laughter.

Aisha rolled her eyes at their antics.

"Well, I for one will be watching from the comfort of my nice, warm, comfy bed." Dale winked at them.

At that, Keenan threw the peanut that she had been shelling at him.

* * * *

By the time she was setting up her sleeping bag by the light of her electric lantern, Keenan was very much wishing she were home in her nice, warm, comfy bed, too. *Damn Dale and his hair-brained ideas.*

Although it was a clear night, the chilly air nipped at any exposed skin without mercy. Even with her parka and cable-knitted scarf, she could still feel the cold seeping into her bones.

She exhaled a little puff of air as she gazed up at the night sky. Between the lights from the far-off buildings and the luminous moon high above, she couldn't pick out many stars. And of course, it had to be a full moon on Halloween night.

Keenan turned toward her phone. She had set it up on a portable tripod, and now she adjusted the angle before she hit the record button. It was fortunate that cell reception was still strong out there.

"Hi, everyone. Happy Halloween. So, as I announced earlier, I'm here, live, at the fairy mound. For those of you who don't know, fairy mounds — or fairy forts — are remnants of ancient circular buildings scattered all over Ireland. Usually they're farther out in rural areas, next to farmlands and highways, but I got lucky with one right here at the edge of town."

She leaned back and panned the phone to show the surrounding stones. "As you can see, it's pretty desolate here, except for the camp I've set up. Now, old folklore dictates that fairies will come up from their forts that are built beneath and come dancing on Halloween — or Samhain as it's called around here. So tonight, we'll prove once and for all whether that is true, live here on the MythCheck channel."

Keenan took a deep breath, readjusted her toque and rose from where she sat. She reached down and pried her phone from the stand. "Now, a little more background. The fairies in Ireland are also known by a plethora of other names like 'the Good Neighbors'. If you're superstitious—which a lot of folks are around here—you don't want to offend the fairies or they'll come play mean tricks on you. We're not talking mean like your average April Fool's joke here. We're talking about serious stuff, like a 'make something big and heavy fall on your head' kind of deal. A lot of these stories end up bloody." She didn't know that much about Irish folklore, but she had done some last-minute research, including picking Dave's brain, just for this night.

As she spoke, she walked closer to the stone circle and began to pace around the circumference of the fort. "Let's see what we can find."

The stones were still rough on the surface, but time had smoothed away many of the edges. She ran her hand along one and sucked in a breath.

"Oh, this is a treat." She dug into her pocket and shone an extra flashlight over at the rock before bringing the camera closer. "You see these? Triple spirals are etched into the stonework. You see loads of these on the bigger, more famous mounds like Newgrange, but this means that this mound is likely much older, and the ancients may have built it for religious reasons. Maybe it was the druids…but who knows?"

She could go on, but she had already overloaded the audience. "Okay, I'll let you all get back to enjoying your trick or treating. I'll report in again in two hours with another update. If you're watching this live, thanks for tuning in. I'll be posting a compilation later for your viewing pleasure as you're recovering from your hangovers. Anyway, signing off for now."

Probably shouldn't have said the last piece. Her dry humor didn't always endear her to her audience.

She guessed that Dale was likely watching, but she had also promised to check in, so as soon as she hit the stop button, she brought up the dial pad and texted Jonathan to let him know she was okay.

Wait! Is that…music?

She blinked and looked around in confusion. Who the hell would be playing music out in the middle of nowhere? Keenan returned to her small camp, then grabbed the lantern to shine it in the direction the sound was coming from. It was some wind instrument. And by the sound of it, the player was skilled.

Someone must have seen her stream and decided to prank her. She squared her shoulders and, with the lantern still in her hand, she strode with purpose toward the player.

Her breath caught as she beheld a most beautiful man sitting under a hawthorn tree, leaning against it. It was not a word she often used to describe a guy, but there was something about his androgynous look that made him almost pretty. Long silver hair glittered in the moonlight as his sharp features remained composed while he played. But the strong jawline definitely said male, while the full, broody lips curved in a small smile against the pan flute made him appear unearthly, despite the pair of skinny jeans and simple black hoodie he was sporting.

Fairy.

No way. She was being set up.

The man set his instrument in his lap and looked up at her. There was something odd about his eyes, but she couldn't quite place what it was just yet. He parted his lips and spoke in a singsong tone, so dulcet she thought she could listen to it forever.

"Come away, O human child!
To the woods and hills run wild
With a faery, as your guide,
For the world weeps by and by, filled with sorrows you
Cannot understand."

He was still smiling as he finished, amusement clear in his expression. But there was something else in that smile, like he was almost patronizing her.

It jolted her from her wonder, and she rolled her eyes. "Really? Quoting Yeats? Or trying to… A little obvious, don't you think? Besides, would a fairy use a poem by a human? And horribly mangling it at that." On purpose, she used the more common, pop-culture term rather than the more respectful pronunciation with an *e* in the word like he had. In general, only believers and neo-pagan worshippers used that more formal pronunciation.

He raised a brow then laughed. The sound reminded her of tinkling wind chimes. She shook her head lest she succumbed to his spell again. Figuratively, of course.

"You think I'm fae."

"I think you want me to believe you're fae," she shot back.

"And what makes you think I'm not?" He tucked his instrument into a messenger bag that was slung over his shoulder then stood up with a grace that made her feel like a clumsy oaf in contrast.

"Science." She braced her hands on her hips.

He stepped closer, undeterred by her defiance. "Such fiery red curls hidden beneath the darkness," he murmured, raising slender fingers to stroke strands escaping from her toque and curling down her neck.

"And yet such skepticism. There was a time when your kind held ours in unshakeable belief."

She should brush his hand away and take out the pepper spray, no matter how good-looking he was. But something stayed Keenan's hand and stilled her tongue. She could feel her resistance melting away. *No, something is wrong.*

"Would you like to see? That's what your science requires, correct? Observable proof. I can give you that, if you dare to follow."

Keenan swallowed hard. She shouldn't. This was all kinds of stupid. But the challenge in his eyes galled her.

"Fine. Bring it on."

He smiled then, triumph glittering in his eyes, and she wondered just what trap she'd fallen into. But it was too late. Her body moved of its own accord. It wasn't until she followed him, stepping somehow into the tree, that she realized…

She had left her phone back at camp.

About the Author

Award-winning author P. Stormcrow has always been an avid reader across the fantasy and sci fi genres but early on, found herself always looking for the love story in each book. Coming to terms with her love for love later in life, she now writes steamy romances that examine social norms and challenge conventional tropes of the genre, usually on her phone. And yes, she has walked into walls and poles doing so.

When she's not reading or writing (or even when she is), she enjoys copious amounts of tea, way too much sugary treats, one too many sci fi / fantasy / paranormal TV shows (team Dean all the way) and every otome game she can possibly find.

P. Stormcrow loves to hear from readers. You can find her contact information, website details and author profile page at https://www.totallybound.com

Home of Erotic Romance

Sign up for our newsletter and find out about all our romance book releases, eBook sales and promotions, sneak peeks and FREE romance books!

www.ingramcontent.com/pod-product-compliance
Lightning Source LLC
Chambersburg PA
CBHW020558260626
47157CB00003B/754